The INSIDER

OTHER BOOKS AND AUDIO BOOKS
BY SIAN ANN BESSEY

Forgotten Notes

Cover of Darkness

Family Is Forever

Kids on a Mission: Escape from Germany

Kids on a Mission: Uprising in Samoa

Kids on a Mission: Ambushed in Africa

Teddy Bear, Blankie, and a Prayer

Deception

Within the Dark Hills

You Came for Me

The INSIDER

A NOVEL

SIAN ANN BESSEY

Covenant Communications, Inc.

Cover images: *Capitol Building before Sunrise* © Klaas Lingbeek-van Kranen, *DUI Crash Series* © wh1600

Cover design copyright © 2014 by Covenant Communications, Inc.

Published by Covenant Communications, Inc.
American Fork, Utah

Printed in the United States of America
First Printing: May 2014

20 19 18 17 16 15 14   10 9 8 7 6 5 4 3 2 1

ISBN 978-1-62108-763-2

For Kent,
who took me to Maui

Acknowledgments

I'D LIKE TO GIVE SPECIAL thanks to my husband, Kent, and my children, for their unwavering love and support. Throughout all the writing deadlines I've put them through, they've never once complained—even when dinner had to be leftovers again.

Thanks also to my parents, Noel and Pat Owen, who are (and always have been) my greatest fans, and to my sister, Emily Manwaring, who willingly reads all my first drafts and consistently gives me constructive suggestions.

During the writing of this book, I entered previously uncharted territory, and I'm indebted to my brother-in-law, Aaron Olsen, for sharing his understanding of the legal world. His help was invaluable, and any mistakes are most definitely my own.

I am also grateful for my association with all the people at Covenant Communications, particularly the opportunity to work with my wonderful editor, Samantha Millburn.

One of the biggest blessings of writing for the LDS community is the opportunity to meet other authors who are not only gifted writers but also amazing people. I'm grateful for those friendships. Similarly, I am grateful for the many readers I've met or corresponded with over the years. You have touched my life for good. Thank you all.

Prologue

THE TEMPERATURE WAS DROPPING FAST. Snow that had been falling softly an hour ago was now swirling in wild eddies as the storm intensified. An icy layer coated the pines, boulders, and canyon road. Daylight was gone, and in its place, pitch-black night extinguished almost all visibility. It was perfect.

Inhaling one last, long drag from his cigarette, he cracked open the window of his truck and tossed the stub outside. He glanced at the phone on the passenger seat beside him and felt his adrenaline surge. Anytime now.

As if on cue, the phone began to vibrate. He picked it up.

"What've you got?"

"He just passed the mile marker. There's no one in front of him and no one behind. Should reach you in about four minutes."

The man gave a smug smile. "I'm on it."

He dropped the phone into his jacket pocket, turned on the headlights, cranked the steering wheel to the left, and pulled onto the road. Snow was accumulating in drifts, and visibility was even worse once he was away from the protective canyon wall. He inched forward until the hairpin bend lay immediately ahead. Then he angled the truck diagonally across both lanes of traffic, his high beams illuminating nothing but swirling snowflakes where he knew the huge drop into the base of the canyon should be.

Quickly, he pulled his dark knit cap down over his head and opened the truck door, ice crystals hitting him in an arctic blast. Covering his face with his arm, he stumbled across the road to crouch behind a large boulder. He glanced back once. He hated that he had to use his truck. He'd had it customized after the last job. But that was part of the deal this time. Any scratch on his truck and the boss got to buy him a new one. He grinned. Whatever happened in the next few minutes, he'd come out ahead.

The storm masked the sound of the approaching car but could not cover the squealing brakes, spitting gravel, and thunderous crunch of a heavy vehicle rolling down the precipice. The air reverberated with the harrowing sounds of destruction, and then there was nothing. Nothing but the relentless, howling wind.

He paused only a minute before running back to the truck. He'd have to wait until daylight to assess if any damage had been done. All that mattered now was that it was still running. He climbed into the cab, tore off his snow-covered hat, and put the truck in gear. Backing up a couple of feet, he carefully turned the vehicle until it was heading downhill. Taking the corner slowly, he took the phone out of his pocket and pushed the speed-dial button.

"Looks like you owe me some money," he said. Then he disconnected and tossed the phone onto the passenger seat. He needed to concentrate on the road.

Chapter 1

ANNOUNCEMENTS OF INCOMING AND OUTGOING flights crackled across the JFK International Airport loudspeaker system. The buzz of people talking, punctuated occasionally by a child's cry or a cell phone ringing, filled the crowded terminal. Wearily, Ben Cooper navigated the maze of backpacks and carry-on cases strewn at the feet of the many waiting passengers and made his way to a vacant chair beside the far window.

Grateful to escape the milling crowd at the terminal desk, Ben sat and tucked his duffle bag between his feet before rubbing his hand across his face. It had been a long, grueling journey—and it wasn't over yet. He glanced at the overhead monitor. So far, his flight into Salt Lake City was still showing as an on-time departure. Through the window, he could see the large jet parked at the gate. Thirty more minutes until boarding began. Compared to the time he'd already spent in the air, another half hour was nothing.

He sighed. It was surreal to be back in the U.S. His mind and body were still coming to terms with this new reality. His eyes, aching from lack of sleep, felt as though they were full of Afghan sand. He was sure his clothes, hair, and even his scraggly beard still carried dust from the desert that had been his home for the last two months.

Leaning forward, he rested his elbows on his knees, lowered his head to his hands, and shut his eyes. It had all happened so fast. Too fast. Less than twenty-four hours ago, he'd hitched a ride with an Afghan villager and ridden through a barren mountain pass in a dilapidated truck until he made it to the Kabul office, where he hadn't been for weeks. But he'd done nothing more than sit down at his desk and turn on his computer when his editor-in-chief, Pete Segal, had walked in. Ben could still picture Pete's grim expression. He'd immediately misinterpreted it.

"I know. I know," he said. "I'm late. But I promise I'll have the article to you before deadline."

Pete handed him an oblong piece of paper. "Your deadline's just been extended."

With mounting concern, Ben took the proffered paper. "What's this?"

"A ticket on the first available flight home," Pete said. Then, averting his eyes from Ben's, he continued. "We heard over a week ago but had no way of reaching you. Your brother, Jed, died in a car accident almost two weeks ago." He cleared his throat awkwardly. "I'm very sorry, Ben."

"What do you mean, 'Jed died in a car accident'?" Ben rose to his feet, his voice hoarse.

A look of genuine sorrow replaced Pete's habitually hardened expression. "I don't know the details," he admitted. "We received a phone call from an officer in the Utah Highway Patrol, who wanted to let you know as next of kin. Other than that, all we know is what we've picked up online."

Ben's grip on the airline ticket tightened. "Show me."

Pete shook his head. "Take your laptop. You'll have time at the airport. But if you don't leave now, you'll miss the flight." He picked up Ben's grimy duffle bag and thrust it at him. "I had Achmed call for a taxi as soon as you walked in the door."

It was as though he'd been punched in the stomach—and hours later, the deep ache was still there. Even after reading press releases and news reports about the accident until his computer battery died and trying to process the facts all the way across the Atlantic, Ben still couldn't believe his twin brother—his archrival as a child and his best friend as an adult—was really gone.

Their parents had waited a long time for children and had been thrilled to go from a childless home to one filled with the noise and chaos that accompanied two rambunctious boys. Their father, who had been the editor of their small-town newspaper, had been proud of the fact that when they entered college, both boys decided to major in journalism.

Jed had secured an entry-level job with *ABC News* in New York City right after graduation, and with the optimism of youth, Ben had followed his brother to the Big Apple and pounded the pavements for weeks, dropping off résumés at every newspaper, magazine, or broadcast office in Manhattan until he was contacted by the monthly news magazine *Our World*. They were looking for a new investigative reporter, and Ben finally had his foot in the publishing door.

His latest project was an article on life within an Afghan village—and he'd been living like the villagers long enough that his own life in New York now seemed like a dream. With the news of Jed's death, however, the dream had turned into a nightmare.

A wheeled carry-on case bumped against Ben's leg, and its owner muttered a halfhearted apology, bringing Ben back to the present. Reluctantly, he opened his eyes, reached for his duffle bag again, and pulled out his laptop. Then he dug deeper into his bag to retrieve the power cord. Scouring the area for an available outlet, Ben spotted one a few feet away. There were no vacant chairs nearby, but for an outlet, he was willing to sit on the floor. He'd had two months practicing sitting cross-legged in the dirt. Sitting on the airport's industrial-strength carpet would be relative luxury.

Once he'd claimed the spot and plugged in his computer, it didn't take long for it to boot up, and Ben watched with growing dismay as he accessed his e-mail account and the unread message count sped upward. At 1,034, it finally came to a halt. Sorely tempted to delete the messages en masse, Ben gritted his teeth and started scrolling through them. Party invitations were easy to ignore—especially since the events had occurred weeks before. He similarly dismissed ads flaunting Broadway attractions and not-to-be-missed sales. Ben skipped over the e-statements of his utility bills, cell phone charges, and rent payments, assuming that his bank's direct withdrawal system was functioning as it should. He noticed a couple of messages from friends at his New York office but continued scrolling down, past something from his elders quorum president (undoubtedly checking on whether or not he'd done his home teaching from Afghanistan) and something from . . . Ben's hand froze over the touchpad. There was a message from Jed.

He glanced at the date. It was sent the day before Jed's accident. Ben clicked the touchpad, and immediately, Jed's message filled the screen.

Hey, Ben.

One of my contacts in the city called me last week. Not sure why he picked me since I'm no longer there. On second thought, maybe that's why. He probably figured I wouldn't already be involved. Anyway, if there's any truth to what he told me—and my gut tells me there is— there's something big and ugly going down on Wall Street. I've done some checking from here, and I'm hitting roadblocks at every turn. Someone's done a really good job of covering their tracks or has enough

power to shut people down. Let me know when you get back in town.
Maybe I could make use of those investigative skills you like to brag
about. :)
    Jed
    P.S. Zoe's been asking about you. I think that means you're overdue
for a visit.

The ache in Ben's chest intensified. He could hear his brother's voice in
the e-mail—his teasing tone and genuine caring, along with his conviction
that Ben would share his desire to get to the bottom of a story. And Zoe.
She'd been living without her father for two weeks already. How was
she coping? Would she understand why Ben hadn't been there when she
needed him the most?

The crackle of the loudspeaker interrupted Ben's painful thoughts. He
raised his head as the woman at the terminal desk announced the initial
boarding of Delta flight 1783 into Salt Lake City. With one last glance at
Jed's e-mail, Ben shut down his computer, wound up the power cord, and
put everything away. Drawing his ticket out of his shirt pocket, he stood
and heaved his duffle bag off the floor. The initial shock over Jed's death
was slowly giving way to a terrible emptiness. He'd missed the funeral, but
he needed to go to his brother's home. He needed to hold Zoe and allow
himself time to grieve.

Chapter 2

It was late evening by the time Ben finally pulled off the canyon road and entered the long, curved driveway that led to Jed's home. He brought the small rental car to a stop beside the battered green truck parked in front of the house. Turning off the engine, he sat quietly for a moment. The last time he'd been there, the meadow beside his brother's mountain home had been green and dotted with multicolored wildflowers. The towering pine and aspen trees had been alive with the songs of birds and the rustle of forest creatures. Now, a thick layer of snow blanketed the ground. Ice crystals glistened in the moonlight. The stately trees and large, log home were frosted white. And silence hung in the crisp, cold air.

A thin trail of smoke floated above the chimney and fresh footprints in the snow leading from the pickup truck to the front door suggested that someone was home. Ben knew he should feel relieved, especially since he'd not contacted anyone about his arrival. But relief was not a good description of his current emotions. Deep sadness was better, along with a large dose of apprehension. Perhaps even something that bordered on dread. But definitely not relief. Despite the many happy memories this place should invoke, at that moment, it was impossible to overcome the aura of mourning.

Steeling himself, Ben opened the car door. He reached over to grab his duffle bag from the backseat before stepping outside and locking the car. He was within about ten yards of the porch when the motion-sensitive lights flashed on and a dog started barking. Ben looked up at the solid front door and shook his head. No matter what else had changed in the household, it sounded like Jed's crazy dog, Turbo, was still in residence.

Turbo's barks crescendoed as Ben reached the door and pushed the doorbell. He heard a man's voice calling the dog and the scuffle of the animal's paws on the tile. Then the door opened, and a slightly stooped, gray-haired man stood in the doorway, clutching Turbo by the collar. He looked at Ben, muttered a soft exclamation, and stepped out onto the porch. Ben ran a hand over his unkempt beard, suddenly conscious of his disheveled appearance.

"I came as soon as I heard," he began. "I . . ."

"Ben!" The man's voice was hoarse with emotion. "It's good to have you back."

He let go of the dog, which gave a joyous yelp and bolted for the meadow. Then the man grasped Ben's right hand in his and drew him in for a hug.

"We've missed you, boy," he said. "We've been praying that you'd get here soon."

Ben swallowed the lump in his throat. "I'm sorry, Bert," he said. "I was in the desert. No contact with the outside world until today . . . yesterday . . ." He paused, trying to sort out the time zones. "I got here as fast as I could."

"Didn't stop to pick up a winter coat, I see," Bert said, stepping back and assessing Ben's thin cotton khakis.

Ben shook his head. "Nope. And no shower or shave either."

"You're a sight for sore eyes, boy. I'll tell you that!" Bert slapped him on the back. "A marvelous sight for sore eyes." He turned toward the door. "Come on in before you freeze. There's someone else who wants to see you."

Bert gave a piercing whistle, and with a flurry of legs, Turbo charged past the men and into the house, sliding out of control on the tile as he entered.

"Fool dog," Bert muttered under his breath, and Ben caught himself smiling for the first time in over twenty-four hours.

His smile didn't last long, however. Bert led him into the spacious family room and there, sitting in a wheelchair beside the fire, was Bert's wife, Dorothy. Angry red scratches covered her face, and the surrounding skin was mottled shades of yellow, green, and purple. A bald patch above one ear exposed a row of stitches. One arm was tucked against her chest in a sling, and her left leg was cast all the way to her hip. It rested on a horizontal bar that protruded from the wheelchair, preventing her from sitting very close to the small table, where a mug of steaming hot chocolate sat.

She looked up as the men walked into the room, and Ben saw surprise, followed almost immediately by pleasure, cross her battered features.

"Ben!" she cried, holding out her one functioning arm.

Ben stepped forward. "Dorothy." Shock filled his voice. "I read that there was another passenger, but I had no idea . . ."

"Tsk!" She brushed off his distress. "None of that! Those fussy doctors wouldn't have let me come home yesterday if they hadn't been sure I was on the mend—especially living this far from the city. Besides, Bert, here, is waiting on me hand and foot. Who could ask for more than that?"

Ben could think of many things Dorothy could ask for, but he didn't dare voice them. Dorothy had been a best friend to his mother and had stepped in to help when Jed's marriage had dissolved and he'd returned to Utah. Dorothy and Bert had never had children of their own but had been willing to leave their old home and take on the roles of Jed's housekeeper and handyman, along with becoming Zoe's surrogate grandparents. They had become family, and Ben hated to see Dorothy so badly hurt.

Dorothy gave him a gentle smile and patted his hand with her own. "When did you find out?" she asked.

Ben raked his fingers through his dark hair. "Today. Yesterday. I was in Afghanistan. Living in a village out in the boonies. No running water, no electricity, no communication with anyone else. The deadline for my article was looming, so when I found out that one of the village leaders was heading to Kabul, I bribed him into taking me along. I left him at the outskirts of the city and made my way to the bureau alone. I'd barely walked into the office when my editor told me about Jed and handed me my airline ticket. I've been traveling ever since." He took a deep breath and looked at Dorothy. "I've read every report I could access on my computer, but I need to know . . . did he . . ."

"I really don't think he suffered," Dorothy said, squeezing Ben's hand reassuringly. "It all happened so fast, and the coroner said he died instantly."

"Can you tell me about it?" Ben asked.

Behind him, Ben heard Bert take a step toward his wife. Dorothy looked over at him and shook her head. "It's all right, Bert. I've gone over it again and again with the police—and a million more times in my mind. Ben needs to hear it from me."

Bert's expression remained troubled, but he took a seat next to her without a word. Turbo trotted across the room and collapsed in a heap at Bert's feet. The older man leaned over and absently stroked the dog's head, his eyes never leaving his wife's face. Dorothy leaned back in the wheelchair, collecting her thoughts.

"We knew the storm was coming," she began. "They'd been forecasting it for days, but Bert had the Stowells' boy up here chopping wood with him all week, and I didn't want to interrupt them to have Bert drive me down the canyon to the grocery store, so we made do until Saturday. That day, Jed had been working on something on his computer and said he needed to go back to the studio to pick up some papers. I asked if he'd drop me off at the grocery store on his way. It didn't seem like it was any bother, and even though the sky was overcast, there was still no sign of the storm." Dorothy gave a small smile. "Jed even joked that the station weatherman was the only person he knew who could be wrong 75 percent of the time and still keep his job."

Ben gave an answering smile, knowing full well how Jed felt about some of the more-flash-than-substance weathermen he'd worked with.

"Zoe stayed here with Bert," Dorothy continued. "Snowflakes were beginning to fall by the time we reached the valley, but Jed was confident that we could get back before the roads got too bad. He dropped me off and promised to return in half an hour. Forty-five minutes later, the groceries were in the trunk and we were heading home again.

"It had gotten dark while I was shopping, and the snow was much heavier. What made matters worse was that once we entered the canyon, the wind picked up and the snow started drifting across the road. The conditions were bad, and I confess, I was a bit anxious. But Jed knew the canyon road like the back of his hand and was taking it slowly."

Dorothy paused, and Ben saw her grip on the arm of the wheelchair tighten. "We came to the bottom of the bend right below Angel Falls. Jed turned the corner, and suddenly there was a bright light."

Ben sat forward. "There was another car?" he gasped. "Why didn't it say that in any of the reports?"

Dorothy shook her head. "I don't know if it was a car," she said helplessly. "There was so much blowing snow, it was hard to make out anything, and it didn't seem like the lights were moving. It wasn't like headlights coming at us—it was more like a floodlight." She looked at Ben, her face stricken. "I've tried to remember—every day I've tried, Ben. But it all happened so fast. There was the light. Jed braked. The car slid. I can still hear the sound of crunching metal and broken glass, branches hitting the car as we fell . . ." Her voice broke. She lifted a shaking hand to her face.

Bert rose from his seat and moved to stand behind the wheelchair. He placed his hand on Dorothy's shoulder and gave it a gentle squeeze. "I'll take you to your room," he said, the gruffness in his voice not quite masking his emotion.

"No!" Dorothy lowered her hand and uncovered her tears. "No, Bert. Let me finish." She looked over at Ben. "When the rescue team found us, Jed was gone, and I was unconscious," she said. "I have no memory of anything after the fall until I woke up in the hospital two days later.

"I've told the police everything I've told you, but since there were no reports of any other accidents in the canyon that night and no one else has come forward with information, I think they've explained my statement of seeing a light as confusion caused by head trauma or a near-death experience—depending on which officer was writing the report."

"But haven't they gone back to look for evidence?" Ben asked. "If Jed's car impacted before it went off the road, there'd be broken glass or something there."

Dorothy shook her head. "Detective Roman was the only officer who kept questioning me about the light. I asked if they'd found anything, and he said that by the time Bert found us and the rescue crew reached us, the snowplows had been through twice. If there'd been evidence left on the road, it was plowed into the canyon with the rest of the wreckage."

"But you think there was another car?" Ben pressed.

"I don't know what to think anymore," Dorothy confessed. "I know that something made Jed brake. I don't remember seeing a car coming toward us, but I do remember light."

"And you think you hit something before going off the road?" Ben asked.

"I remember the sound more than anything," Dorothy said. "The grinding of metal and then falling."

She grew silent. Bert shifted but didn't move from his position beside his wife. Ben stood and paced over to the fireplace.

"It took us four hours to find 'em," Bert said quietly, taking up the story. "I planned on 'em taking extra time to get home 'cause of the weather, but when they were an hour late, I started callin'. When neither one of 'em answered, I called 911, put Zoe in the truck, and headed down the canyon. The police checked the TV station and knew that Jed had come and gone. The store clerk even remembered seein' Dorothy. I reckon the storm stopped most people from going in after she left.

"Once we knew they'd started back, we got to searchin' the canyon road. But conditions were real bad, and I drove past the place they'd gone off the road two times before I saw all the broken trees.

"I left Zoe in the truck and went to check it out. The truck's high beams picked up the destruction, and even with all the blowin' snow, I could tell there was somethin' down in the gorge. Search and rescue got there within twenty minutes—along with the police. One of the lady officers took care of Zoe in her squad car until Sister Stowell arrived. Zoe left with Sister Stowell before the rescuers had anyone out of the car. I stayed and went to the hospital with the ambulance."

Ben could only too easily envision how awful that night had been for everyone involved. With no one else to care for Zoe at home, Ben was grateful his brother's neighbor had been willing to take her, but it was hard to imagine that the little girl could make it through an experience like that unscathed.

He glanced over at the dimly lit hall that led to his young niece's bedroom. "How's she doing?" he asked.

Bert cleared his throat and looked down at Dorothy. Ben watched with growing alarm as tears began to roll down Dorothy's face again.

"We don't know," she whispered. "She's gone."

Chapter 3

RACHEL HAMILTON STEPPED ONTO THE lanai and into paradise. It had been dark when she'd arrived at the hotel the night before, and although she'd been vaguely aware of lush tropical foliage, balmy warm temperatures, and the rhythm of distant waves, she'd been too tired to do more than accept her key at the hotel's front desk, locate her room on the sixth floor, and collapse, gratefully, into bed. Now, however, with the sun coming up in the cloudless sky, she took a few minutes to soak in the view before her.

Just below, tall palm trees lined a cobblestone path that meandered between manicured grassy areas and decorative ponds. A narrow, slow-moving stream linked the ponds, and the path cut back and forth across the stream via low wooden bridges, eventually reaching a large swimming pool surrounded by rows of white chaise lounges. A thick green hedge, dotted with brightly colored yellow and hot-pink flowers, separated the swimming pool area from the white-sand beach beyond. And then as far as the eye could see was the sparkling blue ocean. It was a breathtaking view in Technicolor brilliance—and a far cry from the wintery-gray world she'd left behind in Washington, DC.

When she'd first opened her eyes this morning, Rachel had stared up at the bamboo ceiling fan for all of two minutes before deciding that no measure of you-need-more-sleep reasoning could overcome her first-morning-in-Hawaii excitement. That's when she'd abandoned the bed for the lanai. And now, as she watched dawn paint the sky, she was ready to abandon the lanai for the beach.

It didn't take long for Rachel to put on her running shoes, T-shirt, and shorts. Tucking her cell phone into her pocket, she left her room and made her way to the elevator. The hotel was quiet, and she didn't see anyone until she reached the main lobby. A couple of young men dressed in bright blue

Hawaiian-print shirts were working behind the desk. An older Polynesian woman was tending to a huge planter full of flowering orchids. Her dress matched the men's shirts, and she wore a lei of purple plumeria flowers.

Rachel crossed the marble-tiled floor, passing the small fountains and stunning flower displays and stepping through the pillared entryway. There was a slight chill to the early-morning air, but she barely noticed. Cutting through the hotel's manicured grounds, she reached the winding path that followed the coastline. The view was breathtaking, and she quickly turned off the path and scrambled down a sandy trail to the beach.

Slipping off her shoes, she walked to the water's edge. Her feet sank slightly in the cold, wet sand, and as she stood waiting for the froth of the incoming waves to reach her, she thought back over her experiences of the last few days and wondered for the millionth time what she was doing in Hawaii.

Despite the fact that she'd worked for Arizona Senator Troy Sheldon for over a year, up until now, her responsibilities had been menial. She knew the senator was in Hawaii to facilitate a trade agreement between the U.S. and Japan—specifically, he was representing a fledgling biomedical company headquartered in Arizona. But other than Rachel and the senator both having a vested interest in Arizona, Rachel wasn't sure why she had been singled out to aid with the negotiations. The fact that she had been singled out was undeniable—and unfortunately, the entire staff at the DC office was aware of it.

Two phone calls—that was all it had taken to have her on the first flight out of Dulles and into Maui. The first call came to Senator Sheldon's office in the midafternoon. She was filing newspaper articles about the senator's recent trip to the Far East when Kelly, the office receptionist, called Rachel over to her desk and handed her the phone. She was surprised to hear the voice on the line.

"Rachel, this is Karl Trost," the senator's personal secretary said. "I'm calling to confirm some information in your personal bio."

"Okay," she replied, trying to hide her bewilderment.

"I have you listed as a Latter-day Saint," he went on. "Is that right?"

"Yes," she said.

"I gather you've never been married, but do you come from a large family?"

"I'm the oldest of seven children," she replied, confused by the direction Karl's questions were taking.

"Thank you," Karl said. "That's all I needed to know. I'll be in touch."

And with that, he ended the phone call. Rachel handed the phone back to Kelly, and at Kelly's upraised eyebrows, Rachel just shook her head.

"I have no idea what that was all about," she said.

Kelly shrugged, and Rachel went back to her filing. But it wasn't as easy to file away her concerns. Why had Karl called to ask about her religion and her family? Did the senator have issues with either of them? As far as she knew, none of her little brothers had gotten into any trouble—at least nothing that would concern a senator. And as a native of Arizona, Senator Sheldon would be well aware of the large LDS population in the state. She'd be surprised if he would take umbrage with her religious views—he wouldn't want to ruffle the feathers of that portion of the voting populace. Karl's questions made no sense. But Rachel couldn't deny that she found them unsettling.

Two hours later, the second phone call came in. Once again, she took the call at Kelly's desk, and once again, it was brief.

"Rachel, this is Karl. The senator would like you to join him in Hawaii. I've booked you on a flight leaving from Dulles tomorrow morning at 6:10, and I'll have a driver meet you when you arrive at the Kahului airport. You'll be getting in late, so we'll expect you at the senator's hotel suite at 8:00 a.m. the next day."

Rachel listened in stunned silence, and Karl must have taken her lack of response for agreement because he continued. "Oh, and plan on being here for about a week—we're not sure exactly how long our meetings will go."

"I fly out tomorrow?" she finally managed to say.

"That's right. Check in at the Delta desk. They'll issue you an e-ticket."

"Is there . . . Is there anything from the office that you need me to bring?" she asked.

Karl laughed. "Nothing from the office. But sunscreen and a swimsuit would be a good idea."

"Uh, okay." Rachel didn't know how to respond to that.

But Karl apparently wasn't expecting anything more from her. "Great. I'll see you the day after tomorrow," he said.

"Eight o'clock at the senator's suite," she repeated. But Karl had already hung up.

Kelly took back her phone. If it were possible, her eyebrows were even more raised than they had been the first time.

"The senator wants me in Hawaii," Rachel told her.

"What for?" Kelly asked.

"Your guess is as good as mine," was all Rachel could say.

Kelly frowned and turned back to her computer in stony silence.

Unfortunately, it seemed that Kelly's silence hadn't lasted long. By the time Rachel left the office that day, word had spread. The rest of the office staff had also been frowning.

Rachel sighed at the memory and began walking along the water's edge. The sand was already warming under the sun's morning rays. She heard voices and turned her head. More early risers were arriving, hauling deck chairs, umbrellas, mats, and totes overflowing with brightly colored toys. Pulling her cell phone out of her pocket, Rachel glanced at the time and quickened her pace. She had an eight o'clock appointment to keep.

Chapter 4

BEN STARED AT BERT AND Dorothy. "What do you mean Zoe's gone? Where is she?"

"Whitney took her," Bert said.

"Whitney?" Ben was having a hard time thinking clearly.

"Her mother," Dorothy added in a whisper.

The fingers of dread that Ben had sensed in the car now had him in a stranglehold. Somehow, he made it back to the chair and sat down heavily. "Whitney's had nothing to do with Zoe for over four years," he said. "What happened?"

"Jed's death happened," Bert said shortly.

Ben felt as though he'd been punched—again. "I know that, Bert," he said through gritted teeth. "And I'm doing my best to come to terms with it. What I don't know is why his four-year-old daughter is now living with the woman who left her at eight weeks old and hasn't wanted anything to do with her since!"

"Because you were in Afghanistan, Dorothy was in a coma, and I'm an old man who was livin' at the hospital," Bert said bitterly. "You have no idea how bad it was, Ben! I know your name and our names are on Jed's will for Zoe's care. Dorothy has cried every night over the fact that she's gone, but when Whitney showed up sayin' she wanted her daughter, no one could stop her."

"But why?" Ben said. "Why, after all these years, would she suddenly show up wanting Zoe? It makes no sense."

"Maybe she's finally ready to be a mother, have a family," Dorothy suggested.

"Not unless she's done a complete overhaul of her priorities over the last few months. Last time I saw her name, it was in the society pages. She was partying with celebrities, not hanging out with stay-at-home moms of preschoolers!"

"Well, she did just get married again," Dorothy offered.

Ben's eyes widened. He tried to remember the names of the men he'd seen linked to Whitney in the gossip magazines. "Who did she marry?"

"Some senator," Bert said. "That was her big thing when she was here. As a married woman, she could give Zoe a good home with two parents. I reckon she thinks Dorothy and I are too old and feeble for the job and that you're not around enough."

Ben groaned and raked his fingers through his hair. The thought of Whitney raising Zoe made him sick, but he couldn't deny the fact that his current career left little room for anyone else in his life—especially a child. For the first time, he entertained the sobering thought that perhaps *his* priorities needed to be revamped as much as Whitney's.

With sudden, unexpected clarity, Ben realized that as of that moment, his focus had to change. It might require some fast-talking with his managing editor, perhaps even a leave of absence from *Our World*. Whatever it took, he was going to do everything in his power to honor his brother's last wishes and care for the people he loved.

"We'll get Zoe back," Ben said, rising to his feet again. "Whitney relinquished custody years ago. Zoe belongs here with us."

He saw hope flare in Dorothy's eyes, but Bert's expression remained grim.

"You're goin' to need a good lawyer," Bert warned. "That was one determined woman who came here for Zoe."

"Well, she may not know it yet," Ben responded with feeling, "but she's about to meet her match."

* * *

When Ben entered the kitchen the next morning, he looked and felt like a new man. Complete exhaustion had finally overcome the maelstrom of emotions he'd experienced the day before, and he'd slept for almost eight hours. A warm shower, a thorough shave, and some clean clothes had worked their magic too. He was a man with a mission, and waking up with direction was easier than simply waking up to grieve.

Bert was at the kitchen table working on a stack of pancakes.

"Help yerself," he mumbled through a mouthful as he pointed at a plate of pancakes on the counter.

"Thanks." Ben picked up a plate. "Did you make these?"

"Yup." He nodded. "But don't get yer hopes up. Pancakes and opening a can of soup are about my limit. We're going to have to go pick up some frozen dinners if we want to survive until Dorothy's back on her feet."

"Nah . . . I can do grilled cheese sandwiches, nachos, and Pop-Tarts. We're going to live like kings!"

Bert snorted. "If you think Dorothy's going to let us get away with that, you've got another thing comin'. She may not be movin' real fast right now, but she's still the boss of the kitchen."

"Thanks for the reminder," Ben said with a smile. "Maybe we'd better get a grocery list from her this morning. I'm going into town to see Jed's lawyer; I can pick stuff up while I'm there."

Bert nodded and carried his plate over to the sink. Opening a nearby drawer, he pulled out a cream-colored business card.

"Jed's lawyer," he said, handing Ben the card.

Ben took it and read *Blaine Thompson, Attorney-at-Law* embossed in gold letters above a Salt Lake City address and phone number.

"Tell me this is not who I think it is," Ben said, giving Bert a piercing look.

"Depends on who you think it is," Bert responded with a shrug.

"Blaine-the-Pain Thompson."

"Pretty sure I heard Jed call him that once or twice," Bert admitted.

Ben shook his head in disbelief. "Are you kidding? What was Jed thinking?"

"I dunno." Bert shuffled his feet uncomfortably. "Seems like he said somethin' about it being what yer mother would have wanted him to do."

"Not if it meant losing his daughter!"

"Well, I reckon that's true," Bert said. "But he had no way of knowin' that, now did he?"

Ben thought back to the awful junior high year when Blaine-the-Pain had moved next door to them in their small hometown. Blaine's mother had confided in their mother that Blaine felt ostracized by the youth in the area. She'd made it sound like the youth were being purposely exclusive, when in actuality Blaine had no interest in the fishing, tubing, or dirt biking the other boys loved.

Unfortunately, their mother had taken the conversation to heart. Despite their protests that Blaine didn't want to hang out with them, she'd insisted that her boys include Blaine in all their summer activities. It had been the longest summer vacation of Ben's life and the only time he ever remembered being grateful for the beginning of another school year.

By the time the next summer rolled around, Blaine had become friends with another boy who preferred being at home on the computer. Jed and Ben's vacation had been saved.

"How did Jed find him?" Ben asked.

"Don't think he did," Bert said. "More like the other way round. Seems like Blaine came to see Jed at the TV studio. Told him he'd just started a new law firm and was lookin' for business."

Ben groaned. "I always told Jed he was a pushover."

"Well, then, it's a good thing you're the one having to talk to this Blaine fellow today, isn't it?" Bert said.

Ben grimaced. "Did Blaine do anything when Whitney took Zoe?"

Bert shrugged again. "He showed up after the funeral. Whitney was already here with some social worker lady. Blaine told them Jed had a will and he'd listed you as Zoe's guardian, and if you weren't able to take her that she was to stay with Dorothy and me. The social worker said somethin' about you being gone and Dorothy being in the hospital, making Whitney the only good choice. Seems like she threw in something about a mother's rights too."

"And he just accepted that?" Ben asked incredulously.

"Don't reckon he knew quite what to say," Bert said. "From that point on, those two women took over. The social worker had Zoe's bag packed in about ten minutes, and they were gone in another five."

Bert tossed the frying pan into the sink with a little more force than necessary. "I should've stopped them since that lily-livered lawyer didn't. But just coming off Jed's funeral and with Dorothy barely alive herself, I wasn't even thinkin' straight."

"The timing was too perfect," Ben said. "It wasn't an accident that Whitney came for Zoe when she knew she'd meet the least resistance."

Another dish got a beating in the sink, but Bert didn't look up. "Well, she had her moment, then," he said gruffly. "Now you go find our little girl. Make sure she's all right. Then bring her back home!"

Chapter 5

RACHEL STOOD OUTSIDE THE SUITE door and took a deep breath, then she ran a hand down her navy-blue pencil skirt to smooth out all the imagined wrinkles. Her navy flats and white, short-sleeved blouse completed her outfit, and she hoped she appeared professional despite her nervousness. With her purse over her shoulder and a notebook clutched in one hand, she raised the other hand and knocked.

She heard footsteps, and Karl Trost opened the door.

"Rachel," he said with a welcoming smile. "Glad you made it. How was the flight?"

"Fine, thank you," she replied, stepping into a large sitting room.

Two sofas and an armchair surrounded a coffee table and a large flat-screen TV on one side of the room. The coffee table held a couple of glasses, a takeout box, and a teddy bear dressed in a Hawaiian shirt. Two men, silently thumbing through magazines, sat on either end of one of the sofas.

On the other side of the room, there was a large dining table complete with six matching chairs. Papers stood in small stacks on the table next to two open laptop computers. Senator Sheldon was sitting in front of one of the laptops, and as Rachel walked in, the senator rose and stepped forward to shake her hand. "Thank you for coming at such short notice, Rachel," he said.

"It's my pleasure," Rachel said. "I think most of your office staff in DC would have traded me in a heartbeat. Hawaii has a lot more appeal than Washington in early February."

Senator Sheldon smiled. "You have a point," he said. "I hope the pleasant surroundings will make your job here a little easier."

Rachel recognized the segue she'd been hoping for. "I'm sure it will," she said. "Although, to be honest, Karl was rather vague about my assignment."

She did not miss the look that passed between the two men. At the senator's nod, Karl turned to her.

"You were brought here because you are a trusted member of Senator Sheldon's staff," he began. "You've already passed the necessary security screenings, and hopefully, we need not remind you that any information you are privy to—whether it be in relation to the senator's work or his private life—remains private."

"Of course," Rachel said.

"As you know," Karl continued, "Senator Sheldon and his wife were married a few months ago. What you may not know is that this is Mrs. Sheldon's second marriage. Although her first marriage didn't last long, she does have a daughter by that marriage. Up until a few days ago, the child was living with her father. Two weeks ago, he was killed in a car accident. Mrs. Sheldon was apprised of the situation and was immediately concerned for the welfare of her daughter. She flew to Utah, where she reclaimed custody of the little girl."

Rachel's eyes flew to the teddy bear on the coffee table. "And her daughter is here with you now," she said.

Karl nodded. "Yes. Her name is Zoe. She's four years old."

"It must have been very difficult for her," Rachel said, her heart going out to the little girl who had lost so much so young.

"I believe it has," Karl said. "Which is why we've brought you here."

Rachel looked at him blankly. "What can I do to help?"

"Zoe's arrival was obviously unexpected," Karl said, circumventing Rachel's question. "Mrs. Sheldon has many engagements in Hawaii. Engagements that she cannot attend accompanied by a child. Unfortunately, Zoe is too young for the hotel's kids program. She does, however, require childcare. The senator and his wife feel that leaving Zoe with an assortment of babysitters supplied by the hotel would not be in Zoe's best interest—or for that matter, in the senator's best interest, given the confidential nature of his work here."

Rachel knew she was staring. She hoped her mouth wasn't actually gaping as the reason for Karl's lengthy explanation about Whitney Sheldon's daughter finally became clear. "You brought me here to be a babysitter?" There was no denying the accusation in her voice. She took a step back toward the door as another thought hit her. "Those questions on the phone about my family . . . ? You just wanted to know if I had any experience taking care of children."

"You're right, Rachel." Senator Sheldon spoke now. "But I wish you would take it as a compliment, not an insult."

"A compliment!" Rachel swung to face the senator. "I came here believing I would finally have the opportunity to use the political science degree I spent so long acquiring, that I would finally be making a real contribution, not only within our own political system but internationally too. And you expect me to be complimented that I was chosen to babysit a four-year-old instead?"

"Perhaps I *should* have you look over some of the treaties we're attempting to broker this week," Senator Sheldon said. "A pair of fresh eyes and another perspective are always a good thing. But I'll be honest with you, Rachel. There are several members of my staff with more experience who could do that. However, based on all the personal bios I reviewed, you are quite possibly the only one who would know how to cope with a young child." He paused, then said, "This is not a trivial assignment. Apart from the fact that Zoe is adjusting to a new situation, her security is a factor. Her father was a well-known news anchor. Interest has been high in his death and in his daughter. It's vital for Zoe's well-being that reporters not have any access to her."

"It sounds like you'd be better off with someone trained in security," Rachel countered.

"We thought of that," the senator agreed. "But my security detail is already stretched thin covering Mrs. Sheldon and me—especially as we're often at different locations. And the fact remains, none of them are qualified to care for a young child."

"I don't think I'm qualified to do that either," Rachel said.

"I realize you've had no formal training in childcare," the senator said, "but I know enough about large LDS families to know that you've had more experience than most single women your age."

In one of the rooms off the sitting room, a child began to cry. The two men on the sofa, Karl, and the senator all turned toward the sound. When Senator Sheldon turned back to face Rachel, there was desperation in his eyes.

"An all-expenses-paid week in Hawaii, and I'll pay you time-and-a-half to take the assignment."

Rachel's thoughts flew back to the brief magical moments she'd spent on the lanai and at the beach that morning, and her indignation began to waver. She was being offered a week full of moments like that, and she wouldn't have to pay a penny for them. Not to mention the fact that returning to cold, gray Washington, DC, tomorrow and facing an office full of questions held little appeal.

"Can I study the notes from your negotiation meetings when I'm not with Zoe?" she asked.

"As I said before, you already have security clearance," Senator Sheldon said. "I'll list you as a political aide. I don't think there will be any problems with that."

The sound of crying coming from behind the closed door intensified. Rachel glanced that way. One week. Surely she could do one week. Especially if it meant a chance to review the treaty with Japan firsthand, to be—even minutely—involved with history in the making.

Rachel took a deep breath. "Okay," she said, "I'll do it."

Senator Sheldon gave her one of his vote-winning smiles and reached out to shake her hand again.

"Thank you, Rachel. You'll be an invaluable member of our team here in Hawaii."

Rachel waited for the heaviness of heart that should accompany selling herself short—but it didn't come. Instead, she experienced an unexpected surge of excitement. This would be a new adventure. Certainly not what she'd originally envisioned, but if making a difference was really important to her, she could do that. Even if it was only for one very sad little girl.

Karl reached over, picked up a manila envelope from the table, and handed it to Rachel. "This has all the information you should need," he said. "A copy of your tentative schedule, the senator's schedule, and Mrs. Sheldon's schedule; a copy of the suite key; and a prepaid credit card. Any purchases you need to make within the resort for either you or Zoe can be charged to Senator Sheldon's room. Other purchases can be made using this credit card. Its current balance is $2,000."

Rachel's eyes widened.

"Transportation, entrance fees, tours, meals . . . you name it," Karl explained. "They'll add up quickly."

"You're okay with me doing those things?" she asked.

Senator Sheldon gave a short laugh. "We don't expect you to entertain Zoe in the hotel suite all day, every day. Spending time at the hotel pool and the beach is obvious, but if you want to take her to the aquarium or something, that's fine."

"Can Zoe swim?" Rachel asked, scanning the papers in the folder and not finding any information on the child. "Food allergies? Bedtime? What about those kinds of things?"

For the first time, Senator Sheldon looked uncomfortable. "There's a great deal we don't know. We're all functioning on a high learning curve when it comes to Zoe."

"I see," Rachel said.

And she did. She was going into this job blind, and there was no one who knew any more than she did. She glanced at the schedule in her hand. It looked like her new duties were to begin immediately. Taking a deep breath, she pinned a smile on her face. "Then I guess it's time Zoe and I met each other," she said.

Chapter 6

BLAINE THOMPSON'S LAW OFFICE WAS part of a small strip mall in an older part of Salt Lake City. Ben pulled into the almost empty parking lot and looked around. Immediately in front of him was a glass door that read *Blaine Thompson, Attorney-at-Law* in the same gold lettering printed on the business card in Ben's wallet. The suite next door had a bright yellow sign advertising cash advances, and the one after that appeared to be a chiropractor's office. With no one in sight, the lights shining through the office windows were the only indication that the businesses were open.

After two months in the Afghan desert, stepping out of the car into Utah's frigid winter temperatures was still a shock. Ben zipped up the coat Dorothy had made him take from Jed's closet and was grateful for her insistence. Quickly, he walked over to the gold-lettered door and pulled it open. As he walked in, a young woman sitting behind a desk raised her head. Whatever she'd been about to say froze on her lips, and she stared at Ben as though seeing a ghost.

In fact, Ben realized instantly, she probably thought he really was a ghost. As identical twins, he and Jed had gotten used to being confused for each other. They had often found it easier to answer to the other one's name than to explain the mix-up. Not anymore. Tamping down the sorrow that thought evoked, Ben stepped forward. "Hi. I'm Ben Cooper, Jed's brother," he explained.

"You're Jed Cooper's brother," the young woman repeated as though trying to convince herself of its truthfulness.

"Yes," Ben said. "I'd like to speak with Blaine Thompson, please."

Color was returning to the receptionist's face. She took one more long look at Ben before lifting a telephone receiver. "Let me see if he's available," she said.

It took only a moment. "Mr. Thompson will be right with you," she said, lowering the phone.

"Thanks," Ben said as a man entered the reception area from a room behind the receptionist's desk.

"Ben," he said, extending his hand. "Good to see you again." Lowering his voice slightly, he continued. "Please accept my heartfelt condolences on Jed's passing."

Ben shook the hand extended to him and tried not to show his shock. Time had not been kind to Blaine Thompson. Gone was the skinny, spectacled kid with a thatch of dark brown hair. Standing in front of him was a balding man with a rounded belly barely hidden by his suit coat. He looked ten years older than he should be, and if it hadn't been for the distinctive blue eyes peering back at him through dark-rimmed glasses, Ben would have been sure he had the wrong Blaine Thompson.

"I arrived late last night," he told Blaine. "I gather you're the person I need to speak to about Jed's will."

Blaine cleared his throat awkwardly and nodded. "Let's talk in my office, shall we?"

He led the way into a small room furnished with a large, dark wooden desk, a desk chair, two wingback chairs, three large filing cabinets, and a narrow bookshelf loaded with large tomes. Ben shook off a feeling of claustrophobia at the cramped quarters and slid into one of the wingback chairs. Blaine took a seat behind the desk.

"I'd like a copy of Jed's will and any other legal papers he left with you," Ben began.

"I have them here," Blaine said, opening a green folder and handing Ben a sheaf of papers. "On the top is Jed's will. Then there's the deed to his house. The other documents are related to his stock market purchases and sales. Any current holdings along with earlier transactions are listed. Jed was his own accountant, but he had me keep all the certificates with his other papers. The assets Jed liquidated over the last couple of years were deposited into a trust fund for Zoe. The particulars regarding the trust fund are also there."

Ben flipped through the papers, noting the various documents as Blaine itemized them before returning to the will at the top of the pile. His name was listed in bold font as Zoe's guardian.

"Do you want to explain to me why you let Whitney take Zoe when you knew Jed had given me guardianship?" Ben asked.

"I didn't have much choice." Blaine squirmed under Ben's look of disbelief. "We failed to reach you in Afghanistan. Jed's housekeeper was in no position to take care of anyone. And to be honest, neither was her husband. It seemed providential that Mrs. Sheldon would arrive and want to take her daughter—certainly preferable to having the child go into foster care."

"Oh yeah, it was providential in that it saved you from any kind of legal entanglement or paperwork." Ben was having a hard time keeping his temper in check. "But it was hardly providential for Zoe. You have no idea what a non-mother you've just sent that little girl to live with—a little girl who has now lost her father and everything and everyone remotely familiar to her. I'm pretty sure this is *not* what Jed was paying you the big bucks for!"

Blaine's face turned an ugly shade of red. "I have personally met Senator Sheldon. He's a very impressive man. I have no doubt that someone of his standing will do right by the child. Besides which," he blustered, "Jed did not hire me as a custody lawyer."

"You're right," Ben said, placing the documents back into the folder and coming to his feet. "And neither will I."

Blaine stood too, the color now draining from his face. "I would be happy to help . . ."

But Ben was already at the door, the folder in his hand. He turned to Blaine, surprised at the desperation in the lawyer's eyes. "Do you know where she took Zoe?" he asked.

Blaine shook his head. "Senator Sheldon's from Arizona, but they must have a house in the DC area too."

"Well, that's a start," Ben said and walked out of the office.

As soon as he was in his car, Ben scrolled through the contacts in his phone until he found Zach Bennett's number. He pushed the call button and was filtering onto the main road when Zach answered the phone.

"Hey, Zach. This is Ben."

"Ben! Where are you calling from?" Zach asked.

"Utah," Ben replied.

"I didn't know you were back from Afghanistan," Zach said.

"I got back yesterday. My brother was killed in a car accident two weeks ago, but I only just got word."

There was a pause before Zach's voice came over the phone again. "Hey, man, I'm really sorry."

"Thanks," Ben said. "It's been a rough few days, and I'm facing another big problem here, so I'm calling *Our World's* big-shot in-house lawyer for help."

Zach gave a short laugh. "You must be desperate! What do you need?"

Ben told him about Jed's will and explained what had happened with Zoe and Whitney. "I just left Jed's lawyer's office. I'm wondering if I can fax you some documents. Take a look at them and tell me what you think."

"You don't trust this guy?"

"I'm not as worried about his honesty as I am about his competence," Ben said. "This is too important to mess up with a lawyer who doesn't know how to do his job. I have to get Zoe back."

"I'll take a look at the documents and get back with you," Zach promised.

"Thanks," Ben said. "I'm pulling into a copy shop now. You should have the fax in the next few minutes."

Ben faxed a copy of every sheet in the green folder to Zach before heading to the grocery store with Dorothy's list. Aware of many stares, several pointed fingers, and a few whispers directed his way, Ben made quick work of the shopping. Looking like his TV anchor brother had never been such an uncomfortable experience, and he was relieved when he was back in the car, heading up the canyon.

He'd almost reached Jed's home when his phone rang. It was Zach.

"Wow! That was fast!" Ben said by way of greeting.

"It was interesting reading," Zach said.

"Only a lawyer would say that," Ben said, and he heard Zach chuckle. "Anything I need to know?"

"Do you want the good news or the bad news?"

Ben sighed. "I'm going to need both, aren't I?"

"'Fraid so," Zach said cheerfully. "The good news is that the will is probably legally enforceable. The bad news is, it's about the weakest piece of legal writing I've ever seen."

"Give me the bottom line," Ben said. "How is weak writing going to impact what happens to Zoe?"

"The will has you listed as Zoe's guardian unless you're unable to care for her, in which case, Albert and Dorothy Dickson have guardianship. It then states that the money in Zoe's trust fund is to be dispersed at the discretion of her caregiver."

"That makes sense," Ben said.

"It's a legal minefield," Zach exclaimed. "An iron-clad will lists one person as the trustee who oversees the trust fund and disperses the money at specified times in the child's life. In almost all instances, the trustee is someone other than the caregiver. That protects the child from reckless spending by the caregiver and possible misuse of the trust fund." Zach let that sink in. "What you have in your brother's will is an open invitation for abuse. Whoever is appointed as Zoe's caregiver will have free rein over her trust fund. Since she's currently with her mother, I would assume her mother intends to contest. If she wins, not only will she keep Zoe, she'll also keep the money."

"But what are her chances of winning with my name on the will?" Ben asked.

"To be honest," Zach said, "her chances are good. There's a basic constitutional right that parents have over their biological children. Her lawyer will probably argue that the constitution trumps a will. It's likely he'll also use the "best interest of the child" standard. In that case, the judge will pit having Zoe live with a happily married mother against her having an occasional visit with a bachelor uncle who spends three-quarters of his time living in third-world countries."

Ben pulled up next to Bert's truck in front of Jed's house, his earlier concern now blossoming into full-fledged fear. His fingers tightened around the steering wheel. "Why is she doing this, Zach? Why, after over four years, does she suddenly want Zoe so badly?"

There was a pause on the line. "You didn't read those papers before you faxed them, did you?" Zach finally said.

"No. I sent them off as soon as I left the lawyer's office," Ben said.

Zach let out a deep breath. "As far as I can tell, the cash balance in Zoe's trust fund currently sits at $2.5 million, but that figure will undoubtedly go up as interest accrues. Two point five million dollars at the discretion of Zoe's caregiver, Ben." Zach's voice had risen. "Does that give you a motive for Whitney's change of heart?"

Chapter 7

Senator Sheldon knocked lightly on the door that separated him from the crying child before stepping into the other room. Rachel heard the murmur of voices and the renewal of cries before he reemerged with Whitney Sheldon beside him.

Rachel had seen Whitney once before and was amazed yet again by her striking appearance. From her long, blonde hair to her exquisite features, flawless skin, and perfect figure, Whitney Sheldon rivaled a top model. Even now, dressed casually in a turquoise and lavender swimsuit cover-up, she looked elegant. She immediately homed in on Rachel and stepped toward her, her arms extended.

"I'm so glad you're here," she gushed, taking Rachel by both hands. "I'm afraid Zoe is being a little difficult, and I have an eight thirty appointment I simply cannot miss."

Rachel glanced at the clock on the wall. It read eight twenty-three.

"Do you have any instructions for me before you go?" Rachel asked uncertainly.

"No, no. I'm sure you're very capable. My husband would not have brought you on if you weren't." She paused for a moment. "There is one thing. The lady who packed Zoe's bag obviously didn't realize we were coming to Hawaii. She has a suitcase full of long pants and sweaters. Would you be a sweetheart and see if you can find her some suitable clothes?"

Whatever instructions Rachel had expected, this was not it. She swallowed hard.

"There's a nice shopping center right next to the hotel," Whitney continued. "I'm sure you could find something there." Without waiting for a response, she turned to her husband and gave him a kiss on the cheek. "I've gotta go, honey. I'll see you later."

She picked up her Gucci purse from the floor beside the table and headed for the door. From across the room, one of the men stood, nodded almost imperceptibly at Senator Sheldon, and followed Whitney into the hall.

Karl glanced at the clock. "If you wish to speak with Senator Langford before the meeting begins, you'll have to leave in the next few minutes, Senator," he said.

"Thank you, Karl," Senator Sheldon said. "If you'll gather my things, I'll take Rachel to Zoe, and we can be on our way."

Numbly, Rachel followed the senator to the bedroom. He opened the door and led her inside. The blinds were closed, leaving the room dimly lit. Two twin-size beds and a chest of drawers were the only pieces of furniture, but the quilts had brightly colored tropical prints on them, and a large painting of an ocean scene hung on the wall. A suitcase lay open, with clothes strewn haphazardly across the floor.

Huddled in the corner of one of the beds was a little girl. Her face was buried in a pillow, and her body was shuddering from crying so long.

"Zoe," Senator Sheldon said, "this is Rachel. She's going to stay with you now. Tell her what you need, and she'll help you."

If Zoe heard him, she gave no indication. Senator Sheldon frowned. "Zoe? I don't have time for this!"

Zoe gave a stubborn growl and shook her head, rubbing it back and forth against the pillow. The senator took a step toward her, stopped, seemed to reconsider, and walked back to the door.

"I hope you can reason with her," he said, annoyance resonating in his voice.

Then he turned on his heel and marched out of the room. Rachel heard him say something to Karl, and moments later, the main door to the suite slammed shut. She looked over at Zoe. The little girl still hadn't moved. Placing her purse and notebook on the unoccupied bed, Rachel knelt on the floor beside the open suitcase and started gathering the scattered clothing.

As she folded the small sweaters and pairs of jeans, she wondered about the little girl who wore them. Zoe liked bright colors, she guessed. There was an especially good selection of pink and purple, and when Rachel picked up a handful of socks and started pairing them, she smiled at the assortment of Disney princesses they represented.

"I lost the other *Tangled*." A sad little voice spoke from the corner.

Rachel looked up and saw two feet elevated above the bed. One foot was covered in a purple sock with the face of a smiling Rapunzel from Disney's movie *Tangled*. The other foot was bare. Rachel hurriedly sorted through the unmatched socks.

"Ta da!" she said, waving the missing sock in the air. "Look what I just found."

As two short legs lowered to the bed, a tousled dark head came up. Rachel watched in silence as the little girl groped all over the pillow until she found a tiny pair of thick-lensed glasses and put them on. Then she peered at the sock in Rachel's hand and gave a watery smile.

"You found it!"

"Yes, I did," Rachel said with a smile. "Would you like to wear it?"

Zoe nodded, and Rachel crawled over to the bed and slid the sock onto Zoe's foot.

"Is Rapunzel your favorite princess?" she asked.

"Yes. Tangled and Belle and Cindayella and Ariel," she announced.

Rachel smiled, noting Rapunzel's new name. "Those are my favorites too."

This time Zoe's smile lit up her face, erasing the misery that had filled it only moments before.

"What would you like to wear today?" Rachel asked, noticing that Zoe was still in her pajamas.

"Um, how 'bout my princess shirt?" Zoe suggested, wiggling to the end of the bed and gazing down at the growing pile of clothes, her earlier tears momentarily forgotten.

Rachel pulled a gray sweatshirt covered in Disney princesses out of the pile. "Hmm. I think you might be a bit hot wearing this today. It's going to be a warm, sunny day. See?"

She walked over to the window and opened the blinds. Sunlight streamed in. Zoe blinked, her dark brown eyes huge behind the thick lenses of her glasses. She scrambled off the bed and walked over to the window. Pushing her nose up against the glass, she gazed outside.

"Can you see the ocean?" Rachel asked gently.

"I see blue," Zoe said.

"That's it," Rachel said, instinctively crouching down and putting her arm around the little girl. "How about we go to the store and find you some T-shirts and shorts and maybe a swimsuit? Then I'll take you to the ocean, and you can put your feet in the water."

"A T-shirt with princesses on it?" Zoe asked hopefully.

Rachel laughed. "If we can find one."

* * *

Two hours later, Rachel understood why she'd been given a $2,000 prepaid credit card. She'd never seen money disappear so fast. Whitney had been right. The *Shops at Wailea* did have a large selection of beautiful stores, but the price tags were out of this world—at least, they were out of any world Rachel had ever lived in. At first, she wandered from one store to another trying to absorb the sticker shock. But when she finally realized she wasn't going to find Walmart prices in Wailea, she took Zoe back to the store with the most colorful children's clothes and started buying.

They left the store with four pairs of shorts, four T-shirts, two sundresses, and a swimsuit. They didn't find any Disney princess T-shirts, but in the neighboring beachwear store, they found bright pink flip-flops with a selection of detachable Disney princess decorations. Zoe was thrilled and insisted on wearing them out of the shop. Rachel, who knew enough about sun and water from her growing-up years in Arizona, also purchased Zoe a purple rash-guard shirt and a matching lifejacket. Zoe had looked at Rachel blankly when she'd asked her about swimming, and Rachel wasn't going to take a chance.

Loaded down with purchases and lacking a spare hand for Zoe to hold, Rachel was grateful that Zoe reached out to hold on to the strap of her purse as they made their way through the shopping center. She wasn't sure if the little girl's desire to stay close stemmed from insecurity brought on by unfamiliar surroundings or from the limitations of her obviously poor eyesight. Either way, Rachel was glad that she didn't need to worry about Zoe wandering off and getting lost during their first outing together.

In fact, Zoe had been remarkably well behaved. Gone was the sulking, uncooperative child who had been crying inconsolably when her mother left. In her place was a little girl who had overcome her initial shyness and was showing signs of being quite talkative. She'd already asked Rachel many questions, including whether fish liked people in pink swimsuits better than blue ones, whether there were any crabs on the beach, and whether Ariel the mermaid lived in this ocean or another one.

Rachel had answered as best she could but was grateful for the current lull in conversation. She was tired and suspected that Zoe was too. She led the way to the exit, and as she stepped off the curb, she felt a jolt along her purse strap as Zoe stumbled.

"I'm sorry, Zoe. Are you okay?"

Rachel silently berated herself. It was at least the third time Zoe had tripped over an unseen obstacle. She needed to recognize obstructions before they did their damage. Somehow, she had to discover just how bad Zoe's vision was and then how to work with it. She crouched down and brushed the grit off Zoe's outstretched hands as the little girl began to sniff.

"You're being very brave," Rachel told her.

"I need a treat," Zoe said with a hint of a whine in her voice.

Rachel bit back a smile. "Me too. Let's go back to the hotel to get something to eat."

"How 'bout right now?" Zoe asked, pointing to Rachel's purse. "Maybe there's a treat in there."

Ruefully wishing she was carrying her mother's purse, which always contained something edible, Rachel deposited the shopping bags on the sidewalk and rooted through her purse. A breath mint and stick of Juicy Fruit gum were all she could find. She held them up. As Zoe strained to see, Rachel moved them closer.

"A mint or a piece of gum," she said. "That's all I have until we get to the hotel."

Zoe frowned and took the piece of gum. "You need some more snacks," she said, peeling off the gum wrapper. "Gramma Dory always has lots of snacks in her purse."

"You're right," Rachel said, making a mental note to buy some fruit snacks or granola bars before the end of the day. And then, because she was curious, she asked, "Who's Gramma Dory?"

"She's just Gramma Dory," Zoe said as though that explained everything. "She lives in my house." Behind the thick lenses of her glasses, Zoe's eyes suddenly filled with tears. "But now she's in the hospital. And Grampa Bert said she's too sick to see me."

Rachel rooted through her purse again and found a clean tissue. She removed Zoe's glasses and wiped her eyes before replacing the glasses again.

"I bet she's feeling better now," Rachel said comfortingly.

Zoe looked up, her eyes searching Rachel's face. "Then why can't I go home?"

Rachel took a deep breath. "Because right now you get to be with your mommy in Hawaii."

"Are you my mommy?" Zoe asked, confusion evident in her voice.

Rachel shook her head, surprised at the girl's question. "No, Zoe. Your mommy is Whitney Sheldon. She was in your hotel room this morning."

"But I'm not with that lady," Zoe pointed out. "I'm with you."

"For a little while," Rachel said, realizing how lost Zoe must be feeling surrounded by strangers. She gave the child a reassuring hug. "Your mother will be back soon. But until then, let's go get something to eat. Then we'll put on your new swimsuit and go to the beach."

Zoe gave an especially big sniff. "Okay," she said.

Rachel stuffed four bags into two and grasped them both with one hand, purposely leaving the other one free for Zoe. Then she reached out and took Zoe's hand in hers.

They walked in silence, cutting through the parking lot until they reached one of the footpaths that led across the Grand Wailea Hotel's grounds to the main entrance. As they drew closer, Rachel noticed a small cluster of people gathered around several tripods. High-powered cameras and microphones were pointed toward the hotel. It was possible they were reporting on the ongoing summit, but Rachel wasn't going to take a chance. Without a word, she steered Zoe onto another path that ran around the west side of the building and back to the rear of the hotel and a less visible entrance.

A young family passed them. They were on their way to the beach, the father carrying two boogie boards and the children running ahead.

Zoe watched them go by. "I miss my daddy," she said quietly. "And I want to go home."

Chapter 8

BEN STOOD IN THE KITCHEN, staring down at the small pile of grocery bags sitting on the counter, wondering fleetingly how they'd gotten there. He had no memory of unloading his car or of taking off his snow-caked shoes at the door. Only one thing filled his mind. Where had Jed come up with $2.5 million, not to mention the money needed to completely pay off his exclusive home in the canyon? What had he done to bank that kind of money?

He knew his brother had taken a significant pay cut when he'd moved from ABC in New York to take the anchor job in Utah, but at the time, the change in lifestyle had been worth it. Ben would have staked his life on Jed's integrity. He'd seen it in action time and time again. But millions of dollars didn't simply show up in a bank account for no reason. He and Jed shared the same background. There was no sudden inheritance, no family money. Ben leaned against the granite countertop and bowed his head. How had this happened? And more to the point, how had Whitney known of it while he had not?

The whir of wheels against the kitchen floor caused Ben to raise his head. Dorothy, dressed in a floral housecoat and sitting in her wheelchair, entered the room, with Bert pushing her from behind. The discoloration around her eye looked better, and she'd been working on her hair. Three lone rollers were pinned in among the loose white curls on her head. She looked over at Ben before turning to her husband. "Bert! What did you feed this boy?" she said. "He looks terrible."

"All we had was pancakes," Bert replied defensively. "I ate what he had, and I'm feelin' just fine."

Ben shook his head. "There was nothing wrong with the pancakes."

"It's Zoe, isn't it?" Distress was obvious in Dorothy's voice. "Bert said you went to see the lawyer. What did he say?"

Ben sighed. "Did Jed tell you anything about a trust fund he set up for Zoe?"

"Just that there was one," Bert said with a shrug. "He said there'd be enough money to take care of her."

"The trust fund doesn't matter," Dorothy said. "Even if there's no money, we can manage. We just want Zoe back home."

Ben looked at Dorothy. If there were two women more polar opposite than Dorothy and Whitney, he had yet to meet them. He stepped forward and took her uninjured hand in his. "Zoe's trust fund contains over $2.5 million," he said. "The money goes where Zoe goes—which probably explains why Whitney suddenly wants Zoe back in her life."

"Two and a half million dollars!" Dorothy gasped.

"Where would Jed come up with money like that?" Bert said incredulously.

Ben ran his hand across his face. "I was hoping you could tell me."

Bert shook his head. "He never said anything. It was just work as usual at the TV station, as far as I could tell."

"You don't remember any unusual visitors, phone calls, mail . . . anything like that?" Ben pressed.

"He called someone in New York quite a bit before the accident," Dorothy said. "I only know because there were a few times he'd come home from doing the ten o'clock news and say something about it being too late to call the East Coast. Not that calling New York was unusual, mind you. He kept in touch with a few people there. But these calls seemed to worry him."

Ben stared at her. Something was niggling at the back of his mind. What had Dorothy said to make him feel like he was forgetting something important? He wracked his brain. Something about Jed calling someone in New York. Why would that trigger anything?

And then it came to him. With a groan, Ben sprinted to the guest bedroom, pulled his laptop and its cord out of his duffle bag, and returned to the kitchen before Bert or Dorothy had time to question his disappearance.

"Jed sent me an e-mail," he said as he plugged in his computer and turned it on. "He was working on something and wanted my help."

Ben waited impatiently for his computer to boot up, then accessed his e-mail. He scrolled through the messages until he came to the one he'd opened from Jed at JFK airport. He glanced over at Bert and Dorothy. They were waiting, silently watching.

"Read this," Ben said, turning the computer screen to face them.

Bert pushed Dorothy's wheelchair closer to the kitchen table and leaned in as Dorothy read the letter out loud.

Hey, Ben.

One of my contacts in the city called me last week. Not sure why he picked me since I'm no longer there. On second thought, maybe that's why. He probably figured I wouldn't already be involved. Anyway, if there's any truth to what he told me—and my gut tells me there is— there's something big and ugly going down on Wall Street. I've done some checking from here, and I'm hitting roadblocks at every turn. Someone's done a really good job of covering their tracks or has enough power to shut people down. Let me know when you get back in town. Maybe I could make use of those investigative skills you like to brag about. :)

Jed

P.S. Zoe's been asking about you. I think that means you're overdue for a visit.

Dorothy stopped reading and stared at the screen as if willing Jed to say more. Bert looked at Ben.

"What are you thinkin'?" he said.

Ben shrugged. "I don't know. Maybe if we can get ahold of Jed's contact, we can find out what he was up to. It might have nothing to do with the money in Zoe's trust fund, but perhaps it would—"

Turbo interrupted him, barking loudly seconds before the doorbell rang.

"Are you expecting anyone?" Ben asked.

Dorothy shook her head.

"Stay here," Bert said. "I'll check it out."

Bert took his time. From the kitchen, Ben heard the door open. Turbo gave a few more friendly barks before the door closed and the sound of a man's voice reached them. Then footsteps headed their way—Bert's slow shuffle and someone else's brisk step. As they entered the kitchen, recognition lit Dorothy's face.

"Detective Roman!" she said. "What are you doing all the way out here?"

"Dorothy," the man said. "It's good to see you looking so much better."

"Thank you," she said. "It's slow, but I'm heading in the right direction." She turned to Ben. "Detective Roman, this is Ben Cooper, Jed's twin brother. Ben, this is Detective Roman of the Salt Lake PD. He spent a good deal of time with me at the hospital after the accident."

Ben shook the detective's hand, sizing him up. He was tall, with broad shoulders, and his dark hair was flecked with gray. His handshake was firm, and Ben got the impression that the detective was a man who got things done. "Nice to meet you," he said.

"My condolences on the loss of your brother," Detective Roman said. "He was well respected in the community and at the police department— one of the few reporters who knew when to push for information and when to back off if more than a story was at stake. He'll be missed."

"Thanks," Ben said. "I appreciate that."

Detective Roman nodded. "I gather you're a newsman too."

"Yeah. I'm an investigative reporter for *Our World.*"

"Well, if you're anywhere near as good at getting to the bottom of things as your brother was, I could use your help," Detective Roman said.

Ben gave him an inquiring look. He'd reported undercover enough to recognize when things were not as they seemed. This was not a social call. He could feel it. He pointed to one of the kitchen chairs.

"Take a seat," he said, pulling a chair out for himself.

Detective Roman sat down, and Bert followed suit, positioning himself beside Dorothy's wheelchair.

"What have you got?" Ben asked.

"Stretch chrome—metallic blue," Detective Roman said.

Bert and Dorothy stared at the detective blankly.

Ben raised his eyebrows. "Care to elaborate?"

Detective Roman gave a thin smile. "I've been on the force long enough to trust my gut," he began. "And no matter how many times I went over the reports of your brother's accident, I couldn't get rid of the feeling that we were missing something. I kept coming back to Dorothy's description of lights. What if there was something on the road? Another vehicle involved?" He looked at Ben. "After wrestling with it for a few days, I made a call to a buddy in forensics and persuaded him to take a look at the wreckage. The results came back a few days ago. On the front left panel of your brother's red Mercedes, he found trace evidence of stretch chrome, a product that can be wrapped over a vehicle's existing paint job to create a chrome-like finish—in this case, metallic blue."

Detective Roman turned to Bert and Dorothy. "To the best of your knowledge, were there any scrapes on Jed's car before the accident?"

Bert snorted. "If that car had as much as a half-inch scratch from a shopping cart, Jed took it to the body shop to have it buffed out. There's no way he'd sleep at night with metallic blue paint on it. That Mercedes was his pride and joy."

Detective Roman nodded as though he'd expected as much. "Well, there are definitely marks on it now," he said. "Which means that before he left the road, he hit something that had been given a highly specialized paint job."

"Highly specialized, as in highly unusual?" Ben asked.

Detective Roman gave a slow nod. "That would be a good assumption."

Ben leaned forward. "Which means that it should be pretty easy to identify, right?"

Detective Roman's smile quirked up a fraction. "Also a good assumption," he said. "I contacted all the body shops in the valley, asking if anyone had brought anything in with that type of finish. I thought it likely that someone who cares enough about their vehicle to give it that kind of facelift isn't going to let it sit in the driveway completely banged up. It would raise too many questions."

"And have you found it?" Dorothy asked, looking considerably paler than she had earlier.

Detective Roman faced her. "Yes," he said solemnly. "But it wasn't at a body shop."

"Where was it?" Bert asked.

"The junkyard."

"The junkyard?" Bert repeated.

Detective Roman nodded. "A guy at one of the body shops had just gotten back from the junkyard when my partner stopped by. He'd seen the truck sitting there and said he'd noticed it because of its metallic blue body. My partner called me, and I met him at the junkyard. The right front panel of the heavy-duty GMC truck is completely buckled. Some of the lights are broken, the bumper's bent, and the right side of the cab is covered in streaks of red paint. The forensic team is working on it, but I'm pretty sure we're going to get a match for the paint on Jed's car."

Dorothy raised her uninjured hand to her mouth as tears welled in her eyes. "They were truck lights," she whispered. "I wasn't imagining things. They were truck lights."

Bert put his hand on Dorothy's shoulder and squeezed it gently. Ben jumped to his feet and paced over to the kitchen counter.

"Do you have a name?" he asked, swinging around to face the detective.

Detective Roman looked grim. "The truck was dropped off at night, abandoned just outside the range of the junkyard's security cameras. The vehicle has been completely wiped clean. The guys at forensic are going over it with a fine-tooth comb, but they haven't found as much as a crumb yet. The truck's Nevada license plates were reported stolen from a Honda Civic in Las Vegas three weeks ago."

Ben swallowed the bile rising in his throat. He was pretty sure he knew where this new information was taking them, and it wasn't a good place.

"You don't think Jed's death was an accident, do you?" he said.

Detective Roman gave him a long, thoughtful look. "What I need to know," he said, "is whether you or the Dicksons can think of any reason that someone would want Jed Cooper dead."

Ben closed his eyes as his world tilted once again. When he opened them, tears were flowing down Dorothy's cheeks and Bert's gray pallor had aged him by a decade. Detective Roman was still waiting.

"I think you'd better take a look at this," Ben said, walking back to the table and turning his laptop around so the screen faced the detective. "Jed sent me this e-mail the day before he died."

Chapter 9

"It's coming! It's coming!" Zoe squealed as the roar of the oncoming wave intensified.

Rachel laughed and tightened her grip on Zoe's hands. "One, two, three . . . jump!" she yelled, lifting Zoe off her feet as the wave reached them.

"Yeah!" Zoe cried as the wave receded and Rachel lowered her to the sand. "Again! Again!"

Rachel shook her head. "You've worn me out, little wave jumper. I need to rest for a few minutes."

"How 'bout one minute?" Zoe suggested.

"How about ten minutes, and we'll go sit on the big towel?" Rachel said.

Zoe's shoulders slumped. "Okay," she said with a sigh.

Rachel laughed. "Come on. We'll see if we can find a stick and make some holes in the sand."

"Why?" Zoe asked, her interest piquing slightly.

"Because it's fun," Rachel said, crossing her fingers that the little girl would believe her.

She took Zoe's hand and led the way through a maze of deck chairs, rattan beach mats, and blankets. The beach was crowded, and Rachel hoped she'd be able to relocate the canvas bag and bright red-and-white-striped towel she'd spread on the sand an hour before. When she spotted it about six yards away, she paused. "Zoe," she said. "Can you see our towel? It's red and white."

Rachel watched as Zoe turned slowly, straining to differentiate objects in the kaleidoscope of colors and shapes on the beach.

"Right there!" she cried at last, pointing to the towel. She released Rachel's hand and skipped forward.

"Good job!" Rachel said, experiencing a thrill that she didn't quite understand as Zoe reached the towel all by herself.

Once Zoe was happily poking holes in the sand to make houses for crabs and worms, Rachel reached into her bag and drew out her notepad, a pen, and a handful of brochures she'd picked up at the concierge's desk. She started flipping through the brochures, looking for activities that might interest Zoe and jotting them down on paper. When she finished, she had five places listed, but each one was a considerable distance from the hotel. She tapped the end of her pen against her chin, thinking.

The simplest solution would be to rent a car. That way she and Zoe could come and go without waiting for taxis. It would also enable them to shop where the locals shopped. She started a new list: snacks, water bottles, toy shovel and pail, child-strength sunscreen. She glanced over at Zoe, who was now poking a piece of seaweed with her stick. With a smile, Rachel added "princess T-shirt" to the shopping list before putting the notepad down and pulling out her own sunscreen.

"Zoe," she called. "I need to put some more sunscreen on you before you burn."

Zoe gave the seaweed a couple more jabs before crawling over to Rachel, trailing sand all over the beach towel.

"I'm not burning," she said.

Rachel remembered saying the exact same thing to her mother during childhood outings to the pool in Arizona. Once, she'd evaded her mother's ministrations all afternoon and had suffered a sleepless, pain-filled night because of it—but she had learned her lesson.

"I know it doesn't feel like it," she said, sliding Zoe's glasses off and applying lotion to her nose and forehead, "but sometimes it sneaks up on you."

"Like Daddy?" Zoe asked.

Rachel hesitated. "Did your Daddy sneak up on you?"

Zoe nodded emphatically. "When Gramma Dory helps me make cookies, she says we have to watch for Daddy. He's good at sneaking cookies." She paused. "And he tickles."

Rachel smiled at Zoe's serious expression. "Did he sneak up and tickle you sometimes?"

"Yes," Zoe said. "And then he ate my cookies."

"I bet it was because they tasted sooo good," Rachel said, rubbing sunscreen on Zoe's arms and trying to hide her sadness from the little girl.

Zoe had obviously been close to her father, and Rachel wondered what he'd been like. Other than the fact that she was beautiful, Zoe bore little resemblance to her mother. Perhaps she looked more like him.

Rachel hugged her. "Thank you, Zoe. You've been a good girl today."

"Maybe I need a treat," Zoe said.

Rachel laughed. "How about this? How about tomorrow we go to the store and you can pick out some snacks. Then we'll go to the aquarium."

"What's the kwarium?" Zoe asked.

"It's a place people can go to see all kinds of different fish," Rachel said.

"Can I see them too?"

Rachel's throat tightened. "We'll get really close," she said. "I'm sure you'll be able to see lots of them."

"Okay," Zoe said happily. "Now can we go jump in the ocean again?"

Rachel rolled her eyes. This child was not to be deterred. "All right, silly goose. One more time."

"I'm not a silly goose," Zoe said, scrambling to her feet. "I'm a girl!"

They jumped the waves and walked along the water's edge, following the gentle arch of the beach. It was a long walk. At first Zoe splashed wildly as the waves lapped at her feet, but by the time they turned around and began their return trek, she was showing signs of tiring. Her chattering had stopped. Twice, a wave caught her off-guard and knocked her off her feet. The first time, Rachel pulled her back up without difficulty. The second time, Zoe began to whimper, refusing to get up. Rachel crouched down in three inches of water beside her.

"Come on, Zoe. We're almost there. I can see the towel."

"I don't want the towel," Zoe cried.

"But we can get you dried off," Rachel said.

Zoe's sniffles increased. "I don't want dried off."

"You want to stay wet?" Rachel asked.

"I don't want to stay wet."

Rachel sighed. She'd seen her brothers do this when they were young and their efforts to keep up with older siblings had worn them out. She didn't know Zoe well enough to have seen it coming but was frustrated that she'd let it happen anyway. Zoe had entered the overtired and completely unreasonable zone. Rachel didn't relish the thought of hauling a screaming child all the way back to the hotel, but at this point, trying to talk things out was useless. Instead, she tried bribery. "Would you like a shaved ice?"

"No ice." Zoe's voice was becoming a wail.

"How about an ice cream?" she tried.

This time she saw a flicker of interest. Rachel seized it. "I bet if you walk back to the hotel, we could find you an ice cream," Rachel said, praying it was true.

"Can I have a banilla one?" Zoe asked, scrambling to her feet.

"I'll ask for one as soon as we get there," Rachel told her with relief, grabbing Zoe's hand before she changed her mind. "Let's cut across the sand. It won't take us long."

Rachel towed Zoe back to their belongings. She shook the sand off the towel and stuffed it into her bag while Zoe reclaimed her stick. Then, taking Zoe's hand again, Rachel followed the path toward the hotel swimming pool and its concession stand. By the time they reached the pool deck, Zoe was flagging and Rachel was beginning to think she'd have to carry her after all.

"Hi, Zoe! Have you been swimming?"

Startled by the unexpected voice, Rachel and Zoe both swung around. Rachel instinctively put a protective arm around the little girl as Senator Sheldon's warning about reporters filled her mind. Zoe squinted into the sun, then shook her head and buried her face in Rachel's leg. Rachel stared at the woman stretched out on the chaise lounge a few feet away. She wore a sparkling white bikini, the color accentuating her tan arms and legs. The large lenses of her sunglasses covered most of her face, but her long blonde hair and the lavender and turquoise cover-up tossed casually over the back of the chair identified her immediately.

"We were at the beach, but we didn't swim," Rachel said.

Whitney lowered her sunglasses and studied Rachel. "Oh, you just seem a bit wet."

"We were splashing," Rachel said, feeling like a grungy piece of driftwood under Whitney's gaze. Her two-year-old navy swimsuit had twenty times the fabric of Whitney's tiny bikini but none of the glamour. On top of that, she was covered in sand, and half of her hair had escaped its ponytail.

"That sounds fun," Whitney said rather unconvincingly.

"I didn't know you were available this afternoon," Rachel said, feeling irrationally irritated that Whitney had chosen to sunbathe by the pool rather than spend time on the beach with her daughter. "You could have come with us."

"Maybe next time," Whitney said as Zoe began yanking on Rachel's swimsuit.

"Ice cream!" Zoe whined. "Ice cream now."

"Zoe! That's enough!" Whitney snapped.

Zoe gave a howl and collapsed on the tile in tears. Whitney put her sunglasses back on and glanced around in embarrassment. "Zoe!" she hissed. "Stop that at once!"

Rachel shouldered her bag, bent down, and picked up Zoe. "She's overtired and hungry," she said. "I promised her ice cream."

"That's hardly an excuse for this kind of behavior," Whitney said sharply. "I will not tolerate it."

Rachel stared at the senator's wife in disbelief. She put her hand on Zoe's head, stroking it gently as the little girl sobbed on her shoulder. "I'll take her to her room," she said, then turned her back on Whitney Sheldon and carried Zoe into the hotel.

Zoe was almost asleep by the time they reached the suite. Rachel struggled to dig the key out of her bag and unlock the door, but once she was inside, she lowered Zoe onto the sofa, dropped her bag on the floor, picked up the phone, and called room service.

She wasn't sure if the speedy delivery was because she called from Senator Sheldon's suite or because the entire order consisted of one bowl of vanilla ice cream. Either way, Rachel was grateful. Zoe rallied at the sight of her treat and consumed the entire thing in less than five minutes. Her disposition improved with every bite, and by the time she'd finished, she was willing to hop into the tub to wash off the sticky mixture of sand and ice cream.

Once Zoe was clean and dry and wearing some of her new clothes, they relocated to Rachel's room. Zoe was content to sit in front of the television and watch a cartoon while Rachel washed, changed, and called the front desk to request a rental car for the next morning. Then, with Zoe excitedly asking questions about their upcoming outing to the aquarium, they went in search of dinner.

Chapter 10

DETECTIVE ROMAN READ THE E-MAIL twice.

"And you have no idea what this is all about?" he said.

"Nope," Ben said. "I've been in Afghanistan and haven't had phone contact with Jed for two months. I didn't have Internet access until yesterday either, so I only just read it. It sounds like it was a fairly recent development, but that's all I have."

"Tell me about his New York connections. He worked for *ABC News* before coming to Salt Lake, right?"

"Right," Ben said. "By the time he left, he was their chief financial correspondent, so he spent a lot of time on Wall Street and had a pretty good network of people who fed him information on what was happening in the markets—along with what was projected to happen."

Detective Roman nodded, took an iPhone out of his jacket pocket, and made some notes. "Do you know any of his contacts?"

Ben shook his head. "I might recognize a few names from years ago when we shared an apartment in New York, but those were the early days of his career, and his network would have been much wider and deeper by the time he left."

The detective turned to Dorothy. "Did Jed keep a list of phone contacts anywhere in the house?"

"All his contacts were on his cell phone and laptop, and they were both destroyed in the accident," she said. "I guess it's possible that he has some of them written down somewhere in his home office, but I don't know for sure."

"Can you get his cell phone records?" Ben asked. "Dorothy said Jed called someone in New York several times the week before he died."

Detective Roman nodded, making another notation on his phone. Then he paused as though weighing his words carefully. "I'd like to keep this investigation under wraps for as long as possible. If Jed was murdered, someone did a really good job of making it look like an accident. As of now, he thinks he got away with it. All reports indicate that Jed Cooper died in a tragic accident caused by bad driving conditions. If we can keep it that way, this guy might relax enough to make some mistakes. The right kind of mistakes will lead us to the killer, and if he was hired out, the killer will lead us to whoever is behind this."

Dorothy's hand trembled as she took a tissue Bert offered her. "What do you want us to do?" she asked.

"The most important thing you can do is act normal," Detective Roman said. "If you and Bert continue as if your sole focus is on recovering from your injuries and adjusting to life without Jed, no one will suspect we're considering foul play."

"Now, wait a minute," Bert interrupted. "You can't go and tell me someone killed Jed and almost killed my wife and expect me to sit around doing nothing."

"I didn't say do nothing," Detective Roman corrected him. "Go about your regular daily activities, but on top of that, I want you to go through the house looking for anything that might help with the investigation. A scrap of paper with a name or a phone number, an unfamiliar address, a note Jed wrote to himself, a message from someone else, financial transactions . . . anything that strikes you as unusual. My partner is over at the TV station right now going through whatever was boxed up when they cleared out Jed's office. We'll be looking for those same things there. And we'll follow up on any clues we gather from the abandoned truck."

"I want to know what you find," Ben said.

"I'll keep you informed," Detective Roman promised. "If we need to bring in the Feds, we will." He glanced back at Ben's computer screen. "It looks like we may need some assistance in New York City."

"I can do some quiet checking back there," Ben said. "You give me some names from Jed's phone record, and I'll check them out."

Detective Roman raised an eyebrow. "I understand your desire to be involved, Ben, but that's not how it works. You have no authority to . . ."

Ben raised his hand. "Don't even go there," he said. "I'm an investigative reporter. This is what I do. I know enough not to step over the line. You give me the names; I check them out and pass on the information. The Feds take over. It's that simple."

"I can't authorize you to do that," Detective Roman said.

"Fine," Ben said, leaning forward across the table. "I'll do it without authorization. The bottom line is I'm going to know some of Jed's contacts and they're going to know me. Those who've never met me before are going to think they have because I look and sound just like Jed." He paused to let that sink in before adding, "And I'm pretty sure those contacts will talk more freely to Jed's twin than to an unfamiliar FBI agent."

"Unless one of them is behind Jed's death," Detective Roman said coldly.

Ben met his eyes. "I'm not going to risk my life," he said. "I just need to do everything I can to find out why my brother's was taken."

Detective Roman held Ben's gaze for a few moments longer before tossing two business cards at him.

"Keep one. Write your cell phone number on the other, and I'll be in touch."

Ben wrote down his number and passed the card back to the detective. "Thanks," he said. "I'll be gone for a couple of days, but I can head back here or to New York as soon as you've got something."

Detective Roman looked at him warily. "Mind telling me where you're going?"

"I need to see my niece," Ben said matter-of-factly.

"Jed's daughter?" the detective asked. "Where is she?"

"Figuring that out is my first priority," Ben said.

"You don't know?" The detective couldn't quite mask his astonishment.

"It's a long story," Ben said.

Detective Roman leaned back in his chair. "Ben Cooper, you of all people should know that I'm in the business of long stories."

So, with Bert's and Dorothy's help, Ben told him of Whitney's arrival after Jed's funeral and of Blaine Thompson's inability to prevent Zoe's removal from the house—despite the fact that Ben and the Dicksons were listed as Zoe's legal guardians on Jed's will. He went on to tell him about his meeting with Blaine Thompson that morning and of his friend Zach Bennett's assessment of Zoe's trust fund. He ended his account by sliding the green folder full of legal papers across the table.

"That's the folder Blaine Thompson gave me," Ben said.

The detective opened the folder and started flipping through the papers. "And you have no idea where your brother came up with $2.5 million?" he said.

"No," Ben admitted. "I was talking it through with Bert and Dorothy when you arrived. None of us have any idea."

"I see," Detective Roman said. "And when exactly were you planning on telling me about this?"

Ben raised his eyebrows. "I don't know. Probably about the time you gave me that list of New York City contacts."

Detective Roman frowned. "Finding a large amount of money that you had no idea existed is a significant piece of evidence to withhold, Ben."

"I wasn't withholding evidence," Ben said, his indignation rising. "Jed was the most honest man I know. I may not know where that money came from, but I know it wasn't acquired illegally."

"I'm not accusing your brother of anything," Detective Roman said. "I knew him as an honest man too. But that's not the point. If there's one thing I've learned in over thirty years of investigations, it's that you don't overlook anything. If you weren't emotionally invested, you'd have recognized that yourself."

Ben's heart sank as he realized the truth of the detective's words. He'd been so concerned that uncovering the source of Jed's money would somehow besmirch his brother's reputation, he'd almost brushed aside what could be a vital clue to uncovering the reason he was killed. He raked his fingers through his hair. "I'm sorry," he said. "You're right. Take the folder and make whatever copies you need."

"I'll get it all back to you." Detective Roman said. He flipped the folder open again. "Is Jed's lawyer's name in here?"

"It should be," Ben said.

Detective Roman nodded. "I think maybe I'll pay the guy a visit." He gave a ghost of a smile. "It wouldn't do to give him too much time to recover from your visit, would it?"

Ben looked slightly chagrined. "I told him I wouldn't be needing his services anymore."

"And how did he respond to that?"

"I didn't give him a chance to say much of anything," Ben admitted. "But from his expression, I'd say he was pretty concerned."

Detective Roman looked thoughtful as he added yet another notation to his iPhone.

"Thank you," he said. "You've given me a lot to go on."

He turned to Bert and Dorothy and handed Bert another of his business cards. "Get started on Jed's home office as soon as you can. If you need help, let me know. If you find anything, however insignificant it may seem, call me."

"We will," Bert promised, shaking his hand.

"Take care of yourself, Dorothy," he said.

"Thank you, Detective," she said. "And thanks for listening to a broken old woman."

Detective Roman squeezed her hand. "You're the hero here, Dorothy. If you hadn't fought to keep living and told your story so consistently, no one would have suspected the accident wasn't what it seemed. My job is to make sure your efforts weren't in vain."

Ben walked Detective Roman to the door and shook his hand. "I look forward to hearing from you soon," he said.

The detective paused as though measuring his words carefully. "Over the last couple of years, Jed found a witness or the evidence needed to close three of my department's toughest cases. In each instance, he called to pass along his information—giving us time to do our job before his story ran. The department owes him; I owe him. I'll keep you in the loop, Ben, and we'll find whoever killed your brother."

"Thanks," Ben said. "I'm counting on it."

"But until then," Detective Roman continued, "let me give you a word of warning. I know you're worried about Zoe. And I know Jed would want her with you, not his ex-wife. But in law enforcement, we're taught to keep the peace. If you rush in and take Zoe back by force or harass the Sheldons in any way, Whitney's going to use it against you. Your chances of getting custody will be virtually nonexistent. She's already got motherhood and marriage on her side. Don't give her any more ammunition."

"I understand," Ben said, accepting the detective's counsel in the spirit it was given. "But I have to know that Zoe's okay."

"I can't argue with that," Detective Roman said, pulling a pair of gloves out of his pockets and putting them on as Ben opened the door. "I'll be in touch."

By the time Ben returned to the kitchen, Bert and Dorothy were gone. He heard voices coming from the direction of Jed's home office and guessed they were already at work sorting through files in there. He sat down at the kitchen table and drew his laptop closer. While the Dicksons looked for information about Jed, he would look for information about Zoe.

Thirty-five minutes and four phone calls later, Ben had what he needed. He was grateful for Google and his credentials as an *Our World* reporter that had helped him uncover the information he sought. Senator Sheldon and Whitney were in Hawaii, where Senator Sheldon was part of a small delegation of U.S. politicians spearheading a trade agreement with their counterparts in Japan. The meetings were taking place at the Grand Wailea Hotel and were projected to last another week.

Ben assumed that if Whitney was in Maui, Zoe was too. He booked the first available flight out of Salt Lake City and into Kahului, turned off his computer, and went to tell Bert and Dorothy that he'd be leaving for the airport within two hours.

Chapter 11

WHEN RACHEL KNOCKED ON THE door of the senator's suite the next morning, Karl opened it and invited her in.

"Ah, Rachel," Senator Sheldon said when he saw her. "I'm glad you're here. Whitney and I were just reviewing our schedules."

Whitney stepped toward Rachel from her position beside her husband. "I'll be in Lahaina all day today," she said. "The dignitaries' wives are being given a special tour of the old whaling town. Our husbands will be joining us in the evening for a luau."

"We'll need you to put Zoe to bed and stay with her until we return," Senator Sheldon explained. "I'll leave some documents on the table for you to look at once Zoe's asleep, if you're interested."

"Thank you," Rachel said. "I'd like that."

"Very good," the senator said. "I'm sorry it'll be such a long day for you, but tomorrow we have no commitments until the late afternoon, so you can have the morning to yourself."

"That would be great. Since tomorrow's Sunday, I was hoping to go to church," Rachel admitted.

Whitney gave her a skeptical look before picking up her capacious designer handbag. "I need to go," she said.

Senator Sheldon slid his laptop into its case. "I'll walk you to the lobby," he told his wife. "Are you ready, Karl?"

Karl nodded and moved a pile of papers from the table into a briefcase. The two security men rose from their seats and moved to stand beside the suite door until Karl and the Sheldons joined them. Just before she stepped into the hall, Whitney paused and turned around.

"Oh, by the way, Zoe's still asleep," she said. "Just call room service when she wakes up. They can deliver her something for breakfast."

The door closed behind them, and Rachel realized they'd left before she'd had a chance to tell them she was taking Zoe to the aquarium. With a sigh, she plopped down on the sofa. Perhaps this was commonplace for celebrities, but she'd never seen a family function this way before. Senator Sheldon and Whitney seemed happy to spare no expense when it came to buying Zoe whatever she needed—including a caregiver—but she had yet to see either of them express any real affection for the little girl or even spend any time with her.

She realized they were still adjusting to having Zoe in their lives and that the sudden inclusion of a four-year-old was sure to add a new level of stress, but was it normal for a mother to keep an appointment at the spa when her child desperately needed clothing? Or to remember only as an afterthought that her daughter hadn't risen or eaten breakfast? They hadn't asked a single question about how the previous day had gone or what they had done together (other than what Whitney knew from their brief encounter at the poolside). No one seemed to really care what she did with Zoe. In fact, Rachel realized with sinking surety, no one seemed to really care about Zoe.

Rachel leaned back against the sofa cushions and stared up at the twirling bamboo ceiling fan. Her heart ached for the little girl. She wished she could transport her to the home she herself had grown up in, a home full of noise, chaos, and spats between siblings but also one full of laughter, the light of the gospel, and unconditional love. She wondered what Zoe's life had been like when she'd lived with her father. She wasn't sure how Gramma Dory and Grampa Bert fit into the picture, but she got the impression that they might have genuinely cared for Zoe.

The bedroom door clicked, and Rachel looked over to see a tousle-headed Zoe emerge. She stood uncertainly in the doorway, looking anxiously from side to side, her little glasses already in place.

"Hi, sleepyhead," Rachel said, getting to her feet.

Zoe turned toward her voice, a smile lighting up her face. "Hi, Wachul! I'm hungry."

Rachel smiled too. She should have known that even if Whitney had forgotten to tell her about breakfast, Zoe would have made sure it happened.

"What would you like to eat?" she asked.

"Grampa Bert's pancakes," Zoe said.

"Grampa Bert's not here right now," Rachel said gently. "But I bet the hotel makes good pancakes. D'you want to try them and see?"

Zoe frowned. "Can they make them look like bears and moose?"

"Probably not," Rachel conceded. "But after you're done, we'll go see some real sea creatures instead."

"At the kwarium?" Zoe asked, hopping up and down with excitement.

Rachel couldn't help laughing. "Yes, at the aquarium, smart cookie," she said.

Zoe giggled. "I'm not a cookie. I'm a girl!"

An hour later, Zoe was fed, dressed, and ready for her adventure. Rachel led her to the hotel front desk. A Polynesian young man in a red Hawaiian-print shirt smiled at them.

"Aloha! Can I help you?" he asked.

Rachel glanced at his nametag. "Hi, Tomas," she said. "I ordered a rental car and was told to come to the front desk this morning."

"Ah, yes," he said, reaching for a piece of paper on the counter. "I have it here. A car for Miss Rachel Hamilton, with child car seat and GPS. One week's rental to be billed to suite eight. Is that correct?"

"That's it," Rachel said with relief.

He slid the paper toward her and offered her a pen. "I just need your signature on the line at the bottom," he said.

Rachel signed the paper and handed it back to him.

"Mahalo! I'll have the car brought around for you," Tomas said, picking up the telephone and dialing as he spoke.

Zoe reached up and put her hands on the edge of the counter, standing on tiptoes to try to see Tomas. "We're going to the kwarium," she said. "To see fish."

Tomas leaned over the counter and grinned. "That's great! Maybe you'll see humuhumunukunukuapua'a."

Zoe gave two long blinks before turning to Rachel. "What's that thing?"

"I have no idea," Rachel said.

Zoe turned back to Tomas. "We're not seeing that," she said.

Tomas laughed. He reached down, pulled something out of a cupboard under the counter, and held it up. It was a long stick with a small plastic fish bobbing up and down on the top. The fish was multicolored—blue, white, gold, and black, with striking striped markings.

"What's your name?" Tomas whispered to Zoe.

"Zoe," she said.

"Humuhumunukunukuapua'a, meet my new friend, Zoe. Zoe this is Humuhumunukunukuapua'a, but you can call him Humu for short.

He's the Hawaiian state fish, and I bet you'll see him and many of his cousins swimming around at the aquarium today."

He leaned over the counter and handed the bobbing fish on a stick to Zoe. Zoe grasped the stick with a huge smile.

"Look," she cried, waving the plastic fish as she hopped around. "It's called Humu!"

"Careful!" Rachel warned, reaching out as Zoe danced her way into another young man who was hurrying to the desk.

The man steadied Zoe as she stumbled. Like Tomas, he was wearing a red Hawaiian shirt, but his nametag read Kai, and he carried a set of car keys.

"Aloha! This must be the *keiki* who is going for a ride in the car parked outside," he said.

"This is Zoe," Tomas told him. "She's taking Humu to the aquarium today."

"Great idea," Kai said with a smile. He handed the keys to Rachel. "It's a dark green Audi coupe, and it's parked outside the main entrance. When you come back, drive it into the multilevel parking garage. There'll be someone there to direct you."

"Thank you so much," Rachel said, accepting the keys. She reached for Zoe's free hand. "Say good-bye, Zoe."

Zoe waved the stick, making the fish gyrate wildly. "Bye! Thank you for Humu."

Both men smiled and waved.

"Aloha! Have fun at the aquarium," Tomas called.

Rachel led Zoe past the water fountains and flower planters to the columned main entrance. Parked to one side of the circular driveway was a dark green car. As she moved closer, her footsteps slowed. It gleamed in the sunlight. She was pretty sure she'd never sat in a car as luxurious as this, let alone driven one, and she experienced a brief moment of apprehension before her sense of adventure took over.

"Let's go, Zoe," she said, excitement conquering her nerves.

Zoe needed no second bidding. She clamored into the car seat as soon as Rachel opened the door.

Rachel took a few minutes to familiarize herself with all the buttons and gadgets on the dashboard. She pushed one lever and watched with delight as the sunroof opened above her, then she entered the address of the Maui Ocean Center into the onboard GPS. After putting the car in gear, she pulled away from the curb. The engine purred, humming with barely repressed power. She thought of her brothers and of how envious they'd be if they could see her now—and she couldn't hold back her smile. Pointing the car toward Kihea, she merged into traffic and sat back to enjoy the ride.

Chapter 12

THE RED-EYE FLIGHT WAS APTLY named, Ben thought ruefully as he glanced at his reflection in the rearview mirror of the Toyota Corolla he'd rented from Kahului airport. His eyes were bloodshot, his dark hair tousled, and his face covered in a heavy evening shadow. He ran his hand over his bristly chin, willing himself to stay focused.

The early hour meant the roads were quiet, and it hadn't taken him long to exit Kahului on the Mokulele Highway and cross to the other side of the island through fields of waving sugar cane. Now he was starting to see signage for Kihei and Wailea, and he had a decision to make. Did he go straight to the Grand Wailea Hotel to find Zoe, or did he check into his hotel first and try to make himself look a little more presentable? With another glance at himself in the rearview mirror, he took the turnoff for South Kihei.

The Comfort Inn was modest, clean, and, most importantly, had a room ready for him. With gratitude, Ben entered his room, tossed his carry-on bag onto one of the twin beds, and threw himself onto the other one. In two minutes, he was asleep.

It was almost eleven o'clock when he awoke. Although his initial reaction was to kick himself for losing the morning to sleep, he knew that facing Whitney and Senator Sheldon in his previously exhausted state would not have been the wisest move. He slid off the bed and lowered himself to his knees. After giving thanks for his safe arrival, he prayed for Zoe—for her welfare and for help in locating her. Then, feeling a little more fortified, he headed for the shower.

* * *

The Grand Wailea was definitely a step up from the Comfort Inn. Passing the opulent furnishings and lush tropical flowers as he entered the lobby,

Ben couldn't help but contrast his current location with the poor, barren desert he'd walked through less than a week before. They were two different worlds.

As he approached the front desk, his tension seemed to increase with each step.

"Hi, Tomas," he said, glancing at the young man's nametag. "I'm here to see one of your guests. Could you give me the room number?"

"What's the name, sir?" Tomas asked, fingers poised over the computer keypad.

"Whitney Sheldon," Ben said. "She's staying here with her husband, Senator Sheldon."

Tomas entered something on the computer, then picked up the phone. "I'll call their room for you, sir."

Ben nodded. He'd thought it unlikely that hotel protocol would permit the front desk to give out room numbers, but he'd held on to a slim hope that he was wrong. He didn't want to talk to Whitney on the phone. It would be too easy for her to simply hang up and refuse to see him. But he had to make contact somehow.

After a few moments, Tomas hung up. "I'm afraid there's no reply," he said. "Would you like to leave a message?"

Ben thought quickly. "I'll stick around for a little while," he said. "If she doesn't show up soon, I'll leave a message with you."

"Of course, sir," Tomas said. "Make yourself comfortable."

Ben turned and walked over to the nearest grouping of elegant chairs and sat down. He should have come earlier. Waiting patiently did not come easily for him at the best of times. And this certainly didn't qualify as the best of times. He picked up one of the travel magazines on the nearby table and flipped through it, wishing he were here to relax and enjoy the tranquility of the Maui advertised on the pages.

After watching people come and go through the lobby for almost an hour, Ben rose to his feet. If he was going to have to wait all day, he'd have to move around or he'd go crazy. Another young man wearing the hotel uniform hurried past, giving him a friendly "Aloha" as he headed toward the front desk.

"Hey, Tomas," Ben overheard the man say. "I'm covering for you while you go for lunch."

"Mahalo," Tomas said, patting his solid girth. "It's been a long time since breakfast!"

The young man grinned. "Is your new girlfriend back from the aquarium yet?"

Tomas smiled too. "Zoe? No. Not yet. I'm guessing she'll be there most of the day."

Ben held his breath. Were they talking about his Zoe? How many Zoes could there be at this hotel?

"A very cute *keiki*," the young man said, slipping behind the desk.

"Uh huh," Tomas agreed. "And her mother was quite easy on the eyes too."

The men laughed, but Ben didn't wait to hear more. A cute child with an attractive mother. Whitney had many failings, but even he could not deny that she always looked good. It had to be them. With new purpose in his step, Ben hurried back to his car.

It took only a few minutes with his smartphone for Ben to find the name and address of the Maui Ocean Center. With a quick glance at the directions printed on his screen, Ben maneuvered his car out of the parking lot and onto the Pi'ilani Highway and headed for Ma'alaea.

The drive was beautiful. Ben passed stunning beaches, blue seas with whitecaps, acres of sugar cane shifting in the breeze, and colorful flowers thriving in every nook and cranny. But it was wasted on him. His attention was completely centered on following the correct road, on finding the aquarium, and on reaching it before Zoe left.

When at last he saw the sign announcing the Maui Ocean Center, he pulled into a parking lot full of cars and tour buses, took the first available stall, and looked around. He was pretty sure Whitney would not resort to going to the aquarium by tour bus, but he had no idea what kind of car she was using.

A handful of people were cutting through the parking lot, but most activity was at the aquarium's main doors. A quick study of the people there convinced Ben that the entrance also doubled as the exit. If Whitney and Zoe were still inside, they would leave through those doors.

Not wanting to waste any more time, he grabbed his camera from the backseat of the car and hurried over to an unoccupied bench about fifty yards from the aquarium's entrance. From this vantage point, he could clearly see the men, women, and children milling around the ticket counter, along with the slow trickle of people leaving the aquarium and heading for the parking lot. He attached the telephoto lens and raised his camera to his eye. The faces at the exit became clear. Ben took a deep breath and forced himself to relax. If Zoe walked through that door, he'd spot her immediately.

* * *

Their visit to the grocery store in Kihea was a success. A large insulated bag filled with fruit, baby carrots, string cheese, granola bars, muffins, and bottled water now filled the passenger seat. They were all Zoe-approved snacks, and she was wasting no time making a dent in the new supply. Rachel smiled at Zoe's reflection in the rearview mirror as she drove. The little girl was concentrating on finding every last one of the princess fruit snacks stuck to the bottom of the small bag in her hand.

By the time they arrived at the Maui Ocean Center, Zoe's snack consumption qualified as lunch and she was raring to go see humu's cousins. Rachel barely had time to eat one muffin before Zoe grabbed her hand and pulled her toward the aquarium's entrance. The little girl's enthusiasm was contagious, and Rachel found herself paying the exorbitant entrance fees with barely a qualm. To see Zoe this excited was worth the price.

They took their time wandering through the exhibits. At the touching pool, Zoe ran her little fingers over starfish and shells of all shapes and sizes. Fish tanks covered the walls of the aquarium's rooms. With her palms and face pressed against the glass, Zoe watched in fascination as the brightly colored fish flitted by. Rachel found a tank full of humuhumunukunukuapua'a and pointed it out to Zoe. Zoe spent ten minutes waving her own humu fish at them.

When they entered the large Perspex tunnel that cut through an enormous fish tank, Zoe clung to Rachel's hand, anxiously watching the dark shadows float overhead. Even though they were not close enough for her to identify them, Zoe sensed the ominous presence of the sharks and stingray as they silently glided by. Her unease passed quickly, however, when they moved away from the shark tank to a pool full of green sea turtles.

Their final stop was the Maui Ocean Center's gift shop. It was full of treasures. Zoe hopped from one enticing item to another and was thrilled when Rachel told her she could choose one thing to take home. After much deliberation, Zoe picked a pink T-shirt with a line of brightly colored humuhumunukunukuapua'a fish swimming across the front and back. Rachel chose a children's book full of large pictures of sea creatures to add to the pink T-shirt, and Zoe waited impatiently at the checkout counter so she could carry them in a bag by herself.

She gave her fish on a stick to Rachel and was holding on to Rachel's other hand, skipping happily by her side when they exited the gift shop and found themselves back at the entrance of the aquarium. Rachel paused momentarily to get her bearings and locate the car.

"Zoe!"

Rachel looked up and saw a dark-haired man lower a camera and leap from a nearby bench. As he began running toward them, Rachel felt Zoe's hand tremble.

"Daddy," she whispered. "I hear my daddy."

Rachel took one look at Zoe's frantic expression, swept her into her arms, turned, and ran back the way they'd come. The exit through the gift shop was a one-way system. A quick glance at the heavy blue door confirmed that there was not even a door handle on the outside. An archway next to the blue door had a sign above it that read *Women*. As the sound of running feet got closer, Rachel bolted for the restroom entrance.

The large, handicapped-accessible stall was vacant, and Rachel rushed inside and locked the door behind her before lowering Zoe to the ground. Then she crouched down beside the little girl and put her arms around her.

"I want my daddy." Zoe was whimpering, tears starting to fall.

"That wasn't your daddy," Rachel said, trying to sound calm despite the fact that her heart was racing and her breath was coming out in gasps.

"But I heard my daddy." Zoe's voice was starting to break with sobs.

Rachel held her close. "It's okay, honey. The man may have sounded like your daddy, but he wasn't. That man's a reporter. He called your name because he wanted a photograph of you."

"No photograph! I want my daddy!" Zoe cried, pushing away from Rachel and backing into the corner of the cubicle.

Rachel looked over at Zoe's tear-stained face and felt her indignation rise. She was kneeling in a public bathroom, trying to console a traumatized child—all because of the thoughtless actions of an aggressive reporter. It wasn't right. She wouldn't let one offensive man affect her or Zoe this way. Tearing off a piece of toilet paper, she leaned over to wipe Zoe's eyes and nose before coming to her feet.

"Your daddy's not here, Zoe," she repeated gently. "But I'll make sure no one takes a picture of you."

She reached out her hand and waited. Zoe turned away, still sniffling.

"Come on, honey," she said with growing determination. "Let's go back to the hotel, and if Tomas is still there, you can tell him humu saw his cousins."

Zoe glanced over her shoulder at the plastic fish now lying on the restroom floor. Slowly, she turned around, bent down, and picked up the stick, giving the rather limp humu a halfhearted wave.

"I think he's getting tired. What do you think?" Rachel said softly.

Zoe nodded.

"Shall we let him rest in the car?"

Zoe gave a shuddering breath and nodded again. Then she stepped forward and placed her other hand in Rachel's.

Rachel gave Zoe's hand a gentle squeeze. Then picking up her purse and the bag from the gift shop, she unlocked the door.

A woman and her daughter were washing their hands at the sinks, but there was no one at the restroom entrance. Rachel moved slowly to the left, pausing a few feet from the archway to study the floor. The restroom tile gave way to concrete, and the Maui sunshine outside created flickering shadows as people walked past the entrance. But there was one shadow that did not move—a long human shadow with a bulge just where a camera would lie against a man's chest. Taking a deep breath, Rachel backed up a few steps.

Suddenly, to the right of the toilet cubicles, she heard voices. She turned to see two women walk around the corner, followed closely by another. An unexpected glimmer of hope filled her. Was it possible that the women had come in through another entrance? Praying that she was right, Rachel turned and walked out the way the women had come.

They turned two corners before she saw the second entrance. It had a similar arched opening to the one they'd used earlier, but there didn't seem to be as much noise or movement outside. Was the reporter aware of this exit? Was he trying to monitor both? She looked down at Zoe standing so trustingly beside her.

"We're going out this way, Zoe," she said, trying to sound more confident than she felt. "Even if that man calls your name, we're not going to stop and talk to him. We're going to keep on walking until we get to the car, okay?"

Zoe looked up at her. "Okay," she whispered.

"Good girl," Rachel said with an encouraging smile. "Let's go."

They stepped out into the bright sunlight. No one stopped them. Rachel shaded her eyes and scanned the parking lot in front of them. She saw their car right away. It was closer to this exit than it was to the other one. With her heart pounding, she tightened her grip on Zoe's hand and hurried across the sidewalk. She purposely didn't look back. Zoe was running to keep up with her but didn't complain. Rachel knew the girl sensed her urgency.

Within seconds, they'd reached the vehicle. Rachel fumbled for the keys, wishing she'd had the foresight to get them out in the restroom. At last, she had them in her hand, unlocked the door, and lifted Zoe into her car seat. She kept her head low as she buckled Zoe in, slammed the door shut, jumped into the driver's seat, and hit the automatic lock on all the doors. Her hand was shaking as she put the key into the ignition, but the engine roared to life, and with a quick check for oncoming cars and pedestrians, she pulled out.

Only when she was almost out of the parking lot did Rachel glance in the rearview mirror at the Maui Ocean Center's main entrance. The reporter was standing outside the entrance to the women's restroom, his camera slung around his neck, frustration evident in his rigid stance. A small smile crossed her lips. She hoped he waited there a long time.

Chapter 13

THE NEXT MORNING, BEN SLIPPED into the Kihea ward chapel and took a seat at the end of a bench near the back. Because of his stint in Afghanistan, it had been more than two months since he'd attended church. He'd missed it. He'd missed the association with other Church members, but more than that, he'd missed the renewal that came from partaking of the sacrament and feeling the uplifting spirit intrinsic to that meeting. Certainly, if there was ever a time he needed uplifting, it was now. The loss of Jed still felt like an open wound. And unless the next few days in Hawaii were better than the last, he faced the very real possibility of losing Zoe too. Ben could barely stifle a groan as he thought back on the disastrous events of the day before.

He'd waited outside the women's restroom at the Maui Ocean Center for almost an hour before a friendly mother of three blonde girls had asked if he needed help. He'd told her he was missing a dark-haired little girl. She'd assumed he'd lost his daughter, and her maternal instinct had kicked into overdrive. She'd entered the restroom and had not returned until she'd checked every stall. Zoe was not there. Stifling his own frustration, it had taken him at least ten minutes to assure the worried woman that he was sure his missing child was safe and was with her mother.

Only after the lady had taken her daughters into the aquarium had he been able to walk to the other side of the building where he'd immediately discovered the other restroom entrance. Zoe's disappearance had been explained. But he still didn't know the identity or role of the woman with her. He'd driven back to the Grand Wailea Hotel and had hung out in the lobby late into the evening, but he'd seen no sign of Whitney, Zoe, or the mystery woman. At his insistence, the front desk had called the Sheldons' suite at least half a dozen times. Each time was met with no reply, and he'd finally returned to his room at the Comfort Inn tired and discouraged.

He would return to the Grand Wailea Hotel after church, likely for another long wait in the lobby. He didn't savor the idea but hadn't come up with any alternatives. With that rather depressing thought, he turned his attention to the meeting.

He watched the young deacons pass the sacrament. With the exception of one tall, redheaded boy, they were all Polynesians. They each wore a white shirt, and although three boys wore dark pants and ties, five of the eight wore black lavalava skirts and flip flops. As they slowly worked their way through the chapel, Ben noticed other members of the congregation wearing traditional Hawaiian clothing and leis. Some of the women had brightly colored flowers in their hair. It was oddly moving to see the sacrament service he was so familiar with conducted in a way that showed the Hawaiians' respect for their God and their culture.

It was when the shortest deacon passed the tray to a family with very wiggly young children that Ben noticed the woman sitting on the end of their pew. She was six or seven rows ahead of him, and he had yet to see more than a small portion of her face, but there was something familiar about her. He leaned forward in his seat, studying her more carefully. Her light brown hair fell below her shoulders in gentle waves, and she wore an attractive sky-blue dress. He watched as the woman reached around an infant to take the sacrament tray and turned to hand it back to the deacon. And in that moment, he saw her face—and he knew.

Tensely, Ben watched the movement on the woman's bench. Three small heads bobbed up and down between her and the Hawaiian couple seated on the other side of the pew. As the meeting progressed, he saw two dark-haired children relocate from the bench to their parents' laps. The other child remained seated beside the woman, but he noticed that the Hawaiian mother leaned over to pass the child objects every once in a while, and apart from an occasional smile directed to the child beside her, his mystery woman's focus remained on the speakers. By the time the closing hymn began, Ben had come to the disappointing conclusion that Zoe was not there.

* * *

Rachel wasn't sure what prompted her to look back when she rose from the bench at the conclusion of sacrament meeting. General interest in the people around her or basic survival instinct—either way, it served the same purpose. She spotted the reporter immediately, and from the determined way he was forging his way toward her against the flow of traffic, he'd obviously seen her too.

How had he found her? For a split second, shock had her rooted to the spot. Then adrenaline kicked in, and her heart started racing as quickly as her mind. She was not about to have a confrontation with him in the chapel. In fact, she'd rather not have a confrontation with him at all. Shouldering her purse, she turned and hurried up the aisle, weaving around small clusters of chatting ward members, trying to put as much distance as she could between herself and her pursuer.

When she reached the exit, she pushed against the door's metal bar and glanced over her shoulder. The reporter was making headway and was now within four rows of the exit too. Leaving all semblance of reverence behind, Rachel stepped into the bright sunlight and started to run. She'd just turned the corner onto the north side of the chapel when she heard the heavy door slam. Pushing her legs even harder, she raced across the parking lot to the waiting green Audi.

Thankful that this time she'd placed her keys in the outside pocket of her purse, she pulled them out as she reached the vehicle. She pushed the unlock button and slipped into the driver's seat, quickly closing the door and locking it behind her. Fumbling in her effort for speed, it took her three tries to get the key into the ignition. But once it was in, the engine started immediately. She forced herself to take a deep breath before putting the car into gear and turning to look behind her.

He'd almost made it. He was within two cars of the Audi and must have seen her taillights turn on because he suddenly swiveled and started running in the direction of a white car parked a few yards farther down. Rachel backed out and drove as quickly as she dared through the parking lot. She'd nearly reached the narrow lane that led to the main road when a family with several small children stepped off the sidewalk in front of her. She slammed on her brakes. The large Hawaiian father herding his children in front of him raised his hand in thanks, called out "Mahalo," and shuffled slowly to the other side of the parking lot, completely oblivious to the fact that the whiteness of Rachel's knuckles on the steering wheel was intensifying with each of his labored steps.

When she was finally free to go, Rachel glanced in the rearview mirror, and her heart sank. The reporter was right behind her in his white car. With no further need for speed, she drove out of the church parking lot decorously, turned left, and headed for the Pi'ilani highway.

At the traffic light, she had a decision to make. If she turned right, she could return to the Grand Wailea and the safety of her hotel room. But she'd also be leading the man behind her directly to Zoe. If she turned left, she could lead him on a scenic drive and hope that somewhere along the way, she'd lose him. It wasn't a difficult choice. Having him get closer to Zoe wasn't an option. So as the traffic light turned green, Rachel put on her blinker and headed away from Wailea.

She didn't consciously decide to drive toward the Maui Ocean Center. It was more that the route was one she knew, and sticking to it lessened her risk of becoming lost on the unfamiliar island. She changed lanes often, and each time she went through a traffic signal, she hoped the white car behind her would have to stop at a red light. It didn't happen. Every time she checked her rearview mirror, the car was there, not more than a few yards from her rear bumper.

As she approached the turnoff for the aquarium, she noticed a long line of cars coming from the opposite direction. She slowed until they were dangerously close, then without any forewarning, she swung across the line of traffic and onto the other road. Cars honked, but with a silent prayer of thanks that she'd escaped collision and prevented the reporter from turning too, she kept driving.

Rachel passed the entrance to the Maui Ocean Center parking lot and followed the road as it swung down toward the wharf at Ma'alaea. To the right, a few restaurants were serving lunch to customers seated at round tables overlooking the sea. To the left, large sheds housed boats of all sizes, some of them out on makeshift frames having repairs done. A speed bump on the narrow road forced her to slow down, and she scoured the area for any sign of a road that might lead her back to the main highway. Her hope began to falter as she continued downhill and realized the road she was on led directly to the wharf. Now that she was finally free of her tail, she was driving into a dead end.

Several boats were docked at the end of the wharf, some of them tethered beside large signs advertising whale-watching expeditions and snorkeling adventures. Three buses had pulled onto the key and were unloading tourists before they parked along the wharf. Rachel maneuvered around one bus and slipped into a vacant parking spot between a large RV and a tour bus. If she was lucky, the large vehicles on either side of her would make it difficult to see the green Audi from the road.

A crowd of people had gathered on the jetty in front of a gleaming white boat with the name *Maui Magic* painted in blue along its hull. As the white car crested the hill behind her, Rachel frantically searched the area for a place to hide. She slipped out of her vehicle and around the tour bus, quickly weaving her way into the center of a large group of tourists. Concealed by the crowd, she moved with them as they advanced to the waiting boat's gangplank.

When the *Maui Magic* pulled away from the dock with a throb of engines and a surge of water, Rachel sat on deck watching the wharf rapidly shrink to miniature. With the rhythm of the powerful propellers gently vibrating the boat and the sea breeze blowing through her hair, she leaned back against the wooden bench and closed her eyes.

She couldn't understand why the reporter was so doggedly determined to talk to her. She was a nobody. Her understanding of what had happened in Zoe's life—or the Sheldons' lives, for that matter—was tenuous at best. She would be a poor source for any reporter's article, partly because of her lack of knowledge and partly because what little she did know she wasn't about to share with a bloodthirsty member of the paparazzi. She could only hope that by the time the boat returned to dock, he would have given up the hunt and she could return to the peace and quiet of her hotel room.

Chapter 14

THREE HOURS LATER, WHEN THE harbor came into view once more, a little knot formed somewhere deep in Rachel's stomach. She'd soaked in the salty air, seen distant humpback whales spouting and rolling through the waves, and watched myriad multicolored fish swim through the crystal clear waters. It had been a magical—albeit short-lived—escape from reality.

The crew had eyed her strangely when she'd declined their offer of a wetsuit and snorkeling session in the calm water off Molokini, but she had gone below deck and watched the fish through the Perspex portion of the boat's hull instead. The ocean creatures were fascinating, but they brought back memories of Zoe at the aquarium—and the man who had first seen her there. So before long, she opted to stay on the deck and watch the crew navigate their return to Ma'alaea.

They came into dock with a gentle thud, and crewmen jumped on shore to tie up the boat. They attached the walkway, and within minutes, a steady stream of people began exiting the boat. Rachel joined the line behind a group of Japanese tourists. As they stepped onto the wharf, the group moved in unison toward a waiting tour bus.

Suddenly, a man stepped out from behind the sign advertising snorkeling and whale-watching tours and grasped Rachel's elbow, steering her away from the others. "Seems like I've spent a lot of time waiting for you over the last couple of days," he said.

Rachel jumped, her pulse racing as his grip tightened. "You chose to do it," she said. She was tired of running, tired of this game of cat and mouse; it was time for it to end.

"That's true," he conceded. "But I don't want to do it anymore."

She tried to break his grip on her arm. "How did you know I was on the boat?" she asked.

He kept ahold of her and raised an eyebrow. "It wasn't that hard. I found your car and asked around to find out which boats had just left." He glanced at her blue dress and offered a hint of a smile. "Of course, it helped that you were the only one to go on a snorkeling expedition in church clothes."

Rachel frowned but didn't say anything more as he led her toward one of the cafés at the end of the wharf and pointed at a vacant round table with two wrought-iron chairs.

"I've been here long enough that the owner's given up on me. If we sit here, I don't think we'll be disturbed for a while."

"Actually, since you won't let me go, that's not very comforting," Rachel said.

Her captor gave a wry smile. "Maybe not. But I have some questions for you, and I'd like some uninterrupted answers."

Rachel looked up at him for the first time. "I don't have to tell you anything."

"I know," he said, startling Rachel with the intense look in his dark brown eyes. "But I sincerely hope you will."

He pulled out a chair for her and indicated that she sit down. Reluctantly, Rachel took the seat and watched as he claimed the other chair across the table from her. To her surprise, he didn't pull out a notebook, a voice recorder, or even a camera. He leaned his elbows on the table, his eyes never leaving her face. "How's Zoe?" he asked quietly.

"Fine," Rachel said, momentarily nonplussed that he would begin his interrogation by asking about Zoe in that way. She hoped her answer was vague enough to be of no use to him.

He leaned back and raked his fingers through his hair. "Don't try to put me off with platitudes," he said in obvious irritation. "I need to know how she's really doing."

Rachel felt her frustration mounting. "Look," she said grimly. "I don't know who you are or what trashy newspaper or magazine you work for. It doesn't matter. You aren't going to get any information about Zoe from me. No child deserves to be hounded and traumatized by obnoxious reporters—especially a child who's just lost her father. If it weren't for the fact that she doesn't need any more stressful publicity rocking her little world right now, I'd have reported you for harassment already."

He paled. "I traumatized her?"

"Are you kidding me?" Rachel knew her voice was rising. "You yell out her name and chase her down—and don't expect her to think anything of it? She was convinced you were her father. She was in tears over it."

He groaned. "I didn't think . . ." he said hoarsely.

"Well, that's too bad," Rachel said, coming to her feet. "But from here on out, I'd appreciate it if you'd stay away from both Zoe and me."

He also came to his feet. "Wait. Please." He cleared his throat. "I've gone about this all wrong. Will you let me explain?"

"There's nothing to explain," Rachel said. "You're a reporter after a new scoop, and I'm not going to give it to you. End of story."

She turned to go, but the man spoke again. "I am a reporter. But not for the kind of publication you think. I have zero interest in doing an article on Zoe, and I'd never intentionally hurt her. The reason she responded the way she did at the aquarium is that I do look and sound like her father. Jed was my twin brother." He paused to take his wallet out of his pocket, and as Rachel swung around to look at him again, he pulled out two cards and handed them to her. "My name's Ben Cooper, and I'm Zoe's uncle."

With a pounding heart, Rachel reached for the cards. One was for *Our World Publications*, identifying Ben Cooper by name and photograph. The other was a small photograph taken in a wooded area. A slightly younger Zoe was riding on the shoulders of someone who looked just like the man in front of her. Her face was alight with mischief, and the man was grinning at the camera.

"Is this you or Zoe's father?" Rachel asked.

"It's me," Ben said. "Jed took the photo. We were going on a honey hunt in the forest behind their house."

Rachel gave a little smile. "Like the Berenstain Bears?"

"Either that or Winnie the Pooh," he said with an answering smile. "I don't remember for sure."

He extended his hand to her. "Can we start over? My name's Ben Cooper. I've spent the last two months in Afghanistan on assignment for *Our World*. Three days ago, I found out my brother, Jed, had been killed in a car accident. I flew straight to Utah, but when I arrived, I found that my niece, Zoe, had been taken somewhere by the mother who abandoned her as a baby. Since then, my sole focus has been to find Zoe." A look of desperation crossed his face. "I have to know that she's okay."

As Rachel stared at the man in front of her, trying to assimilate what he'd just told her, two things struck her simultaneously. The first was that Zoe's expressive brown eyes were a carbon copy of her uncle's—and therefore, she assumed, her father's. Second, and far more importantly, Ben Cooper was obviously more deeply concerned about Zoe than anyone else Rachel had met since she'd arrived in Hawaii. He genuinely cared about his young niece.

After only a slight hesitation, she accepted his hand. "My name's Rachel Hamilton," she said. "Zoe misses her father, but she's safe and well."

Ben's relief was palpable. "Thank you," he said, giving her his first genuine smile. He pointed to the chair she'd just vacated. "Will you stay—just for a little while?"

Rachel glanced at her watch. "I have to be back at the hotel in an hour."

"I'll take whatever time you can give me," Ben said.

She took a seat and looked down at her hands. "I'm very sorry about your brother."

"Thanks." Ben sighed. "There are times when it hurts so much I can hardly stand it. And other times, it seems so unreal that he's gone that I start to wonder if he is."

Rachel nodded her understanding. "I think that's how Zoe's been feeling too."

"Have you been with her ever since she left Utah?"

"No," Rachel said. "I work for Senator Sheldon—at his office in DC. Two days ago, his secretary called to ask me to join them in Hawaii. I thought I was coming to help with the negotiations. I didn't know until I got here that he was assigning me Zoe duty."

Ben raised his eyebrows. "And you weren't too happy about it?"

Rachel gave a sheepish smile. "Not at first, to be honest. But it didn't take long for me to realize I'd much rather hang out with Zoe at the beach or the aquarium than wade through the boring paperwork I got to read last night."

He grinned. "Yeah. Pretty sure Zoe can never be titled 'boring.'"

She shook her head and smiled. "It sounds like you're pretty close to her."

"Apart from being my twin brother, Jed was my best friend," Ben said. "My office is in New York, and my work takes me overseas for weeks at a time, but whenever I could pull it off, I'd head to Utah to see Jed and Zoe. They're the only family I have." He stopped and cleared his throat as he realized the significance of what he'd just said. "I guess Zoe's the only family I have now. The last time I saw them was the beginning of October."

He looked away, gazing out to sea for a few moments. Rachel waited, instinctively knowing he needed time to collect himself. When he turned back, the sadness in his eyes said more than words ever could. "Is there any way you can arrange for me to see Zoe before I leave?" he asked.

"Isn't that something you should ask Mrs. Sheldon?"

Ben gave a frustrated sigh. "I've tried. I've waited for hours in the lobby at the Grand Wailea Hotel. I've had the front desk call through to her suite multiple times. I have no other way of getting ahold of her. I don't even think my brother had any contact with her after he left New York."

"What exactly . . ." Rachel checked herself, then started again. "Since I used this line on you, it's only fair that you have the same caveat. This is a question you don't have to answer."

Ben's eyebrow tweaked up.

Rachel took a deep breath and plowed on. "What happened between your brother and Whitney Sheldon?"

For a few moments, Ben said nothing. A seagull wheeled overhead, its raucous cry breaking the silence that hung over the table.

"Jed was a very private person," he began. "Even when his marriage was over and he moved from New York to Utah, he didn't talk about what he'd gone through. So I can only give you my take on it—something I wouldn't normally do, especially to one of Senator Sheldon's employees. But I think . . ." He paused as though searching his feelings. "I think it may be important to Zoe that you understand the situation."

"It's probably hard to believe, coming from a virtual stranger," Rachel said, "but I do know how to keep things confidential."

"Apart from the fact that you obviously have some level of security clearance to work on Senator Sheldon's staff, your response—or should I say, your lack of response—when I first questioned you about Zoe would tell me that," he said.

"Thanks," Rachel said, feeling her cheeks color. "I think."

Ben gave a small smile. "Jed and Whitney met at *ABC News*. Jed had been assigned to the Financial News department, and Whitney was one of the secretaries there. Jed was thrilled to learn that Whitney was LDS—"

"Wait!" Rachel interrupted. "Whitney's LDS?" She couldn't hide the disbelief in her voice.

Ben gave her a rueful look. "You'd be hard pressed to know it now, wouldn't you?"

"Frankly, yes," Rachel said. "But does that mean you, Jed, and Zoe are too?"

Ben's eyes twinkled. "Why else do you think I was in sacrament meeting?"

Rachel raised her hands. "I don't know. Incredible stalking powers?"

This time he actually laughed. "I wish I could add that to my résumé," he said, and Rachel found herself smiling too.

"I don't think Whitney was very active before Jed came along, but she started going to the young adult ward with him, and pretty soon, they were dating. I was traveling overseas a lot and missed out on their whirlwind romance. I got home from a three-week trip to Guatemala at Thanksgiving to find them engaged and planning a Christmas wedding.

"After they got married, whenever I was in town, I visited them in the fancy new apartment Whitney had rented not far from Central Park. Jed was always genuinely glad to see me, but I don't think Whitney ever felt the same way.

"I don't really know when things started to unravel. Jed always maintained it was when Whitney became pregnant and their radically different ideas on parenting came to light. I've always thought it was before that—when Whitney realized Jed didn't share her aspirations for fame and fortune and she stopped going to church. She thrived on partying with the elite, and if she couldn't do it on her own merit, going as the wife of one of the upcoming stars at *ABC News* was a great alternative.

"When Zoe was born, things came to a head. Whitney hired a personal trainer to help her regain her pre-pregnancy figure ASAP and then announced that she was going back to work and back to attending late-night, adult-only social gatherings and that she was hiring a full-time nanny for Zoe. Jed was stunned and tried to make up for Whitney's lack of maternal interest by spending extra time with their baby girl.

"Because of that, it wasn't really surprising that it was Jed, not Whitney, who first noticed that Zoe's eyes didn't move normally. When she was eight weeks old, they took her to one of New York's best pediatric ophthalmologists, who told them Zoe's vision was severely impaired.

"He sent them home with their baby girl's first tiny pair of glasses. Whitney went straight to her bedroom and locked the door. An hour later, she walked out of Jed's and Zoe's lives pulling two bulging purple suitcases behind her."

Rachel sat in stunned silence. Ben looked at her, his expressive eyes full of remorse. "I always felt bad that I wasn't there when Jed needed me the most. He called me in India to tell me, and half a world away, I could tell how badly he was hurting—his marriage was over, and his baby would never have normal vision."

"They can't do anything for Zoe?" Rachel asked.

"She's already had two eye surgeries, and she's scheduled for another before she starts school," Ben told her. "Her eyesight is better than it was, but even after the final surgery, the doctors don't think it will be where it should be."

Rachel pictured Zoe at the aquarium, her face pressed against the tanks, patiently waiting for a fish to swim close enough for her to see. She wished for so much more for Zoe. Unbidden, a tear rolled down her face. She tried to wipe it away before Ben noticed.

"It ended up being a blessing that they moved so close to Primary Children's Hospital," Ben said. "For a few months after Whitney left, Jed tried to balance single parenthood with being the weekend anchor for *ABC News*, but when the presidential election coverage hit fever pitch, so did his schedule. He was sent out on assignment so many times that he didn't see Zoe for more than three weeks. It wasn't worth it to him. He left his position at *ABC News* and his home in Manhattan for a Monday-through-Friday anchor job at KSL television in Salt Lake City, and I don't think he ever regretted it."

"It sounds like he was a great dad," Rachel said.

"He did it all," Ben said. "The diapers, the sleepless nights, the teething. Don't ask me how. Pretty sure I would have bailed on the potty training at least."

Rachel laughed. "My mother said the only thing worse than potty training was teaching us to drive."

Ben chuckled. "I'll have to remember that."

Across the wharf, a bell sounded, and a large boat's engines revved up. Rachel glanced at her watch and gasped.

"I have to go," she said, coming to her feet.

Ben rose too and handed Rachel a card. "My number. I'll meet Zoe anywhere, anytime. Please talk to Whitney for me."

"I'll try," she said, tucking the card into her purse. "But I can't promise anything."

"Thank you, Rachel."

She nodded and raised her hand in farewell before hurrying across the narrow street toward the wharf and her waiting vehicle.

Chapter 15

BEN WATCHED THE GREEN AUDI disappear over the crest of the hill before he began walking back to his own rental vehicle. His hands in his pockets, he thought back over the last hour. What had begun as a distasteful grilling had ended as a pleasant conversation, and he found himself wishing he could have talked to Rachel for longer.

To his chagrin, he realized that Rachel had gleaned far more information from him than he had from her. His award-winning investigative skills were obviously no match for a protective woman. And the fact that Rachel's eyes were the same color blue as her dress didn't help either. Ben shook his head. He'd probably shared too much, but he'd sensed that she would not trust him with information if he wasn't willing to do the same. He could only hope that she would be circumspect and use what he'd told her for Zoe's benefit—including finding a way for him to see his young niece.

His car was parked up against the short retaining wall along the wharf. Ben leaned against it, looking out to sea. Molokini Island was a distant smudge on the horizon. A scattering of boats of various sizes dotted the aquamarine ocean, and ubiquitous seagulls sailed overhead. It was a beautiful scene, but the sense of peace it should have invoked continued to elude him. With a sigh, he pulled out his cell phone and dialed Detective Roman's number.

"Roman." The detective answered on the second ring.

"Detective, this is Ben Cooper," Ben said.

"Good to hear from you, Ben," the detective said. "You keeping your nose clean?"

"I'm trying," Ben said.

"Glad to hear it."

"Any developments since I left?" Ben asked.

"Nothing concrete, but we've got a lot of leads. The Dicksons found some New York phone numbers we're following up on. Dorothy also found the combination to your brother's safe and handed over the financial records that were inside. I've got someone looking at them now; I'm hoping it will shed some light on Zoe's trust fund balance, among other things." He took a breath, then continued. "I paid a visit to Jed's lawyer. Nervous guy. Don't think he enjoyed having a police presence in his office very much. He was mopping his face by the time I left. We'll continue to keep an eye on things there. And we're still working through Jed's cell phone records. Nothing unusual yet, but we've still got a lot of numbers to go through."

"What about the abandoned truck?" Ben asked. "Any leads on that?"

"According to the company that makes the stretch chrome, they've got thirteen clients in the Vegas area. Four of them have trucks. I called in a favor to a buddy in the Vegas PD. He's checking on them and is supposed to get back to me tomorrow morning."

Ben raked his fingers through his hair. The tedious process of clue hunting and fact-finding was testing his patience. Logically, he knew these things took time and had to be done right, but simply waiting for something to happen went against everything in him.

The detective must have sensed his frustration. "We're putting together a joint task force, Ben. The FBI's on board. Give them some time. They'll do whatever's needed to find the person behind your brother's death."

"Thanks." Ben sighed. "Call me whenever you have an update."

"I will," he promised. "Have you located your niece?"

"Yes, but I haven't had a chance to talk to her yet."

"You remember what I told you about keeping the peace," Detective Roman warned.

"Yeah, I know." Ben felt a twinge of guilt as he remembered Rachel's threat to report him if he didn't stop harassing her. He'd barely dodged that bullet.

"Well, keep remembering it," the detective said. "I'll be in touch soon."

Detective Roman disconnected the call, and Ben was left standing alone at the wharf, praying for guidance and for a little girl.

* * *

Rachel ran all the way from the Grand Wailea Hotel parking lot to the Sheldons' suite, but a quick glance at her watch as she knocked on the door confirmed that she hadn't been fast enough.

"You're late!" Whitney snapped as Rachel entered the room.

Whitney had on a form-fitting black dress and sparkling high-heeled sandals as well as glittering jewelry at her neck and ears.

"I'm sorry," Rachel began. "The traffic was heavy, and I—"

Whitney cut her off with a wave of her hand. "I'm not interested in your excuses," she said. "Cocktail hour for all the dignitaries and their spouses was at four o'clock. I heard my husband tell you that himself. Because you weren't here, he's had to go unaccompanied, and I'll arrive embarrassingly late."

Rachel didn't think ten minutes qualified as embarrassingly late, and she secretly wondered if Whitney might prefer a later, more dramatic entrance anyway. She knew better than to point that out, however, and opted to stand quietly as Whitney snatched her black, sequined clutch purse off the table and marched over to the door.

"I expect you to stay with Zoe until our return late this evening and will plan on seeing you back here *promptly* at 8:00 a.m. tomorrow."

Fleetingly, Rachel wondered if Whitney expected her to bow or salute following the marching orders she'd just been issued but decided her best response was to ignore the woman's condescending attitude altogether.

"About tomorrow," Rachel began. All the way back to the hotel, she'd been trying to figure out the best way to broach the subject of Ben's seeing Zoe but hadn't come up with anything better than a direct approach. "Would you have any objections to Zoe meeting with—"

"Look," Whitney interrupted her again. "My husband has already told you we don't care what you do or where you go with Zoe while we're here. I can see that I will have to tell him that any instructions you receive will need to be repeated or written down. You seem to have an issue with remembering them. I'm already late. Good-bye, Rachel." Whitney waltzed out of the suite, slamming the door behind her.

Rachel stood staring at the closed door, oscillating between disbelief and fury. She couldn't remember a time when she'd ever been treated so badly. The injustice of Whitney's accusations caused a lump in her throat, and her high-handed manner simply made Rachel angry.

"Don't be sad, Wachul. She gets mad at me too."

At the small voice, Rachel swung around. Zoe was standing beside the TV, her dark hair disheveled, her large brown eyes behind her thick glasses gazing at Rachel with concern.

"Hi, Zoe!" Rachel smothered her frustration and smiled at the little girl. She bent down and held out her arms. Zoe shot into them like an arrow from a bow.

"You were a long time." Zoe's voice was muffled by Rachel's shoulder, but her anxiety was unmistakable.

"I'm sorry, honey." Rachel stroked the little girl's unruly hair. "I didn't mean to be late."

"You didn't come for breakfast or lunch," Zoe stated.

"Didn't your mother tell you I wasn't going to be here until almost dinner time?" she asked, pulling back so she could see Zoe's face.

Zoe shook her head. "Where did you go?"

"I went to church," Rachel explained.

Zoe's face lit up. "Today's church day?"

Rachel felt awful. "Yes. It's Sunday," she said. "I'm sorry, Zoe. I should have taken you to church with me." Rachel paused, wondering briefly how different her day would have been if Zoe had been with her when Ben had spotted her in the chapel.

Zoe looked at her quizzically. "Can I still wear my dress?"

Rachel laughed and gave the little girl a squeeze. "That's a wonderful idea," she said, noticing that Zoe was still wearing her pajamas. She didn't want to think about the possibility that Zoe had spent all Sunday in the hotel room, two feet from the TV. "Let's get you dressed, and we'll go for a walk."

Zoe pulled away, hurried over to the coffee table, and picked up her slightly battered fish on a stick. "Can humu come too?" she asked, giving it a wave.

"Definitely," Rachel said with a smile.

*　*　*

Later that night, Rachel sat at the large desk in the Sheldons' suite and stared at the pile of papers in front of her. She'd read and reread some of them multiple times. She could tell the negotiations were going well. They were drawing up agreements. Already, the future looked bright for more than one Arizonan company. But despite her desire to be involved, she couldn't concentrate. Two minutes after reviewing a page, she could barely remember what she'd read.

She picked up the small business card lying on the polished wood beside the papers and flipped it through her fingers. Zoe was asleep. A long walk along the coastal path followed by a large helping of macaroni and cheese was all she'd managed before bedtime. Rachel smiled at the memory of Zoe's joy as she'd skipped along the walkway in her pink and purple sundress carrying her fish on a stick. She was an easy child to love.

Ben Cooper acted as though he loved Zoe—as though he really cared. If she facilitated a meeting between Ben and Zoe, would he show Zoe the affection she was so desperately lacking right now? Or would seeing her uncle simply bring back the pain of losing her father? Rachel didn't want to shoulder the weight of that decision, but it was obvious that Whitney had jettisoned it. She gazed at Zoe's closed bedroom door, picturing the little girl curled up asleep on the other side. Then she pulled out her cell phone and dialed the number on the card.

Chapter 16

THE ROAD NARROWED AS RACHEL and Zoe drove up the 'Iao Valley. A thick wall of dark green vegetation hung over both sides of the road, broken occasionally by narrow gates leading to homes hidden behind the foliage. They passed a couple of early-morning cyclists and an occasional motorist, but for the most part, the road was quiet, and the morning sun lit their way without the intense heat that would come later.

Rachel slowed the car as a wild chicken ran across the road in front of them. She wanted to point out the bird to Zoe but knew it had already scuttled out of the range of Zoe's vision. She glanced at the little girl in the rearview mirror. Zoe had allowed Rachel to put a couple of ribbons in her hair this morning, but with the sunroof down, the island breeze was making short work of them.

She hadn't told Zoe about her uncle, not wanting to get her hopes up should something fall through with their planned rendezvous.

She'd prayed long and hard the night before, hoping to experience a feeling of confirmation that she'd made the right decision. But she was still unsure. And the closer they got to the 'Iao Needle, the more nervous she became. If she needed to, she'd turn around in the parking lot and drive away, and Zoe would be none the wiser.

The road climbed slightly, then curved to the right before suddenly plateauing into a wide parking area. Quickly, Rachel scoured the area. Two tour buses and half a dozen cars had already claimed positions near a path that led toward the mountain. A few stalls away from the other vehicles was Ben's white car. Rachel pulled into a spot on the other side of the parking lot and turned off the engine. Taking a deep breath, she released her seat belt and looked over her shoulder. Ben had obviously been watching for them. He was now standing outside his vehicle, waiting.

Grateful that he hadn't rushed right over, Rachel got out of the car and opened Zoe's door. Leaning closer, she retied Zoe's hair bows before moving on to unbuckle the little girl's car seat.

"Zoe, I have a surprise for you," she said.

Zoe looked up, wide-eyed. "A surprise?"

A wild rooster crowed, and two more chickens ran past the car in a flurry of feathers.

"I hear chickens," Zoe said with mounting excitement. "Can I see the chickens?"

Rachel smiled. "Yes," she said. "But that's not the surprise."

Zoe stopped straining to see the wild birds outside the car and turned back to face Rachel. "Another surprise?" she asked.

Rachel nodded. "Your uncle Ben is here to see you," she said quietly.

For a moment, Zoe was perfectly still. But before Rachel could act on her rapidly multiplying misgivings, Zoe was yanking on the straps of her car seat.

"Uncle Ben!" she cried. "I want to see Uncle Ben!"

Rachel threaded Zoe's arm out from behind the last remaining belt and stood back as she scrambled out of the car.

"Uncle Ben!" Zoe cried one more time.

That was all Ben had been waiting for. He started to run. In a matter of seconds, he crossed the parking lot and scooped Zoe into his arms. She wrapped her arms around his neck and clung to him as he lifted her off her feet.

"Zoe, I've missed you so much," Ben said, his voice catching.

Zoe released her hold on Ben's neck and moved her hands to touch his face. "Daddy died, Uncle Ben," she said.

Ben's brown eyes didn't leave hers. "I know, Peanut."

"He didn't come home," she said. "Why didn't he come home?"

Ben paused, obviously searching for the right words. "He was in a very bad car accident, Zoe. His body hurt so much his spirit had to leave it behind." He tightened his grip on his niece. "I bet that going to live with Heavenly Father without you was the hardest thing he's ever done."

Zoe buried her face in Ben's shoulder. "But I want him to come back to my house," she said with a sob.

Ben raised one hand and gently stroked her head. "Me too, Zoe," he whispered. "Me too."

He lowered his cheek to rest on top of Zoe's head and held her close. For a few minutes, no one spoke. Then a rooster crowed again, and Zoe's head popped up, curiosity overpowering her sadness. "Did you hear that?" she said with a sniff. "I think it was a chicken."

"Or maybe a rooster," Ben said, his eyes shining with unshed tears and a small smile playing across his lips.

"Or maybe a rooster," Zoe repeated, her head turning every direction to locate the source of the sound.

Ben lowered her to the ground. "How about we go find out?" he said.

"And Wachul too?" Zoe asked.

"Of course," Ben said, looking over Zoe's head at Rachel.

Hurriedly wiping the tears from her eyes, Rachel gave him a weak smile. She was not as resilient as Zoe. "I'd love to go on a rooster hunt," she managed.

Zoe placed her small hand in Ben's and beamed. Rachel's eyes pricked again. She turned away, fumbling with her keys. It may have taken longer than she liked, but she'd just received the answer to her prayers.

Rachel watched Zoe and Ben chase three frantic chickens and one skinny rooster across the parking lot several times before the traffic increased enough that Ben pronounced the activity too dangerous for children or poultry. Then he swung a squealing Zoe up onto his shoulders, and with Rachel beside them, they headed for the path that led to the 'Iao Needle.

The scenery was spectacular. A short footbridge took them across a narrow gorge to the other side of the mountain. Far below, a stream circumvented boulders, collected in pools, and fell in a cloud of water droplets. Zoe turned her head to listen to the running water, laughing as the breeze blew the spray onto her outstretched hands. Rachel pointed out flowers and birds as they passed them. And from her perch on Ben's shoulders, Zoe saw much more than she would have seen on her own.

The path continued climbing up the side of the mountain in switchback fashion until it neared the top, where stairs had been added. At the top of the stairs, a concrete platform formed a viewing area for the 'Iao Needle, and when they drew nearer, the two men who were already there moved aside to share the view.

"Can you see the huge pokey rock, Zoe?" Rachel asked, and Ben swiveled so Zoe was facing the 'Iao Needle.

"It's green," Zoe said, looking confused.

"That's because it's covered in plants," Ben explained.

"Can I touch it?" she asked.

"No. It's too far away," Rachel told her. "This is as close as we'll get."

Zoe squinted at the 'Iao Needle in the distance for a few more seconds. "Okay," she said. "Can we go now?"

Ben chuckled. "So much for sightseeing with a four-year-old!"

Rachel looked up at him. His eyes crinkled just like Zoe's when he laughed, and Zoe's ministrations on her ride up the mountain had given his dark brown hair the same unruly look as his niece's. Rachel smiled. Ben and Zoe were so alike it made Rachel feel as though she'd known Ben far longer than an hour or two.

"Would you like to go down to the river?" Rachel asked.

"Yeah!" Zoe bounced up and down on Ben's shoulders, and Ben seized her legs with a gasp. "Whoa, crazy girl!"

Rachel laughed at the pained expression on Ben's face. She was pretty sure his broad shoulders could handle a lot more than a wiggly young rider, but she opted to take pity on him. "Hop down, Zoe," she encouraged. "I bet you can walk all the way to the river on your own."

Zoe gave a reluctant sigh. "Okay," she said, releasing her grip on Ben as he lifted her up and over his head.

Once her feet were on the ground, Zoe skipped over to Rachel and took her hand. Rachel gave her fingers a gentle squeeze, surprised by how much the little girl's gesture meant to her. Then they turned and headed back down the stairs to the steep path below.

The paved path eventually gave way to a dirt trail that followed the river. Vines hung from many of the trees, and elaborate root systems lay both above the ground and below. Unfamiliar birdcalls and the slowly increasing heat gave the area a junglelike feel. Zoe found a long, thin stick and dragged it behind her until Ben pointed out a large, flat rock beside the river and suggested that she try fishing. He lifted her onto the rock and sat beside her as she dipped the tip of the stick into the fast-moving water, hoping a fish would bite.

Rachel hung back to watch. Ben had a protective arm around Zoe, who had snuggled up against him and was flicking the stick in and out of the river. Rachel felt a lump form in her throat again. Even though Rachel had never seen them together, she knew this picture-perfect moment could have been Zoe and her father. Ben turned his head, and Rachel managed a weak smile.

He smiled in return. "There's room for three," he said, patting the slab of rock beside him.

Rachel stepped over the labyrinth of roots and scrambled onto the sun-warmed boulder. There was not a lot of extra space, and she was uncomfortably aware of Ben's leg next to hers as she sat down. She set her purse on her knee and dug through it until she found a granola bar. After tearing it open, she held it out. "Here, Zoe," she said. "Have a snack."

Zoe reached for it with alacrity. Taking a bite, she mumbled a crumby thank you.

Rachel forced herself to look at Ben. "Would you like one?" she asked.

"Do you have extra?"

She dug a little deeper into her purse, pulled out two more granola bars, and handed him one.

Ben raised his eyebrow. "I'm impressed," he said.

Rachel felt herself blush. "Don't be. Poor Zoe had to have a meltdown on the beach before I got my act together." She shook her head. "You'd think with six younger brothers I'd have remembered that kids need regular fuel."

"You're the oldest of seven? And the others are all boys?" he asked, amusement lighting his eyes.

Rachel sighed. "Yes. Which means I'm much better at playing flag football and basketball than I am at painting nails and doing hair."

Ben laughed at her look of chagrin. "Hey, that's not a bad thing."

"It is sometimes," Rachel said, looking at her unadorned hands and picturing Whitney's glamorous nails, hair, clothing, and accessories. "The high-powered players in the worlds of politics and business care a lot more about a woman's appearance than her skills on the basketball court."

For a moment, Ben studied her as though her words surprised him. "Well, for the record, the Zoe and Ben Coopers of this world would much rather be with a woman who plays games and carries snacks in her purse," he said. Then keeping his tone light, he added, "Of course, if she's pretty too, that's an added bonus."

Color flooded Rachel's face, and she turned away, but not before Ben noticed.

"Hey," he said, reaching out to touch her arm. "I didn't mean to embarrass you."

"Look!" Zoe shrieked. "I caught something." She swung her stick high into the air, showering them all with water droplets.

Ben raised his hand to catch the soggy leaf as it fell off the end of the stick. "Nice work, Zoe," he said, giving Rachel a quick wink. "We'll make a fisherman out of you yet."

Zoe glowed with pride, and Ben commandeered the wildly flailing stick as Rachel gave herself a stern, silent lecture on the importance of controlling her heart rate.

Chapter 17

By the time they reached the parking lot, Zoe's short legs had given out, and she was back on Ben's shoulders. Rachel glanced up at Zoe. Her arms were still wrapped tightly around Ben's head, but her blinks were lasting longer and longer.

"She's falling asleep," Rachel whispered, pointing at Zoe.

Ben smiled. "I wondered," he said. "She seemed to be swaying a lot."

"Can you get her down?"

He gave a small nod. "Go ahead and open the car door. I'll put her in her seat."

Rachel pulled open the door and stepped aside as Ben reached up and drew Zoe off his shoulders and into his arms. He held her close for a few seconds, then reached over to place her in the car seat. As soon as she was seated, Zoe's eyes popped open and a look of panic crossed her face. "Uncle Ben!" she cried, pulling at the restraining straps. "I want to stay with Uncle Ben!"

Ben placed a gentle hand across her torso, calming her frantic movement. "It's okay, Zoe. I'm still here. We're ready to go, but you have to be in your car seat before Rachel can drive."

"Are you coming too?" Zoe asked, tears already forming.

Ben turned to Rachel with a questioning look. "What are you doing for the rest of the day?" he asked.

"I don't have anything specific planned," she admitted.

"There's a big swap meet in Kahului," he said. "Would you be interested in checking it out? We could probably find something to eat there."

Zoe was holding tightly to two of Ben's fingers, not willing to let him go. And truth be told, Rachel had enjoyed having another adult around. Their trek to see the 'Iao Needle would have been difficult at best without

Ben's willingness to carry Zoe, and their morning had been better because he was there.

"You know it won't be long before this growing girl and adult man need more fuel," Ben coaxed, a twinkle in his eye.

Rachel laughed. She couldn't help it. "Do you know the way?" she asked.

"I read about it during one of my long sojourns in the Grand Wailea's lobby," he said. "I think I can find it, but I can plug it into the GPS on my phone too."

"Okay," Rachel agreed. "We'll follow you."

Ben's eyes reflected his gratitude. "Thank you," he said softly. He turned back to Zoe and slowly extricated his hand from her clutches. "I have to drive my car, Peanut. But I'll be with you in a few minutes, okay?"

"I'm not a peanut," Zoe began. "I'm a . . ."

"Monkey!" Ben cut her off and started tickling her.

"No!" she squealed. "I'm a girl!"

"Okay, little girl," Ben relented. "You be good for Rachel. I'll see you soon."

He dropped a kiss on Zoe's forehead and stepped back to let Rachel finish securing Zoe's car seat buckles. When she was ready, he pushed the door closed and turned to face Rachel.

"I still haven't officially thanked you for setting this up with Whitney," he said. "I don't know how you pulled it off, but it means a great deal to me."

Rachel's jaw tightened. The memory of her encounter with Whitney—the unfair accusations and indifference over Zoe's needs—still stung. She looked away, not trusting her voice.

"Did I say something wrong?" Ben sounded anxious.

She shook her head but kept her face averted. "Whitney doesn't know," she finally admitted. "I tried asking her, but she wasn't interested." Rachel glanced at Zoe. The little girl had found a discarded fruit snack bag and was checking it for leftover treats. Rachel swallowed hard. "Whitney said she doesn't care what we do. I was the one who decided to bring Zoe to see you. I was the one who risked hurting a little girl even more than she's already been hurt. I prayed all the way here that I'd made the right decision."

Ben placed his finger gently under Rachel's chin and raised it so she had to look at him. "And what do you think now?" he asked. "Did you make the right decision?"

"This has probably been the best day Zoe's had since her father passed away," she said softly. "But having you leave again may make it her worst."

Ben dropped his hand but didn't break eye contact. "While I'm in Hawaii, I'll take as much time with Zoe as you'll give me. And when I get back to the mainland, I'll do everything in my power to get Zoe back home to the family who loves her."

"I thought you had no other family," Rachel said, confused.

"I don't have any other siblings, and my parents both died before Jed and I graduated from college," he said. "But Bert and Dorothy Dickson have lived with Jed and Zoe since Zoe was a baby. They were good friends of my parents and have taken over the role of Zoe's grandparents. Dorothy was in the car accident with Jed and still has a long recovery ahead, but she loves Zoe like her own."

"Grandpa Bert and Grandma Dory," Rachel breathed. "I couldn't figure out who Zoe was talking about."

"When Zoe was little, she couldn't say Dorothy, so she shortened it to Dory," he explained. "No one's broken it to Dorothy that she has the same name as the loopy fish in *Finding Nemo*."

Rachel managed a smile. "I'd like to hear more about them. All Zoe's told me is that Grandma Dory always has snacks in her purse and Grandpa Bert makes pancakes that look like moose."

Now it was Ben's turn to smile. "I'll tell you more about them at the swap meet." He paused. "Are you still okay with doing that?"

Rachel nodded. "It's getting late enough that the adult woman is ready for some more fuel now too."

Ben chuckled. "I'll lead out," he said and took off toward his car at a run.

* * *

It was perhaps the most eclectic lunch Rachel had ever eaten. Fresh pineapple, dripping with juice; chips and homemade mango salsa; seasoned nuts and kettle corn; homemade donuts; and Hawaiian shaved ice. As they wandered from one food stall to another, Rachel promised herself that she and Zoe would have at least one serving of vegetables at dinnertime, then put aside all worries about balanced meals, tried a little of everything, and loved it all.

Zoe was in heaven. By the time she'd worked her way through all her yummy snacks, her fingers were sticking to each other and to everything else she touched. Ben banned her from riding on his shoulders until she was

clean, and Rachel, laughing at the crusty peaks Zoe had already created in
Ben's hair, decided it was too big a job for the wet-wipes in her purse and
carried the sticky girl into the nearest restroom.

When they emerged again, Ben was waiting for them. He gave Rachel
a slow smile—one that did strange things to her insides. "I'm glad you
didn't escape through another exit this time," he said.

Despite her best efforts, Rachel blushed. "You're a little less scary now,"
she admitted.

Ben looked like he was going to respond, but before he could say
anything, Zoe took his hand and tugged him in the direction of the closest
vendor.

"Come on, Uncle Ben," she said. "I'm all clean. Let's go see more things."

Ben rolled his eyes in Rachel's direction. "I guess we need to keep
moving," he said with a smile.

They meandered through the various stalls. The swap meet was really
a huge open-air market, with tourists and locals alike filling their bags
with fresh produce and household items, clothing, and souvenirs. It was
a kaleidoscope of sights, sounds, and smells.

Rachel found a booth selling Hawaiian hair accessories and bought two
clips covered in yellow artificial plumeria flowers—one for her and one for
Zoe. Zoe insisted on wearing hers immediately. Since she already had two
ribbons in place, she clipped it right on the top of her head. It wobbled
whenever she moved, but she was thrilled to be wearing something so
beautiful. Ben stopped at a booth selling inexpensive jewelry and bought his
niece a necklace with a tiny blue dolphin hanging from it. She donned that
straightaway as well.

Tropical fruits were in plentiful supply and were priced far cheaper
than they were on the mainland. Rachel found herself wishing she had
a refrigerator in her hotel room or a way to ship them home. There was
Hawaiian clothing in every size and style, from gimmicky T-shirts to
authentic sarongs, from button-down shirts to long, flowing dresses. But
after a while, the booths all started looking the same.

At Ben's side, Zoe was beginning to flag. As her footsteps slowed, her
whining increased. Rachel pulled a water bottle out of her purse. The
water was warm, but she offered it to Zoe, who took a long drink before
wrapping her arms around Ben's leg and leaning against him.

"Need another ride, Peanut?" he asked.

Zoe nodded silently. Ben reached down and lifted her onto his shoulders
again.

"Have you seen enough?" he asked Rachel.

"I think so," Rachel said.

"Then let's go." He led the way to the exit.

Zoe's head was lolling by the time they reached the parking lot.

"I don't think Zoe's one-minute power nap at 'Iao Valley was enough," Rachel said softly. "We're losing her again."

Ben looked to the right. A road cut between the parking lot and a green-belt area that fronted Kahului's harbor. The green belt boasted a children's play area, along with several park benches and mature trees. He pointed in that direction.

"Shall we sit in the shade over there for a few minutes? It might give Zoe a chance to sleep a bit longer."

"That sounds great," Rachel agreed. Her feet were ready for a rest, and she could only guess how sore Ben's shoulders must be.

They walked through the parking lot until they reached the road. Vehicles were passing fast and frequently, and there was no sign of a crosswalk. Ben gently lifted a dozing Zoe off his shoulders and repositioned her in his arms. Then he checked the traffic again. "After that red truck," he said.

The truck sped by. Ben grabbed Rachel's hand, and together they hurried across the street.

Chapter 18

BEN LEANED BACK AGAINST THE bench, stretching his legs out in front of him. He couldn't remember when he'd enjoyed a day so much. Spending time with Zoe always lifted his spirits, but this time, it was more. The huge burden of worry he'd been carrying ever since he learned that Whitney had taken his niece had been lifted. He knew Whitney was still not providing the compassion or loving care Zoe needed—something he was determined to change as soon as possible—but she had at least brought Rachel into Zoe's life to make up for it.

Rachel. He couldn't deny that he was attracted to her. There had been a couple of times during the day—when she'd been sitting by the river and later, when she'd smiled at him—that her natural beauty had actually taken his breath away. But it was more than that. She had an inner glow that seemed to radiate from her, a goodness that was as real as it was intangible.

He glanced at her. She was gazing out over the harbor, watching all the activity as an enormous cruise liner came into dock. Zoe was still sleeping on the bench beside her, the little girl's head lying on Rachel's knee. Rachel was gently stroking Zoe's head, her genuine affection for his niece obvious in even her subconscious actions.

Although visiting the 'Iao Needle and the swap meet had been fun, Rachel was the reason this day had been a success. She was the reason it had happened in the first place. She'd put her trust in him, and he hoped he hadn't let her down. He felt that they'd already progressed from new acquaintances to friends.

While Zoe slept, they talked. She told him of her growing-up years in Arizona, her family, and her work for Senator Sheldon. He told her about Dorothy and Bert and Jed and some of his adventures abroad for *Our*

World. She laughed easily and listened carefully. And when they lulled into silence, she was happy just to sit. He would have categorized their current state as companionable silence, if it weren't for the fact that her proximity on the bench seemed to be affecting his pulse.

When he'd taken her hand to cross the street, he hadn't let go until they'd reached the bench. He hadn't wanted to then either, but she'd insisted on taking a turn with Zoe. He still wasn't sure if she was really concerned about his aching shoulders or if she simply needed an excuse to reclaim her hand. The thought bothered him more than it should.

The vibration of his phone interrupted his disquieting thoughts. He slid his hand into his pocket and checked the caller ID. It was Detective Roman. He turned to Rachel. "I'm sorry," he said. "I have to take this."

"You don't have to apologize. It's okay."

Ben nodded his appreciation, stood up, and walked a few yards closer to the sea wall.

"This is Ben," he said.

"Ben. Detective Roman here. We've turned up a few things, and I'd like to run them by you." The detective wasted no time on pleasantries.

"Go for it," Ben responded.

He heard the detective take a deep breath. "First, an update on the truck: Three of the four trucks in the Vegas area known to have had the blue stretch chrome job have been accounted for. The bad news is that officers have gone to the fourth residence multiple times and found no one there. The worse news is that the missing owner, an Eddie Belton, has a police record and has already done time. DUI, drug possession, armed robbery."

"And you're wondering if he's moved on to being a hired killer," Ben stated grimly.

Detective Roman didn't respond. "We have a warrant out for his arrest," he said simply.

Ben gave a frustrated sigh. "Anything else?"

"Yeah. One of the cell numbers your brother called repeatedly over the last two weeks of his life has been disconnected. We traced the owner. Bill Nichols. Recognize the name?"

"I think so," Ben said, struggling to put a face to the name. "Doesn't he work in the city? For one of the big-name brokers down there? I think Jed talked about him a few times. They've known each other for several years."

There was a pause. "He's dead," Detective Roman said. "He died of a heart attack the same day as your brother's accident. Apparently, it was completely unexpected."

Ben stared out at the ocean, seeing nothing. His stomach roiled at the possible implications. What was going on? Had Jed really uncovered information that someone was willing to kill to protect?

"We don't have any evidence of foul play," the detective said.

"Just strange coincidence?" Ben asked, his voice sounding strained even to his own ears.

"FBI agents are looking into it," Detective Roman said.

"I need to get back there," Ben said, unable to look at Rachel and Zoe as he spoke.

Detective Roman's thoughts obviously followed a similar tack. "Have you seen your niece yet?"

"Yes," Ben told him. "She's with me now."

"Well, then, sit tight," he said. "The task force has this end covered. Spend as much time with the little girl as possible. I'll call you tomorrow."

"Thanks," Ben said. "I can be on a plane in a matter of hours if needed."

"I'm counting on it," Detective Roman said.

Ben hung up and shut his eyes. With every new revelation and every unexpected turn he'd been forced to take over the last few days, another portion of his world shattered. And he felt more and more torn apart. A moan escaped before he realized it.

"Ben?" Rachel had moved from the bench and was standing beside him. She reached out to touch his arm. "Is everything okay?"

"Yeah," Ben said, turning to face her. But the concern in her blue eyes was his undoing. He blew out a long breath. "No. Not really," he amended.

She reached out again, this time taking his hand. Their fingers interlocked. "Can I do anything to help?" she asked.

"You're already doing more than you know," he said, glancing back at Zoe, who was still curled up, asleep.

She drew him gently back to the bench and sat down beside him. "I have it easy," she said. "I'm not dealing with the loss of a twin brother or trying to come to terms with how his death radically changes my own life. You only found out about the accident four days ago. It takes time to reach a new normal."

Ben shook his head sadly. "I don't have that time," he said. "Not until I find some answers."

"What kind of answers do you need?"

"One that would explain why Whitney virtually kidnapped Zoe from her own home and legal guardians would be nice for starters," Ben said, bitterness tingeing his voice. "But even more importantly, why someone went out of their way to kill my brother."

Rachel stared at him. "What do you mean? I thought Jed died in a car accident."

"He did. But it's looking more and more likely that someone intentionally forced him off the road. The police are still trying to figure out why."

"Do they have any ideas?" Rachel's voice was barely above a whisper.

He nodded. "The day before he died, Jed e-mailed me to say he was following a tip that something big was happening on Wall Street. It sounded like he'd hit some roadblocks in his investigation. It's now looking like those roadblocks were more like safety walls for whoever is behind all this. Anyone trying to scale them had to be dealt with."

Horror filled Rachel's eyes. "Have others died?"

Ben shook his head helplessly. "It's possible. But the authorities don't know for sure. That phone call was from the detective in charge of the case. The questions are multiplying, and right now, we have very few answers."

"Which would drive anyone crazy, let alone an investigative reporter whose brother was a victim," Rachel said sympathetically.

Ben nodded. "I can't stop thinking that if I did some digging in the city, I might uncover something. Some of Jed's old contacts know me. I could even pass for him if I had to. But if I go back and help with the investigation, I'll be abandoning Zoe—leaving her here with Whitney."

"And me," Rachel said quietly. "I'll be here for her, Ben."

Ben rubbed his thumb across the back of her small hand. "You're the only good thing that's come out of this whole nightmare," he said. "Knowing you're with Zoe is the only reason I can even contemplate leaving."

Rachel dropped her gaze. "What are you going to do?"

"I don't know," Ben said. "Detective Roman told me to stay put until he hears more. He's going to call me again tomorrow."

"Wachul, I'm hungry!"

Ben and Rachel turned as Zoe raised her head off the bench, pressure lines running down her cheeks from the wooden slats. She'd lost one ribbon, and her plumeria clip was even more askew than before. Rachel released Ben's hand and held out her arms to Zoe. "Come here, sleepyhead."

Zoe crawled onto Rachel's knee and accepted a hug. "But I'm weally, weally hungry," she said most seriously.

"Then we'd better weally, weally feed you," Rachel told her with a smile. She straightened Zoe's glasses, smoothed back her hair, and fixed the clip. "What would you like to have for dinner?"

Zoe looked thoughtful for a moment. "How 'bout donuts?"

Ben couldn't help it. He laughed.

Chapter 19

THE LIGHTS WERE ON IN the Sheldons' suite when Rachel unlocked the door.

"Oh. Hi, Rachel." Karl was seated at the large table, his laptop in front of him, a large stack of papers to his right. "I wondered when you'd get back."

"Hi, Karl," Rachel responded with surprise. She hadn't seen him since the day she'd arrived. "What are you doing here?"

He grimaced. "Catching up on paperwork. The senator and his wife are still at dinner. They probably won't be back for a couple more hours."

He rose to his feet and gave Rachel a look of undisguised admiration. "Seems like Hawaii agrees with you. The tan looks good."

To her frustration, Rachel felt herself blush. "We've been outside a lot today," she said awkwardly. After walking the dirt trail by the river, eating sticky food at the market, having Zoe asleep on her knee for at least an hour, and driving back from Kahului with the sunroof down, she could only imagine how rumpled she looked. Her only consolation was that her shirt didn't have a huge ketchup stain like Zoe's did.

"Have you eaten yet?" he asked.

"Yes, thanks," Rachel said, her unease growing as Karl stepped closer. What did he mean by *you*? Did he mean *you* singular? Or was he hoping to have dinner with Zoe and her in the suite? She realized that she didn't feel comfortable with either scenario. She pointed to Zoe's shirt. "As you can see, we stopped at Zippy's on the way back." She forced a smile. "Chicken fingers and lots of ketchup."

"Lucky girl," Karl said, glancing at Zoe. "She seems to be doing better."

Zoe wrapped her arms around Rachel's leg and leaned her head against it. Rachel recognized the gesture of tiredness.

"She's doing great," Rachel said, reaching down to take Zoe's hand, "but I've completely worn her out, and it's late, so I'd better get her in bed."

Karl raised his eyebrow and watched in silence as Rachel led Zoe across the room and into Zoe's bedroom.

Once the connecting door was closed, Rachel hurried into the bathroom and started running Zoe's bath. She helped the little girl into the water, washed her thoroughly, then gave her a few miscellaneous cups to play with while she worked on getting the ketchup off her shirt in the sink.

Rachel smiled to herself as she scrubbed. Zippy's had been a good choice for dinner. The Hawaiian restaurant chain had a vast menu. Ben had chosen their famous chili. True to the promise she'd made to herself earlier in the day, Rachel had opted for a salad and had insisted that Zoe have some steamed vegetables with her chicken fingers and fries.

Ben was the one who'd suggested to Zoe that the steamed vegetables would taste better covered in ketchup. Rachel rolled her eyes at the thought. He should be the one dealing with the resulting spill.

They'd parted ways after their meal. Zoe had clung to Ben in the parking lot until he'd promised to go to the beach with her the next day. They'd decided to meet at Big Beach. Ben wanted to check out the famous landmark with the unimaginative name, and Rachel thought it might be a safer location than Wailea Beach. She still wasn't sure what Whitney's reaction would be if she discovered Ben with Zoe. And she decided she'd rather not find out.

She marveled at the difference twenty-four hours could make. This time last night, she'd been a bundle of nerves, dreading the morning and the meeting she'd arranged between Ben and Zoe. Now she caught herself humming as she thought about seeing Ben again.

It took another twenty minutes to get Zoe in bed. After prayers, reading the fish book from the aquarium, and a good-night hug, Rachel slipped out of the bedroom and closed the door. To her dismay, Karl was still working at the table. He looked up as she entered and smiled.

"How are the negotiations coming along?" Rachel asked, wanting to keep their conversation as work related as possible.

"Great," he replied. "Senator Sheldon's a master at this kind of thing." He lifted the small pile of papers at his left. "All we need now are a few key signatures and we'll have some very happy CEOs in Arizona."

"How many companies is he representing?"

Karl shrugged. "Half a dozen or so. They're all involved in medical equipment manufacture—most of them in the Phoenix area. The products are pretty high-tech; a lot of them are only used for very specialized surgery." He shuddered. "Believe me, we got to watch all the demo DVDs."

Rachel bit back a smile. "A little too graphic for you?"

"Yeah, well, it wouldn't be my first choice of movie viewing," he said. "But they must have impressed the Japanese delegation. Senator Sheldon's sold them on a ten-year contract."

"Nice," Rachel said. She didn't tell him that she'd already gleaned most of this information from her reading each evening.

"Yep." Karl looked pleased that she was suitably impressed. "I daresay we'll be wrapping things up tomorrow."

This *was* news. "So when d'you think we'll head back to DC?" she asked.

He pulled up another screen on his laptop. "Our flights are scheduled for two days from now."

Rachel processed this information. If Ben had to leave within the next twenty-four hours, they wouldn't be too far behind him. Maybe that would make things easier for Zoe. Washington, DC, wasn't very far from New York. She was sure Ben would work out some way to see his niece before too much time passed.

"Good to know," she said. "We'll have to make the most of the time we have left."

"Right," Karl said, a charming smile on his face. "And we'd better decide when you and I can go have a drink together."

Rachel stared at him. Karl knew she was LDS. That was the whole reason she was here. "Uh, you do remember I don't drink, right?" she finally said.

Karl brushed her concern off with a nonchalant shrug. "They have soft drinks and juice at the bar too, Rachel."

"I still don't think it's a great idea," she said, frantically trying to think of an excuse that wouldn't sound rude. "I have an unwritten rule against dating anyone from work."

Karl's eyes hardened. "No drinking. No dating. You must live a really exciting life."

Rachel clasped her hands behind her back so he wouldn't see them tremble. Karl yielded considerable power in the DC office, and she didn't want to get on his bad side. But she refused to apologize for holding to her standards. "It has its share of craziness," she said.

Karl snorted. He rose to his feet and started packing up his computer. "Well, let me know if you change your mind," he said cuttingly.

"I will," Rachel said. "Thanks for inviting me, Karl. It was really nice of you."

A look of surprise flashed across his face, and his rigid stance softened. "You're welcome," he mumbled. Then he walked to the door. He stood there a few seconds before raising his hand in silent farewell and letting himself out.

Rachel dropped to the sofa as relief washed over her. With Karl's blond good looks and fast-track career, it was unlikely that he was ever lacking for female company. She'd undoubtedly wounded his pride, but she hoped she'd managed to avoid any long-term damage.

Just over an hour later, Senator Sheldon and Whitney arrived back. Rachel had checked on Zoe fifteen minutes before, and as there'd been no sound from her room since then, she rose to leave as soon as the couple entered. Whitney breezed past her, a heady mixture of perfume and alcohol lingering in her wake. Senator Sheldon shook Rachel's hand, asked politely how her day had gone, and walked her to the door. The cloying smell of cigarette smoke clung to his dinner jacket, and his face was drawn, his eyes tired. As Rachel wished him good night and headed to her own room, she experienced her first twinges of misgiving about her chosen career.

* * *

Eddie Belton was getting antsy. It was the second time the cops had stopped at his house today, and according to his buddy Neil, they'd been there the day before too. He stood in the shadow of Neil's porch watching the two uniformed men make their way back to their patrol car.

He was glad he'd stopped here before going home. Neil always had some sort of party going on—day or night—and Eddie was ready to join in. He had a wad of bills in his pocket and a flashy, new black truck parked out back. That was reason enough to celebrate. And luck was still on his side. He'd arrived while his friend was still sober enough to warn him about his unexpected visitors.

Hesitating only one minute more, Eddie pulled out his cell phone and punched in a number. It took four rings before anyone answered. "I've got cops at my house," he said.

"I thought you said there were no mistakes."

"No one can trace the truck. The plates are bogus, and it's wiped clean."

"Then don't call me again." Anger sizzled through the phone. "You did your job. You got paid. We're done."

There was a click, and the phone went dead. Eddie swore. He looked across the street again. The patrol car was gone. Everything looked normal, but he wasn't going to take a chance. He'd get in his brand-new truck and go spend some of the money burning a hole in his pocket. Maybe by the time he finished partying, the cops would move on to harassing someone else.

Chapter 20

RACHEL FORCED HER EYES OPEN. The twisted bed sheets were tangled around her legs, and her heart was racing. Ben! She rolled over, groping for the cell phone she'd left on the bedside table. Turning it on, she scrolled down until she found Ben's number. Her hands were shaking, but she managed a brief text.

Are you ok?

She leaned back against her pillow and took deep, cleansing breaths. In the darkness, she could just make out the whirring blades of the ceiling fan, but the gentle puffs of air were doing little to offset the perspiration trickling down her hairline.

It had been a bad nightmare. Ben was in the distance, trying to scale a sheer white wall. She knew that danger lay on the other side, but no matter how hard she tried, she couldn't reach him. And he was too far away to hear her screams. Karl, Whitney, and Senator Sheldon were on the sidelines, talking, laughing, and ignoring her pleas for help.

At last, Ben reached the top of the wall, and just before he dropped to the other side, he saw her. But it was too late. There was the sound of a gunshot, followed by a child's cries. And when she finally made it to the other side of the wall, she found Zoe sobbing beside Ben's broken body.

Rachel released a shuddering breath, then jumped convulsively as her cell phone chirped. With her hands still shaking, she reached for her phone and read the message on the screen.

Yes. Are you?

She stared at the words. Had she lost her mind? She'd actually texted Ben at—she glanced at the clock in the corner of her screen—3:35 a.m.! He probably thought she was nuts. Groaning at her own idiocy, she texted back.

Yes. Had a nightmare. Was half asleep when I texted. So sorry to wake you.

She crawled out of bed and staggered into the bathroom. Without turning on the light, she splashed her face with cool water, then patted it dry. Filling a glass with water and taking a long drink, she returned to the bed just as her phone chirped again.

No problem. It must have been a bad one. Hope you can go back to sleep now. Singing a Primary song always helps me. :)

The thought of manly Ben singing a Primary song in bed to ward off nightmares made Rachel smile.

Thanks, she texted back. *I'll try it. See you later.*

As she lay back down in bed, his reply came in.

For sure :)

* * *

Rachel was helping Zoe out of the car when Ben pulled into the parking lot at Big Beach. Rachel's long hair was pulled into a ponytail, and she was wearing a navy swimsuit with an ankle-length blue floral sarong wrapped around her tiny waist. Ben was pretty sure he wasn't the only man in the parking lot with his eyes on her, and the thought had him hurrying out of the car.

"Hi, Zoe," he said as he reached them.

Zoe, clad in a pink and purple swimsuit and plaid pink shorts, swung around at the sound of his voice. "Uncle Ben!" she cried, wrapping her arms around his legs.

Ben laughed and reached down to give her a hug.

"I have a new shovel and pail, see?" Zoe lifted a mesh bag full of plastic beach toys.

"Awesome," Ben said. "We'll make a great sandcastle with those."

Zoe grinned. "Can we do it now?"

"As soon as we get to the beach," he promised.

He turned to Rachel. She was lifting a large insulated bag out of the trunk. "Here, let me get that," he said. He took the bag and placed it on the ground beside a bag full of towels.

"Thanks," Rachel said. She slid her sunglasses onto the top of her head, exposing the dark smudges beneath her blue eyes.

"Hey," Ben said, instinctively stepping closer. "Are you sure you're okay?"

"I look that bad, huh?" Rachel said, her lips twitching as she fought back a smile.

"You look incredible," Ben said softly, "but it doesn't take a genius to recognize lack of sleep. Did you get any rest after 3:30?"

"A little," she said. "I think it was 'My Heavenly Father Loves Me' that finally did it."

Ben chuckled. "Leave it to the Primary songs." Then more soberly he added, "It sounds like I traumatized you, along with Zoe, if I'm in your nightmares. I'm sorry."

Rachel frowned. "How did you . . . ?"

"You asked if I was okay, remember?"

She shook her head. "I think I was more traumatized by what you may have to do in New York. By those safety walls you're hoping to break down." Color flooded her cheeks. "I don't want you to get hurt."

Ben put his arm around her. "I won't do anything stupid," he said. "I don't want to get hurt either."

"Can we go build a sandcastle now?"

At the sound of Zoe's pleading voice, Rachel pulled away. Ben felt the loss immediately. For a second, her blue eyes met his, and she gave him a hesitant smile before directing her attention back to Zoe. His overwhelming desire to pull her back into his arms caught him off guard. He blew out a long breath. Rachel Hamilton was really getting to him.

* * *

They followed the sandy path that led from the parking lot to the beach. Rachel had Zoe's hand and the bag of towels. Zoe was still holding her toys, and Ben was carrying the insulated bag, beach mats, and Zoe's life jacket. A lifeguard tower marked the entrance to the beach, and from that point, the turquoise-blue water met the sparkling white sand in a gentle arc that stretched as far as the eye could see. Sand dunes, anchored in place by native vegetation, were the beach's backdrop, and out at sea, small boats dotted the horizon. The panorama was as vast as it was stunning.

Rachel's footsteps slowed to a stop, and she realized that despite his heavy load, Ben's progress had halted too.

"Wow!" he said, his gaze traveling along the pristine coastline. "I hadn't expected this."

"It's so beautiful," Rachel breathed.

"Is this where we're going to build the sandcastle?" Zoe asked.

Ben rolled his eyes. "Remind me to come back here without a four-year-old," he said.

Rachel smothered a giggle and gave Zoe's hand a gentle tug. "Let's go a little farther down," she said. "We need to be a bit closer to the wet sand, or your castle won't stand up."

They found a spot not too far from the water's edge. Ben laid out the beach mats, and they set the bags down in such a way that nothing would blow away. Once they were situated, Ben helped Zoe build a giant castle, and Rachel showed her how to use the bucket to collect seawater to fill the moat. When the sand towers started to disintegrate, they took the toys back to the beach mats, and Rachel pulled string cheese and sliced apples out of the insulated bag.

As soon as she finished her snack, Zoe announced that she wanted to play in the ocean. Rachel helped her into her life jacket before noticing that Ben had also changed. He'd taken off the red New York Yankees baseball hat and gray T-shirt he'd been wearing, leaving only his red and black swim trunks. Trying not to stare, Rachel swallowed hard. She'd known he was in good shape before, but now, standing on the sand with the turquoise water behind him, he looked like he'd just walked off a *GQ* magazine cover. She quickly lowered her eyes and fumbled with the knot on her sarong.

"Go ahead, Zoe," she said. "Your uncle Ben's ready, and I'll be right there."

Zoe skipped over to Ben and took his hand, but Ben didn't move. "It's okay," he said. "We can wait."

Feeling horribly self-conscious, Rachel stepped out of the sarong and onto the sand. Ben's other hand reached out and took hers. He drew her closer. "I like your swimsuit," he whispered. "I'm grateful and impressed that you prefer to be modest."

Rachel's heart pounded, but she forced herself to look up. "Thank you, Ben," she said. "I think that might be the nicest thing a man has ever said to me."

He smiled at her, admiration in his eyes. "Well, I meant every word," he said. "So don't get too irritated if I stay close. Someone's got to ward the other guys off."

She shook her head at the absurdity of his statement and allowed him to lead her down to the ocean.

At first Zoe jumped the waves. It was much easier to lift her up and over the foam with Ben on her other side than it had been the other day when she was alone. But after a while, Ben offered to take Zoe into the deeper water. He turned her onto her back so she could keep her glasses on and towed her out until she was bobbing up and down like a purple sea turtle. Rachel waded out until the water reached above her waist, then she stood back and watched Ben and Zoe together, wishing she had thought to bring a better camera than the one on her phone.

She'd not been there very long when a tall, sandy-haired man approached with a snorkel and mask hanging from his neck. He'd just started telling her about the fish he'd seen swimming around a coral reef a little farther down the beach when Ben and Zoe arrived back with considerable splashing and noise. The man made a hasty retreat, and Ben turned to Rachel with a twinkle in his eyes. "I warned you," he said. "And since you flunked the 'I'm not available because I'm here with Ben and Zoe' test, you have to be punished."

He reached out and grabbed her.

"No, Ben! No!" she yelled, her legs flailing as he lifted her off her feet.

"Oh, yes. I think so." He laughed as he spun her and tossed her into the water.

Seconds later, she surfaced right beside Zoe. "Zoe!" she cried, pushing the little girl forward. "Tickle him!"

Zoe wasted no time. With arms outstretched, she reached for her uncle. She managed a few scratch-like tickles before Ben lifted her out of the water too. She squealed with delight as he positioned her on his back.

"Hold on tight, Zoe," he said.

Rachel took one look at the mischief written across his face and started wading as fast as she could toward the shore. Seconds later, Ben pulled her feet out from under her, and she came up spluttering as Ben emerged from the water, Zoe still on his back as though she was riding a dolphin. Ben reached for Rachel and put his arms around her. "You okay?" he asked.

"Are you going to dunk me again?"

He tilted his head to one side. "I'm still deciding."

"As long as you don't dunk me again, I'm okay," Rachel said with a smile, her arms automatically snaking around his neck.

She felt him tense, and for a fleeting moment, his eyes went to her lips. And then the moment was gone. Zoe bounced up and down on his back, and another wave rushed by, pushing them apart.

Chapter 21

BEN AND ZOE WERE DIGGING a hole in the sand next to the beach mats when Ben's phone started ringing. Rachel, who'd been following Ben's orders to rest, opened her eyes and looked over at him. For a second, the small shovel in his hand hung suspended midair, then he dropped it and began brushing the sand off his hand. Rachel rolled onto her stomach and rummaged through the towel bag at her side until she found the still-ringing phone. Without a word, she handed it to Ben. He glanced at the caller ID, gave her an almost imperceptible nod, and rose to his feet as he took the call.

"This is Ben," he said. "Go ahead, Detective."

He moved toward the sand dunes, away from the sounds of people and ocean.

"We've had a few more developments." Detective Roman got straight to the point as usual. "Thought you'd want to know."

"What've you got?"

"Right now we're focusing on the folder the Dicksons found in your brother's safe. One of the FBI's specialists has gone over it, and we now know where all the money in your niece's trust fund came from."

Ben's grip on his cell phone tightened. "Go ahead."

"It looks like your brother was even more financially savvy than the people he reported on. The bulk of the folder is his stocks portfolio. He began purchasing them about the time he was made ABC's financial analyst. All his business was done through the Sterne and Lowe Brokerage House. Not all of his investments paid off, but most of them did. Some of them were huge moneymakers—hundreds of thousands of dollars.

"We've spoken to one of the senior brokers at Sterne and Lowe. He told us Jed was a respected analyst, even among the top brokers. Jed knew who to listen to; he watched trends and knew when to act. He bought smart and sold even smarter."

Relief flooded through Ben as he listened to the detective's account. Notwithstanding severe scrutiny, Jed's integrity remained intact.

"But this is where it gets interesting," Detective Roman continued. "The broker Jed worked through was Bill Nichols."

"The man who died the same day as Jed," Ben said. "Do you think he was the contact Jed mentioned?"

"We think it's likely," the detective said. "Especially since another sheet of paper with Sterne and Lowe's letterhead was clipped to the outside of the folder. This one listed twenty-three companies that seem to have no connection to the ones in your brother's portfolio. Seemingly random dates going back five years are written alongside each company name, and stuck to the paper is a handwritten note that says, 'Let me know what you think. Bill.'"

"Could this be what Jed was working on?" Ben asked.

"Well, we think it's definitely worth checking," Detective Roman said. "The FBI sent a couple of agents over to Sterne and Lowe. The senior broker they talked to couldn't shed any light on the list, but the agents are going through Bill Nichols's files right now, trying to find something that links those particular companies and dates."

They were doing investigative research—a skill Ben had been honing for years. "I'll be there tomorrow," he said firmly.

To his surprise, Detective Roman didn't argue. "We could use your help," he said. "Let me know your flight, and I'll have one of the FBI agents meet you in New York. They can bring you up to speed when you get there."

"I'll call you back as soon as I have a reservation," Ben told him.

"Good enough," Detective Roman said before ending the call.

Ben stared down at his phone and took a deep breath. He'd had this feeling before—a sense of urgency that bordered on panic, the weight of knowing people's lives depended on his recognizing clues and following the most tenuous of leads to expose wrongdoing. He'd experienced it while reporting in multiple foreign countries, but never had it alarmed him as much as it did now. This time it was personal.

He knew they had a narrow window to work in—before time erased both evidence and memories. Discovering Jed's e-mail two weeks after his death had already put the investigation behind. He needed to make up for that now.

Within seconds, Ben had pulled up United Airlines' website on his phone. Two minutes after that, he'd found a flight out of Kahului and into LA, with a connecting flight straight into JFK. There were three seats remaining. Not allowing himself to think about the enormous dent these last-minute flights were making in his bank account, he sped through the screens. He entered the required information on each one before finally hitting the submit button and receiving his confirmation number. He was leaving Maui in under six hours.

His return call to Detective Roman was brief. Ben gave him his flight numbers and scheduled times of arrival at each airport. Only after he'd ended the phone call did he turn around to face Rachel and Zoe. They were still playing in the sand. Zoe glowed with happiness, but Rachel must have sensed Ben's gaze because she looked over at him, her blue eyes full of concern. Ben's chest tightened. He didn't want to tell them he was leaving.

Zoe looked up as he reached the beach mats. "Hi, Uncle Ben," she said. "Look how big my hole is now."

"Wow!" Ben feigned shock. "That might be the biggest hole on the beach!"

Zoe beamed. "I can fit in it. See?" She climbed into the hole, covering her entire body in sand, including her hair. Once inside, she started digging again, singing as she worked.

"What's the news?" Rachel asked softly.

"I fly out tonight," he told her.

Regret flashed across Rachel's face, but she nodded as though she'd been expecting as much. "We shouldn't be too far behind you," she said. "The senator's secretary told me last night that we're scheduled to leave for DC tomorrow evening."

"I'll figure out a way to see Zoe," he said.

"I know you will," she said, and Ben suddenly realized that it was quite possible that Rachel would not play a part in that reunion. Once she returned to DC, she would also return to her office job. The thought made him unaccountably miserable.

"What time do you leave?" she asked.

"The flight's at 9:45 p.m., but since I have to return the rental car, I should probably be at the airport a couple of hours before then." He glanced at the clock on his cell phone. "Do you think we could leave here in about an hour?"

Rachel nodded. "I don't think Zoe will last much longer than that anyway."

"Okay," Ben said, trying to look more cheerful than he felt. "Let's make the most of the time we have left."

* * *

Ben waited until Zoe was strapped into her car seat before he broke the news to her. Zoe was inconsolable. She fought against the car seat restraints like a wild animal, reaching for Ben as if he were a lifeline. No amount of reasoning helped, and eventually, Rachel had to shut the car door on the little girl's sobs. With a brief good-bye to Ben, she hurried into the car and drove back to the hotel, wanting to burst into tears herself.

Zoe fell into a fitful sleep in the car, her breathing punctuated by ragged shudders. Rachel carried her to the suite but woke her once they arrived so Zoe could wash off all the remaining sand in a bath. The little girl was unusually somber, but at least her crying had stopped. Room service brought in a meal, and Rachel was actually able to coax a few smiles out of Zoe before she finished her pizza.

A long day in the sun coupled with a major crying session had exhausted the little girl, and she went to bed right after dinner. Rachel held her a little longer than usual, hoping she'd know how much she was loved, and Zoe responded by wrapping her arms around Rachel's neck and squeezing tightly until sleep overtook her.

As soon as Rachel left the bedroom, she located her phone and sent Ben a text.

Zoe's already asleep. Her tears were worse because she was tired. Please don't worry. She was smiling again before bed.

The reply was almost instant.

Thank you!

To her surprise, Senator Sheldon and Whitney arrived back at the suite soon afterward. Whitney was complaining of a headache, but it was Senator Sheldon who looked the most haggard. He told Rachel they'd be leaving for the airport at 5:00 p.m. the next day and let her return to her room for an early night. Grateful for the time to herself, Rachel showered and changed before slipping away from the hotel to be on the beach at sunset.

As she walked along the shoreline, Rachel marveled at how much had changed since her arrival in Maui less than a week before. She'd entered the fringes of Senator Sheldon's inner circle—both professionally and personally. She'd fallen in love with little Zoe, whose sweet acceptance and example of bravery were gifts Rachel would always treasure, and she'd met Ben. She smiled ruefully as she reflected on the vast spectrum of emotions Ben had elicited over the last few days—from fear and frustration when she'd considered him a threat to her overwhelming desire to stay in his arms at Big Beach.

She sighed. Zoe's meltdown had prevented them from having a meaningful farewell. Her departure had been rushed, and Ben's bleak expression as she'd driven away had reflected her emotions too. She hoped her text had helped put his mind at rest with regard to Zoe. But it had said nothing about her. Would she ever see him again?

The cell phone in her pocket vibrated. Rachel drew it out and checked the caller ID. Her footsteps across the sand faltered.

"Hello?"

"Rachel? This is Ben."

Her heart rate quickened at the sound of his voice. "Hi, Ben," she said. "Are you at the airport?"

"Not yet. I just left my hotel," he said. "I have something for Zoe and wondered if I could drop it off before I go. Perhaps you could give it to her tomorrow since I won't be here."

"She'd love that," Rachel said warmly. "Where shall I meet you?"

"Can you get away, or are you still with Zoe?"

"Actually, the Sheldons arrived back early this evening, so I'm just out walking the beach," she said.

"In front of the Grand Wailea?" he asked.

"Yes."

"Perfect. I'll meet you there in about five minutes." And before Rachel could say another word, he was gone.

* * *

Ben spotted her immediately. She was standing at the water's edge, her long hair and skirt blowing in the breeze, her face turned toward the setting sun. She was silhouetted alone against a fiery yellow and orange backdrop, and the scene was breathtaking. For a moment, Ben could only stare. Then Rachel stepped away from the ocean, and he moved onto the beach to join her.

As he approached, Rachel turned and greeted him with a smile. "That was fast."

"I wasn't very far away when I called," he said, smiling too. He handed her a plastic bag. "It's a dolphin. I thought it might go well with her necklace."

Rachel peeked into the bag at the gray stuffed animal. "She'll love it," she said. "It'll probably go everywhere with her from now on."

"Perhaps it will help her forgive me," he said heavily. "This afternoon's good-bye will definitely go down as one of my top ten worst experiences."

"She loves you, Ben," Rachel said. "She may be a little sad that you're not here tomorrow, but she'll be okay. And you're doing something important. You owe it to your brother—and to Zoe—to find out what happened."

Ben recognized the compassion in her beautiful eyes, and it was suddenly difficult to speak. He reached out and ran his fingers through her hair, loving the feel of it. He hadn't wanted to admit that he'd needed an excuse to see Rachel again. But it was true. This afternoon's wretched parting could not be their last. "It should make it easier to leave, knowing that you're here with Zoe," he said softly. "But somehow, leaving both of you at the same time makes it doubly hard."

She gave him a small smile. "Zoe will be excited to see you as soon as your work in New York is done." Then a little more quietly, she added, "And so will I."

He felt hope flare. "Can I call you?" he asked. "Even when you're not with Zoe?"

A faint blush touched her cheeks. "I've been hoping you would," she said.

Ben put his arms around her, drawing her close. Her floral perfume mixed with the salty sea air was affecting his breathing. She looked up, her lips slightly parted, her eyes shining, and he knew he was lost.

As he lowered his lips to hers, he was vaguely aware of the plastic bag falling to the sand, of Rachel's arms around his neck, and of her fingers in his hair. But it was the deepening sweetness of her kiss that left him reeling. When they drew apart, he moved his hands to gently cup each side of her face. "Forget doubly hard," he said, his voice hoarse with emotion. "Leaving just got one hundred times harder."

And then he kissed her again.

Chapter 22

ZOE LOVED THE DOLPHIN. RACHEL gave it to her after breakfast, and as she had predicted, it didn't leave Zoe's side all day. She held it while Rachel packed their suitcases, placed it at the edge of the deck when they went swimming at the hotel pool, sat it on the chair beside her at lunchtime, and tucked it under her arm at the airport. It wasn't the same as having Ben there, but it was as though he'd left a little part of himself for Zoe to hold. And it made a difference.

For Rachel, there were text messages. She followed Ben's journey home through the messages he sent her from each airport. Their time together on the beach the night before had been too brief, but the memory of Ben's kisses lingered. Knowing that his feelings for her mirrored her growing feelings for him buoyed her as nothing else could have.

She wasn't quite sure what her function would be during her journey home. Whitney had been around most of the day, doing her own packing and spending last precious hours sunbathing at the poolside. But she'd made no effort to interact with Zoe at all. Neither had she given any instructions to Rachel. So Rachel had made sure she turned in her rental car and had her bags and Zoe's bags in the lobby by 5:00 p.m., and then she simply waited to see what would happen.

Once everyone had gathered, it took only five minutes for Rachel to determine that even though Whitney was traveling with Zoe, she had no intention of taking responsibility for her daughter. Because of their excess luggage, they took two cars to the airport. Rachel and Zoe traveled together in one. The Sheldons and Karl were in the other.

At the airport, Karl handed them their tickets, giving Rachel care of Zoe's as well. Rachel walked Zoe through security, took her to the restroom, bought her snacks, and walked her around the terminal when the wait became too long.

Their time together at the airport was a gentle reminder of Zoe's limited vision—and of how much Rachel had learned to adapt to her needs. They spent extra time in the gift shops so Zoe could stand close to the racks of merchandise and study the brightly colored products. Over the last few days, watching for steps, curbs, and uneven ground had become automatic for Rachel, and guiding Zoe over them had become second nature. She always kept Zoe close by, knowing that should she and Zoe become separated, Zoe would be hard pressed to find her way back to anyone she recognized.

The other adults remained seated at the gate. Whitney spent her time flipping through a magazine and checking her phone. Senator Sheldon was busy on his phone too. Karl sat beside him, working on his laptop. Every once in a while, when Rachel was standing in the main traffic area, she would feel Karl's eyes on her. She wasn't sure whether his scrutiny was motivated by censure or interest. Either alternative was disconcerting, so she did her best to ignore him.

Senator Sheldon, she noticed, spent a great deal of time studying Zoe. It didn't seem to matter if Zoe was skipping, chattering, or simply walking quietly with her hand in Rachel's, Senator Sheldon's thoughtful expression did not change. Occasionally he'd glance at his wife, but if she was aware of it, she hid it well.

When they finally boarded, Rachel discovered that they were seated in the first-class section. To her amusement, Karl had been assigned to the seat next to Zoe. She allowed him to sit down next to the excited, squirming little girl just long enough for her to stow their carry-on bags before she took pity on him and offered to trade places. His expression of relief coupled with the eagerness with which he moved spoke volumes. Rachel had to work hard to hold back her laughter.

Zoe ended up being a perfect travel companion. She ate the children's meal offered to her right after take-off, then, still clutching her dolphin, she curled up in a ball on the roomy first-class seat and fell asleep. Rachel covered her with an airline blanket before claiming another blanket for herself and closing her eyes.

Unfortunately, sleep did not come easily for her. A kaleidoscope of recent memories from her time in Hawaii and anticipated difficulties associated with her return to Washington swirled through her mind. Concern for Zoe's future, Ben's investigation, and her position on Senator Sheldon's staff battled her tiredness.

She didn't know what the Sheldons' plans for Zoe were when they returned to Washington—or whether those plans involved her. She cared deeply about the little girl and was committed to being her advocate until Ben returned. But how long would that be? The only thing she knew for sure was that Ben *would* return. And with that encouraging thought, she finally drifted into a restless sleep.

* * *

Ben sat at the large mahogany desk across from two FBI agents. Agent Leavitt and Agent Perez had been working in Bill Nichols's office for more than twenty-four hours, and as yet, they had little to show for it. Ben could sense their frustration; he shared it. He looked down again at the piece of paper in front of him. It was a copy of the one they'd found in Jed's safe.

"So you haven't found another copy of this list in any of Bill Nichols's files?" Ben asked.

Agent Leavitt shook his head. "We've gone through everything in the office—looking for that paper or anything else that might shed light on why those companies are listed." He pointed to the boxes of sorted files on the floor. "We've emptied the filing cabinets, cupboards, and safe. And we've gone through all the bookshelves."

Ben glanced around the sumptuous room. The furniture was all solid wood, the chairs beautifully upholstered. Along with the more generic decorations common in an office, the walls, shelves, and desk were scattered with personal photos of Bill Nichols and his family boating on a lake, hiking a mountain, and zip lining across a canyon. The room felt tidy and well organized.

Agent Leavitt indicated a bare spot on the corner of the desk. "His computer was password protected. We've got some of our computer guys working on it. We should have access to his e-files by tomorrow."

"What d'you know about the companies?" Ben asked.

"They range in size from small, start-up companies to huge, well-established corporations," Agent Leavitt said. "Their products run the gamut from farm supplies to medical supplies to military supplies. They're all headquartered in the western U.S., but some of them have branches back East."

"The most interesting pattern that has emerged in our research involves the dates rather than the names," Agent Perez said, leaning forward on the desk and pointing to the first column of numbers. "The stock prices for each of these companies skyrocketed within about three weeks of the date listed beside their name. If these are purchase dates, someone made bank. Some of these stock prices went up as much as twenty times their predate price."

Ben whistled through his teeth. "Do you think the second date listed beside some of the companies could be a selling date?"

Agent Perez shrugged. "That seems to be the most obvious conclusion."

"Can we get a listing of all stockholders for each of these companies?" Ben asked, studying the list more carefully.

"We're working on it," Agent Leavitt said. "Some of the larger companies have thousands of stock owners, and some are held in offshore accounts, but once we have those lists, the computer guys can help speed up the search for any repeat names."

Ben nodded. The agents had done a good job covering the basic groundwork, but they were going to have to dig a lot deeper to unravel this mystery. He needed time to process the information he'd received, to do some investigating of his own.

"Can I keep this?" Ben asked, lifting the paper off the desk and coming to his feet.

The two agents also rose. "Yeah," Agent Leavitt said. He passed him his business card. "Call if you think of anything that might help us."

"I will," Ben said. "Let me know when you have access to Bill's computer files."

The agents nodded and shook his hand. Then Ben picked up his bag and let himself out of the plush office. He smiled politely at yet another receptionist who was staring at him as though she'd seen a ghost. Looking like Jed had never been such a miserable experience.

* * *

The cab driver dropped Ben off at the curb outside his apartment building. The sky was gray, the temperature low. Piles of dirty snow edged the sidewalk and the steps leading up to the building's main lobby. As Ben hurried to get in from the biting cold, he couldn't help but think that the dreary winter day matched his mood completely.

He took the elevator to the fourth floor, passing a few people en route but recognizing no one. At last he reached the door to his own apartment. He unlocked it and stepped inside, heading down the hall to his bedroom, where he dropped his bag onto his bed before doing a brief tour of the small apartment. Everything was just as he'd left it, except for the chill and stale smell that always seemed to follow his long absences. He adjusted the thermostat and heard the heat kick on. After more than two months, he was finally home—it just didn't feel very welcoming.

His cupboards were even more bare than usual, but he found a can of soup and put it in a pan to heat on the stove before returning to his bedroom to retrieve the piece of paper Agent Leavitt had given him. He read through the list again, pacing back and forth between his small kitchenette and the living area as he considered each name and date. The information the FBI had uncovered about the sudden dramatic rise in each of the stock prices hinted strongly at insider trading. But who would have that kind of information on such a wide variety of companies? Was it the same person who had orchestrated Jed's death—and perhaps Bill Nichols's too?

Something had been bothering Ben ever since he'd left Bill's office. He hadn't been able to put his finger on what it was, but something was off. He reflected on his visit to Sterne and Lowe again, visualizing the office, thinking through everything he and the FBI agents had said and done. The agents had been focusing their investigation on one thing—the list of companies and dates. But what about the people involved? Turning down the heat beneath the boiling soup, he took out his phone and the card Agent Leavitt had given him and placed a call.

"Leavitt." Agent Leavitt answered immediately.

"Hey, this is Ben Cooper," Ben said. "What can you tell me about Bill Nichols's death?"

"His receptionist found him slumped over his office desk at 4:10 p.m. after she'd repeatedly tried reaching him on the phone and intercom. The paramedics were called in. They determined he'd been gone less than an hour and cited heart attack as the cause of death."

"Was an autopsy performed?" Ben asked.

"No. Even though his death was unexpected, at that time, there was no evidence of foul play. Nothing to suggest it was anything more than his heart giving out. Agent Perez contacted his widow when we joined the investigation. He put out feelers about exhuming the body for an autopsy. It didn't go over so well. I don't think it will happen unless we turn up something more concrete."

"I understand," Ben said, completely empathizing with Bill's wife's reluctance. "But a sudden, deadly heart attack seems completely out of keeping with his active lifestyle."

As soon as he said the words, Ben realized what had been bugging him. No one had told him Bill Nichols was fit. He'd seen it. Every single photograph in his office showed Bill and his family doing something that involved physical strength, stamina, and practice. He may have been in his early fifties, but he'd been in prime physical condition.

"I agree," Agent Leavitt said. "According to his colleagues, Bill hadn't taken a sick day in three years."

"Okay," Ben said. "Hear me out as I talk this through. If Bill Nichols is sitting at his desk and a heart attack strikes, what's he going to do? Breathe through the discomfort? Think he's got bad heartburn and ignore it? Maybe—until it becomes too intense. At some point, he's going to realize he needs help. We know he was at his desk, but even if it was a sudden cardiac arrest and he was unable to rise, all he needed to do was lean over far enough to push a button to connect him to the receptionist. One button. I saw the intercom on his desk. It obviously didn't happen. Why? It seems to me that there are two possibilities: one is that the heart attack hit so fast and was so debilitating that he literally died in an instant. The other is that someone watched him die and prevented him from calling for help.

"The first scenario could go two ways. We could lay it at the feet of natural causes, which we've already ascertained to be unlikely. Or we could consider the possibility that someone wanted Bill Nichols dead so badly that he or she administered something to him—something as fast-acting as it was lethal. I'm not a betting man," Ben continued, "but the way I see it, things are stacking up in favor of murder."

The phone was silent for several seconds before Agent Leavitt came back on. "Any theories on what would have been administered?" he asked dryly.

"No," Ben said, ignoring the agent's tone. "Believe it or not, that's a little out of my range of personal experience. A hypodermic needle? Something dropped into his coffee? I don't know. But it seems to me that it would have to have occurred soon before his death. If he'd been feeling bad for a while, he would have mentioned it to someone or left for the day."

"So you're thinking that someone who visited him that day—probably that afternoon—may be his killer?" Agent Leavitt said slowly.

Ben didn't answer. Instead, he threw out another idea. "Maybe that would explain what happened to the information Bill surely had in his office—the information he shared with Jed that's not there anymore. It would be pretty easy to abscond with a folder full of sensitive documents if the person you took them from was already dead."

"Meet me at Sterne and Lowe tomorrow," Agent Leavitt said, all skepticism now gone from his voice. "We'll have the security camera footage and a list of all the scheduled appointments for that day."

Chapter 23

BEN'S PHONE WOKE HIM THE next morning. It had been a rough night filled with disjointed dreams and sleepless hours. Jet lag compounding on jet lag was taking its toll. He fumbled for his phone.

"Hello," he mumbled.

"Ben? This is Detective Roman."

Ben leaned back against his pillow, trying to clear the fog from his brain. "Do you have any idea what time zone I'm in?" he asked.

"Can't say that I've given it much thought," Detective Roman replied, humor lacing his voice.

"Neither have I," Ben admitted. "But it must be the wrong one."

The detective made a noise that sounded suspiciously like a chuckle. "Well, you're gonna want to be awake for this news."

"Go ahead," Ben said, raking his fingers through his hair. "But just so you know, it had better be good."

This time it was definitely a chuckle. "Want to guess who was pulled over and booked on a DUI on the Vegas strip last night?"

Ben raised himself up on one elbow, all sleepiness suddenly gone. "They caught him?"

"Eddie Belton. Drunk as a skunk with more than twenty-seven grand still in his pocket and driving a brand-new black Ford pickup."

"Have they learned anything from him?" Ben asked.

"Once he was sober enough to realize he wasn't simply being booked for a DUI but was looking at a murder charge, he lost some of his bravado. Thankfully, his attorney is encouraging him to cooperate. Belton already has a criminal record, and they both know his chances of going back behind bars for a really long time are high if he doesn't do some serious plea-bargaining. The Vegas PD has supposedly assigned their best interrogator to the job. Let's hope he lives up to his reputation."

"Yeah," Ben said. "It's about time something broke in our favor."

"How did it go yesterday?" Detective Roman asked.

"Fine. Nothing much to report. I'm planning on spending this morning checking out who Bill Nichols was with on his last day."

"Good idea," Detective Roman said. "I'll let you get going."

"Thanks for the call," Ben said. "Keep me posted."

"I always do," the detective said.

Ben made his way to the bathroom and turned on the light. He felt awful, and the mirror corroborated it. His eyes were shadowed. He hadn't cut his hair in two and a half months and his shaggy curls were starting to resemble Zoe's unruly locks. He couldn't remember when he'd shaved last, but it needed to be done.

Leaning against the sink, he hung his head. He'd never felt this alone. The reality of Jed's death was finally sinking in. He wasn't sure that anyone could ever completely fill the void his twin had left, but Zoe and Rachel had helped. Now he was missing them too. Zoe had always had a special place in his heart, and with the innocence of youth, she'd been a balm to him in Hawaii, despite her own tragic loss. Rachel was something else entirely. She'd awakened something in him he'd never felt before. He wanted to be with her—to see her eyes light up when she smiled, to hear her laugh at Zoe's silly antics, to talk to her about his day, to listen as she told him about hers, to hold her close and kiss her. He rubbed his hand across his face and groaned. He was a mess.

A quick glance at his cell phone on the counter confirmed that there were no more messages from Rachel. She and Zoe were in flight. She'd texted him to let him know they'd boarded the flight bound for Dulles airport. They should land soon after lunch. He offered another quick prayer for their safety, then forced himself to focus on what lay ahead at Sterne and Lowe.

* * *

The wait for their suitcases at the baggage carousel at Dulles airport was painfully long. Rachel had woken Zoe upon landing, and now Zoe was beside her, clutching her dolphin and whining about how her eyes hurt and her legs were too tired to stand. Rachel had tried offering her fruit snacks and crackers, but Zoe had rejected both items with a swipe of her little hand and a grumpy grunt. A very short night interrupted by a long layover in LA was not helping Zoe's disposition. But with her own body aching from lack of sleep, Rachel was reluctant to pick up the little girl until she absolutely had to.

The two men were beside the conveyor belt watching for the bags. Whitney stood on the other side of Rachel, her red painted nails drumming a tattoo on the handle of her carry-on bag as her impatience grew.

"Zoe, stop whining!" Whitney snapped as Zoe's complaints escalated.

The little girl stiffened at the reprimand, then took off at a run.

"Zoe!" Rachel called. "Come back!"

Zoe ignored her and disappeared into the crowd. Thrusting Zoe's backpack into Whitney's hands and leaving her own carry-on bag at Whitney's feet, Rachel raced after Zoe. Too far away to help, Rachel saw Zoe stumble over unseen feet and baggage, but with one arm wrapped around her dolphin and her other arm extended in front of her, Zoe plowed on toward the baggage carousel.

Immediately in front of her, a man pulled a duffle bag off the conveyor belt. He obviously hadn't seen Zoe. He swung the bag around, clipping her head with the corner of his luggage, and like a bowling pin, Zoe went down, her dolphin and glasses sliding across the floor in front of her. Rachel reached her as Zoe's crying began.

The man was already on his knees recovering the missing toy and glasses, apologizing profusely and looking more and more worried as Zoe's howling got louder. Rachel gave Zoe a quick inspection, and upon seeing no blood and no obvious sign of breakage, she gathered the little girl into her arms and tried to reassure their fellow passenger that Zoe was fine and to convince Zoe of the same thing.

Once her dolphin and glasses were restored, Zoe began to calm. The man picked up his duffle bag and made a hasty retreat. Rachel positioned Zoe on her hip and walked slowly back to their bags and the waiting, fuming Whitney.

"Could she do anything more to embarrass me?" Whitney said, her whispered words making her sound like a snake.

Rachel looked at her. "I can think of at least half a dozen worse scenarios," she said coldly.

This time, Whitney really did hiss. Then she swiveled on her high heels and marched over to stand beside Senator Sheldon and Karl, who had just recovered the last of the luggage. Wanting nothing more than to hurl Zoe's backpack at Whitney's head, Rachel instead hooked its purple straps and the handle of her own bag over one arm, firmly clasped Zoe in her other arm, and joined the others.

Karl pulled Rachel's case along with his own until they reached the parking lot. At that point, he headed for his own car on level 3, and Rachel followed the Sheldons to theirs on level 1. Zoe was dozing uncomfortably against her shoulder when they arrived at the silver Lexus. Senator Sheldon unlocked the doors and transferred their luggage to the trunk while Rachel slid Zoe into the car seat. She had just finished doing up the buckles when Zoe woke up, and in an awful moment of déjà vu, Rachel recognized the panic she'd seen in Zoe's eyes when Ben had left her at Big Beach. Zoe started pulling on the straps, arching her back, and screaming to get out.

"I want Wachul!" she cried. "Wachul!"

Helplessly, Rachel leaned into the car and took Zoe's hand. "You have to go home with your mom now, Zoe. But I'll see you again very soon, okay?"

It was obviously not okay because Zoe's cries became even more frantic.

"Oh, for goodness' sake!" Whitney's voice cut across the sound of Zoe's shouts. Whitney pushed Rachel aside and reached into the car. "Enough already!"

As if in slow motion, Rachel watched in horror as Whitney drew her arm back and slapped Zoe across the cheek. There was a moment of stunned silence before Zoe buried her face in the headrest of her car seat and started sobbing. Whitney, with her head held high and without so much as a glance at anyone else, walked around the car, opened the passenger door, got inside, and slammed the door behind her.

Rachel turned to a pale-faced Senator Sheldon. "Let me take Zoe," she said.

She knew she had no real claim on her, and she was even less prepared to care for a child in DC than she had been in Hawaii, but she didn't care. "I can look after her until you hire a full-time nanny."

Senator Sheldon shook his head. "She needs to go home with her mother."

"Did you see what her mother just did?" Rachel said, throwing caution to the wind as her voice rose.

"Whitney will not touch Zoe like that again," he said firmly. "I'll make sure of it."

"How can you say that?" Rachel asked, desperation filling her voice. "You won't be with her all the time. Zoe's gone through enough already. She—"

"It will not happen again." Senator Sheldon's voice was icy. "You have my word on it. Just as I have your word that no one else will hear of this incident. I assume that I don't need to remind you of the confidentiality agreements you've signed?"

Rachel realized she'd crossed a line and recognized the veiled threat. She took a deep breath, trying to rein in her emotions. "I haven't forgotten," she said.

"I'm glad to hear it," the senator said, his expression the one he wore when negotiations were at an end.

He turned his back on her and climbed into the car. One minute later, Rachel was alone in the parking lot, watching the silver Lexus's taillights disappear down the exit ramp and still trying to process what had just happened.

She grasped the handle of her suitcase and numbly forced her feet forward until she'd crossed the parking lot and reached her own car. Digging deep into her purse, she pulled out the key. Her hand was shaking so badly she could barely get the key into the lock. She wasn't sure if the shaking was from delayed shock or from fury, and tears blurred her vision as she loaded her bags into the trunk and took her seat behind the wheel. Tossing her purse onto the seat beside her, she let out a cry of frustration.

She hated feeling so helpless. She'd promised Ben she'd be there for Zoe, and she'd failed before they'd even left the airport. But what could she do? She couldn't forcibly take Zoe away. She doubted that even Ben could legally do that.

Her cell phone rang. Rachel leaned over and sorted through the clutter that had spilled out of her purse on the seat beside her. Picking up her phone, she glanced at the caller ID. It was Ben. She couldn't answer it. Her emotions were too raw, and her voice would betray her immediately. If she were to tell Ben what Whitney had done, nothing would stop him. He'd be on the next flight into DC, and things would get ugly. Ugly for everyone—including Zoe. Ben would get slapped with some kind of restraining order, she would lose her job, and Zoe would truly be left with no one but Whitney. As much as Rachel longed to talk to Ben, she tossed the unanswered phone back onto the seat and started the car.

Chapter 24

DETECTIVE ROMAN WAS A PATIENT man, and he'd done his share of long, boring stakeouts, but this was pushing even his limits. And the fact that he was simply waiting for the man to show up to work made it even worse. Surely any self-respecting lawyer would let his secretary know if he wasn't going to make it into the office before noon. An hour and twenty minutes ago, the secretary had assured him that Blaine Thompson was due any time.

If he hadn't been sitting on one of the hard plastic chairs in the lobby ever since then, Detective Roman would have wondered if the secretary had somehow warned her boss of the police presence at his office. But there was no way she would have been able to send off a warning message under his constant surveillance, and her efforts to reach Blaine Thompson by phone had come to naught. He was not answering his phone.

Detective Roman considered leaving and returning another time, but his gut told him to stay—and he'd long ago learned to listen to his gut. With Ben and the FBI now devoting their attention to Jed Cooper's New York connection, Detective Roman had decided to do a little more digging locally. Something didn't feel right about Jed's ex-wife's sudden arrival on the scene right after the accident. And her speedy departure with Zoe was equally odd. He had a feeling Blaine Thompson could shed more light on both incidents.

From his seat in the lobby, he watched an old, cream-colored Chevy Impala pull up outside the lawyer's office. Out of the corner of his eye, he noticed the secretary sit up and straighten her small pile of papers. Then he saw Blaine Thompson exit the vehicle. The balding, paunchy man walked heavily down the short sidewalk and in through the main door. The secretary greeted him as soon as he entered.

"Mr. Thompson, Detective Roman is here to see you," she said.

An expression of shock followed by one of dismay flitted across the lawyer's face as he looked over and recognized the officer sitting in the corner of the lobby.

"I'm sorry to have kept you waiting, Detective," Blaine said.

Detective Roman ignored the apology and came to his feet. "I'd appreciate a few minutes of your time," he said.

"Of course," Blaine said. "If you'll follow me."

He led the way past the secretary's desk to his office. Turning on the light, he indicated that the detective could take a seat as he slid a pile of newspapers to one side of the desk and dropped an empty pop can into the garbage. "How can I help you?" he asked, sitting down across the desk from the officer.

"I'd like to know how Whitney Sheldon knew about Zoe Cooper's trust fund," Detective Roman said, coming right to the point.

Blaine blanched. His clasped hands on the desk could not completely hide the tremor that passed through them. "What makes you think that she did?" he asked.

Detective Roman gave him a disdainful look. "Ms. Sheldon relinquished all custody rights when she and Jed Cooper separated. According to Jed's brother and the Dicksons, she's had no contact with either Jed or Zoe since then. Up until two days after Jed's death, her interest in her daughter's welfare was zero. My research would suggest that Whitney Sheldon is not someone who has spent months hankering over a lost daughter. In fact, I would go as far as to say that having a child around would put a pretty big damper on her social activities and interests. As soon as Jed died, however, she was suddenly adamant that Zoe belonged with her. She did not wait for Jed's brother's return, for the reading of Jed's will, or for any of the normal legal proceedings. She wanted to stake her claim immediately—and she did so by taking Zoe right from under your nose."

Detective Roman could tell Blaine understood where he placed a good portion of the blame for that occurrence. He hoped it would give the lawyer cause to ponder his alternatives carefully, especially as Detective Roman shared his other, more personal findings. "I'm a police officer, Mr. Thompson," he said. "When I see someone do something completely out of character, I immediately wonder about the motive. And of all the motivators out there, I'd say money is at the top of the heap." He gave the lawyer a long, hard look. "Wouldn't you agree?"

Blaine managed to maintain eye contact for only about two seconds before puffing out his cheeks and giving a blustery reply. "There are many other equally compelling motivations, Detective. I could name at least half a dozen, most of them quite honorable."

Detective Roman inclined his head. "Perhaps," he said. "I wish I could assign Ms. Sheldon a more admirable motivation than simple greed, but hours of research have yet to uncover one."

"But she already has plenty of money," Blaine argued. "She doesn't need more."

"True," Detective Roman said. "And so, if she did indeed take Zoe to get her hands on the trust fund, would you consider her actions more reprehensible than if someone did something similar out of financial desperation?" He studied the lawyer carefully. "Perhaps you studied something like this in a legal ethics class at school. For example, would it be less wrong if it were done by a man faced with losing his law practice, home, and everything else of monetary value because debt collectors were calling far more often than new clients?"

It took only seconds for the implication of his words to register, and once they did, Detective Roman watched Blaine crumple before his eyes. The man's shoulders sagged, and he dropped his head into his upturned palms with a groan. "I didn't mean for anything bad to happen," he said, his voice barely above a whisper. "Jed didn't deserve it."

* * *

Ben leaned back in his chair and tried to work the ache out of his shoulders. He'd been hunched over a computer screen for six hours, and it was beginning to take its toll. Beside him, Agent Leavitt reached for his fourth cup of coffee and glanced at the piece of paper in front of him.

"We're getting closer," the FBI agent said.

Ben nodded. Of the forty-four names written on the paper, thirty-nine of them had red lines drawn through them. In the last few hours, the three secretaries who worked at Sterne and Lowe had studied the security tapes from the day of Bill Nichols's death and had managed to identify all but five of the people shown walking in and out of the office that day. Pulling up the schedules for each of the six brokers who worked there had helped, and they'd given special attention to Bill's appointments. The secretaries had even managed to identify some of the walk-ins whose names didn't appear anywhere.

Most of the people on the tape had been eliminated from consideration once the secretaries had verified their appointments with other brokers in the company. Of the men and women who had been scheduled to meet with Bill Nichols that day, all but three had been taken off the initial suspect list because they had come and gone empty-handed. Agent Perez was already making official visits to the three remaining clients. That left the five unidentified walk-ins, all of whom were shown carrying something on the tape.

"We'll bring in each of the brokers, one at a time," Agent Leavitt said. "Someone sat across the desk from each of these people and should be able to ID them." He got to his feet. "Take a five-minute break while I go round up anyone without a client in his office."

Ben gave a tired grin. "Glad you get to be the annoying one."

Agent Leavitt gave a grunt of agreement and stepped out of the room. Ben stood up and walked over to the window that looked out over the busy street below. Despite the high-quality, double-paned windows, the sound of honking horns and squealing tires reached him even on the fifth floor. Vehicles and pedestrians alike were hurrying to their various destinations, anxious to escape the sleet and the dropping temperatures outside.

Ben drew his cell phone out of his pocket and glanced at it. Rachel had sent a short text about three hours ago telling him they'd landed safely in Dulles. He'd tried calling her twice since then, but she hadn't replied. He was trying not to let it bother him, but it did. Even if he'd been mistaken about where their relationship was heading, he thought she'd at least have given him an update on Zoe.

As voices and footsteps sounded in the hall outside the office, he sent her a brief text.

How are things going?

Then he pocketed his phone once more and stepped over to greet the two men entering the office with Agent Leavitt.

An hour later, five of the six brokers had viewed the tapes and had identified three of the unknown walk-ins. The sixth broker had gone home for the day before Agent Leavitt could catch him, but his secretary had been notified that he was to check in with the FBI agent first thing the next morning.

"Perez or I will interview each of these people tomorrow," Agent Leavitt said, raising the paper with the three names circled in red. "We should have his reports on the ones he spoke with today by then too. We'll keep our fingers crossed that our missing broker can provide us names for the last two."

Ben nodded. They'd worked hard today, and even though he knew they'd made significant progress on this part of the investigation, his frustration that there were no obvious clues lighting the way forward was hard to conceal. "What can I do to help?" he asked.

"Get a decent night's sleep," Agent Leavitt told him. "You look like you could use one, and we need everyone operating on all cylinders." He pointed at the security tape video still showing on the computer screen. "This was a great suggestion. I want to hear any more ideas like this. Otherwise, I'll call you when we learn anything new."

Ben put on his coat and picked up his copy of the papers on the desk. He'd made his own notes as the video feed had played and had written even more when the secretaries gave their commentaries. Later this evening, after he'd given his mind time to sift the trivial from the important, he planned on reviewing the pages again. He had a feeling Agent Leavitt thought that his participation in the investigation was now at an end. He didn't bother setting him straight. Doing little to hide his exhaustion, he moved over to the door. "I'll be in touch, then," he said with surety, and he walked out of Bill Nichols's office without looking back.

Chapter 25

RACHEL'S ANSWERING TEXT DID NOT reach Ben until he was back at his apartment.

Been to the grocery store and unpacked. Zoe is with the Sheldons. I miss her.

Ben stared at his cell phone. That was it? He glanced at the time. After almost five hours, that was all Rachel was going to say? He grabbed a couple of frozen burritos from the freezer and slammed them onto the counter a little too hard. The bang helped dislodge the thick coating of ice surrounding them but did little to make him feel better.

What had happened to the warm, easy-to-talk-to Rachel he'd spent the last few days with in Hawaii? She'd seemed happy to communicate with him until she arrived in Dulles. What happened then? Ben stopped midway through unwrapping the first burrito. What happened in Dulles? He shook his head. He'd spent all day looking for clues at Bill's office, and now he was trying to find them in Rachel's text—or lack of texts. He needed his head examined.

The burritos were awful. Ben tried eating around the soggy freezer burn on the first one before giving up on the second and throwing the rest in the garbage. He placed a call to the pizza place on the corner and opted to take a quick shower while he waited for his pizza to be delivered.

Life looked considerably better after he'd showered, put on his most comfortable sweats, and eaten half a large, fully loaded New York–style pizza. Spreading the papers he'd brought home on the table in front of him, he started going over the names and notes he'd written down. Halfway through the second page, he stopped trying to ignore the nagging feeling that something was wrong and grabbed his cell phone. He reread Rachel's message. It bugged him that he couldn't stop thinking about her when she didn't seem to be suffering from the same problem. He put the phone down, hesitated for only a few seconds, and then picked it up again to text her.

Are you ok?

This time the reply was almost instant. *Yes. It's been a long, hard day, but I'm heading to bed soon. Thanks for checking on me. :)*

Need to talk about it? he asked.

Maybe tomorrow.

Ben stared at the message. Even though Rachel's immediate response to his texts was encouraging, he was still convinced that something wasn't right. He may not have spent more than a few days with her, but he felt as though he had come to know Rachel well. Her upbeat personality usually shone through her texts, and it wasn't like her to show no interest at all in what he'd been doing.

Tomorrow starts after midnight, he wrote. *Call anytime.*

Thanks :)

Ben put down his phone and stared unseeingly at the papers before him. Even the most basic level of concentration was eluding him. Maybe Agent Leavitt was right; he wasn't going to be any use to the investigation unless he caught up on some sleep. With a sigh, he headed to bed.

Three hours later, his cell phone's ringing woke him again. Immediately thinking of Rachel, he forced himself onto his elbow and leaned over to grab the phone. "Hello," he said, trying to mask the grogginess in his voice.

"Ben, this is Detective Roman."

Ben collapsed onto his pillow. "Don't you ever sleep?" he asked with a groan.

"Not much," the detective admitted.

"Yeah, well, I can now say the same thing," Ben said. "And it's about killing me."

"Want me to call back later?" Detective Roman asked.

"So you can wake me up again?" Ben said. "No, thanks." With a defeated sigh, he rubbed his hand across his face. "What's going on?"

"I spent a very informative afternoon with Blaine Thompson today," Detective Roman said. "I think you need to hear what he told me. Then you might want to get ahold of that lawyer friend of yours."

All traces of sleep evaporated. "What did he say?" Ben asked.

"Well, first you need to know that I did a little digging into Blaine's background and learned that by the time he graduated from law school, he was almost $300,000 in debt. As if that wasn't enough, he opted to go into more debt by setting up his own law firm and buying a large house in a ritzy part of town. Then he sat back and waited for wealthy clients to come support his financial deck of cards. Unfortunately for him, they didn't come, and it wasn't long before he realized he was going to have to start beating the bushes or lose everything.

"He started working his contacts—however tenuous—and that was how he came to approach your brother, Jed. As far as I can tell, Jed may be the only one who panned out for him. But once he could claim your brother as a client, he started using Jed's name as a marketing tool.

"He went to all the upscale events he could get a ticket for and schmoozed his way around the attendees, dropping Jed's name as an example of the type of clients he represented.

"About four months ago, he went to one of those political fundraiser dinner functions. Pretty sure I saw it advertised as two thousand dollars a plate. Anyway, who should be in attendance but Senator and Mrs. Sheldon. Blaine had no idea Whitney Sheldon had once been Whitney Cooper, so when he noticed her interest in his well-known client, he ramped up the bragging, telling her he'd recently drawn up the paperwork for a trust fund for Jed Cooper's daughter that involved millions of dollars."

Ben could barely contain his disgust. "How did he ever make it through law school? The guy's a total moron and has the moral backbone of a jellyfish."

"You don't have to persuade me," Detective Roman replied. "He gave Whitney one of his business cards that night and left the dinner feeling pretty confident that he'd hear from her again. And he did. The day after Jed's death."

The detective paused, and Ben's grip on his phone tightened. "What did she want?" Ben asked.

"She wanted to know details about Jed's trust fund," the detective told him. "I think at this point Blaine knew he was breaching all kinds of confidentiality laws, but he was desperate. Debt collectors were calling him multiple times a day; if he could secure Whitney Sheldon's patronage, he could get them off his back. So he bent the rules and told her what she wanted to know."

"Bent the rules!" Ben exploded. "How about he violated every lawyer oath out there and should be disbarred?"

"Yep, that too," Detective Roman said in his characteristically calm voice. "He told me he justified it because Jed was dead and the will and trust fund would be made public within weeks anyway."

Ben tossed the covers off his bed, got up, and started pacing across the room. "So when Whitney appeared the next day and took off with Zoe, Blaine knew she was fully aware that Jed's will gave guardianship of Zoe to me and that with that guardianship came $2.5 million?"

"Yep."

"And he let her do it!" Ben had never wanted to punch someone in the face as badly as he wanted to hit Blaine Thompson now.

"Jed was dead, and Whitney was a potential replacement money-maker," the detective said. "That's what it all boiled down to."

Ben took a few deep breaths. "What happens now?"

"We let Blaine contemplate his options as he files for bankruptcy from his empty office. And I make a copy of his statement for your lawyer, along with a paper he signed agreeing to testify against Whitney Sheldon if she takes her custody battle to court."

"He gave you that?" Ben was stunned.

"I think he's finally realized that his law career is over. Jed was pretty much the only person who gave him a shot. He can't undo the damage he's already done, but he does want to try to put things right—for Jed's sake."

Ben let out a long breath. "Well, it's a start," he said. "And I'll take it. The sooner we can get Zoe back where she belongs, the better."

"Maybe just knowing Jed's lawyer will testify against her will make Ms. Sheldon think twice about going to court," Detective Roman said. "It seems to me that most public figures avoid the limelight if there's any possibility that they'll attract negative press."

"If she can ever be persuaded to let the trust fund money go," Ben said.

"That's the lynchpin right there," Detective Roman said. "In my line of work, all too often, money is the root of all evil."

"Speaking of which," Ben said, "any word from the Vegas PD about Eddie Belton?"

"Nothing yet," Detective Roman said. "I was thinking perhaps I could wake you up tomorrow night for that update."

"I'm putting my phone on silent before I go to bed," Ben said. "So you'd better call earlier or leave a message."

Detective Roman chuckled. "Point taken. I'll let you know if I hear anything."

They ended the call, and Ben lowered his phone. He wished he could call Rachel and tell her the news Detective Roman had shared. Despite her reluctance to communicate with him today, he knew she was anxious about Zoe's well-being and would want to know about anything that could impact her situation. But Rachel was undoubtedly asleep by now, and he didn't want to disturb her. And anyway, rather than simply calling her in the middle of the night, what he really wanted to do was to talk to her in person.

An idea began to germinate, and he left the bedroom, flipping on the light as he entered the kitchen. Opening his laptop, he sat down at the table and pulled up JetBlue's website, quickly searching for flights from JFK to Dulles the next day. There was one that left at 9:32 a.m. Ben booked a seat and printed off a boarding pass.

He was going to DC. He wasn't expected at the Sterne and Lowe office, and he could study his papers on the flight as easily as he could at his kitchen table. If necessary, he could contact the FBI from DC and be back in New York before they realized he was gone. He'd see Rachel and do everything in his power to see Zoe too. In fact, he'd call Zach before he left and get the lawyer's opinion on how Blaine's information might impact his options. It was time Whitney knew he was going to reclaim guardianship of Zoe.

As Ben climbed back into bed, he didn't know to what he should attribute the sudden dispersing of the cloud that had hung over him all afternoon and evening; he only knew that for the first time all day, something felt right. With relief and gratitude, he quickly fell asleep.

Chapter 26

RACHEL STOOD BESIDE THE TABLE at the back of Senator Sheldon's main office and gazed down at the overflowing piles of paper in dismay. She didn't want to believe that the rest of the office staff was purposely targeting her because she'd been singled out by the senator to travel to Hawaii, but she was pretty sure this was significantly more than a normal week's worth of filing.

Along with the waiting paperwork, she'd received a pretty cold reception upon her return to work that morning. Kelly had acknowledged her arrival with a sniff. One of the senator's aides had made a caustic comment about her all-expenses-paid vacation and another asked if she'd actually read any of the treaties Senator Sheldon had brokered. Even the naïve young intern hadn't done anything to help her cause when he'd loudly complimented her on her tan. Kelly had looked daggers at him before turning her glare on Rachel.

Swallowing a lump in her throat, Rachel slid her purse under the table, picked up a handful of papers from the top of the pile, and walked over to the tall wall of filing cabinets that separated her corner of the office from the front reception area. She guessed she had at least an hour, maybe two, before Senator Sheldon made his appearance. At that point, she'd need to go pick up coffee for him and Karl. Until then, she'd simply chip away at the mountain of paper without question or complaint. She wasn't about to give the others the satisfaction of seeing how much their unwarranted cattiness hurt.

The only good thing about filing papers was that it gave Rachel time to think. She'd sensed a slow, subtle change in her perspective on life in general and her career, specifically, and she knew it had a lot to do with a sweet four-year-old who'd unknowingly reminded her of what was really important. When she'd first arrived in Maui, she'd been both offended and incensed to discover that the senator wanted her there for childcare duty rather than for any diplomatic acumen she may have developed. Now she'd happily walk away from this office, with its overt and covert politics, in favor of spending each day with Zoe.

As much as she admired the good works of many politicians, she'd spent the last week watching Senator Sheldon play the political game—wining and dining with other leaders, working the system, making connections, and returning to his hotel room exhausted only to start it all over again the next day. It was an artificial existence that left no room for real family life.

There were undoubtedly good politicians out there who made it work—who kept their priorities straight despite the pressure they were under—but Rachel was just beginning to see how difficult it was, and it saddened and scared her. Had she really been working all these years toward a tarnished goal?

As she went back to the table for another stack of papers, she heard Karl's voice coming from the front of the office, followed by the sound of Kelly's girlish laughter. It seemed that her resentment over members of Senator Sheldon's staff spending a week in Hawaii didn't extend to Karl. Rachel sighed and tried to focus on other things.

She wondered for the millionth time how Ben was doing with the investigation in New York. He'd probably been too busy to notice her lack of communication, but she'd missed it horribly. She wished she'd had the courage to call him yesterday, but she'd known he would want to hear about Zoe. Just thinking about the sad little girl had reduced Rachel to tears multiple times during the day. Talking about her—even if she'd refrained from mentioning the traumatic incident at the airport—would have been her undoing. But she had to call Ben soon, if only to hear his voice.

Instead, it was Karl's voice that reached her as he came around the wall of filing cabinets. "Hey, Rachel, what does it feel like to be back in the grown-up world?" he asked, sauntering over to the table and leaning his hip against it.

"It's nowhere near as much fun as being in the little-kid world," she said, continuing to file as she spoke.

"It could be," Karl said, looking at her pointedly. "If you'd just loosen up a bit."

Rachel felt her cheeks color, but Senator Sheldon's timely arrival saved her from having to respond. Kelly's enthusiastic welcome was hard to miss, and Karl immediately stepped away from the table toward the front office.

"Looks like it's coffee time," he said, turning back to face her with raised eyebrows.

Without a word, Rachel dropped the papers she was holding back onto the table and walked past Karl to greet the senator. "I'll have your coffee to you in just a few minutes, Senator," she said.

"Thank you, Rachel," he said, not pausing to look up from an official-looking letter in his hand.

More than anything, Rachel wanted to pull him aside and ask about Zoe, but she knew that with the way their last interaction had ended and with all the office staff currently looking on, this was not the time or the place. So without another word, she walked out of the office.

* * *

Passing through the metal detectors, Ben stepped into the imposing rotunda of the Russell Senate Office Building and paused to admire the century-old architecture. Corinthian columns and elegant archways surrounded him, and overhead, a coffered dome added even more to the stateliness of the building. From every direction, footsteps and voices echoed off the marble floors as sharply dressed government employees cut through the rotunda to go about their business.

Though he wasn't wearing a tie, Ben was glad he'd taken the time to dress up a little. He'd chosen to wear a pair of khaki pants with a light-blue button-down shirt. Pulling off his gloves, he undid the top button of his dark brown overcoat and turned to study the directory hanging near the main entrance. Senator Sheldon's suite of offices was on the second floor. He assumed that would be where he'd find Rachel, so he headed for the wide marble staircase and the upper east wing.

As the suite numbers posted along the hall steadily increased, so did Ben's misgivings about his decision to not tell Rachel he was coming. This morning it had seemed like a good idea to surprise her, but now that he was in her office building, the doubts and confusion he'd experienced when she'd not responded to his phone calls flooded back. Was this impulsive trip a huge mistake? His steps slowed as he spotted Senator Sheldon's name on the wall ahead, and for a moment, he considered walking on by. But then he remembered how good he'd felt when he bought the airline ticket late the night before, and he knew he had to give this a try. He reached for the doorknob and let himself in.

A young woman with shoulder-length, crinkly auburn hair and dark-rimmed glasses looked up from the receptionist's desk as he entered. She gave him a welcoming smile.

"Hi. Can I help you?"

Ben stepped closer. "Yes," he said. "I'm looking for Rachel Hamilton. Does she work in this office?"

For a split second, it seemed as though a frown crossed the woman's face before her professional smile returned.

"Yes, she does," she said sweetly. "Let me see if I can find her for you."

She got up from her chair, walked across the room, and disappeared behind a wall of filing cabinets. Moments later, she reappeared with another woman beside her. The woman wore black high-heeled pumps, a black pencil skirt, and a white blouse covered in tiny black polka dots. A thin silver belt emphasized her narrow waist, and her light brown hair was pulled up in an elaborate twist at the back of her head.

The two women were halfway across the room before he realized that the attractive, sophisticated woman walking toward him was Rachel. He watched her face as she drew nearer and saw her look of confusion turn into one of shock before it melted into a beautiful smile of recognition and warmth.

"Ben!" she said, holding out her hands to him. "What are you doing here?"

He took her hands and held them tight. "Hoping to persuade you to have lunch with me," he said with an answering smile.

She glanced at the clock on the wall behind him. "Can you give me five minutes?" she asked.

"Sure," he said. He released one of her hands and pointed to the three chairs lining the wall beside the door. "If it's okay, I can wait right here."

"That would be great," she said. She squeezed his hand. "I'll be as fast as I can." Then she turned and hurried back across the room, disappearing behind the filing cabinets.

Ben chose the seat that gave him the best view past the receptionist's desk to the office space beyond. Three doors led off the main room; one was closed, and the other two were open. A dark-haired man left one room carrying some papers and knocked on the closed door before entering. He heard male voices before the door closed again. The receptionist resumed her place behind the front desk and shot Ben a few curious glances before a tall blond man exited the second room and made his way over to her desk.

"Hey, Kelly," he said. "Can you make three copies of these forms for me asap?"

He handed her a small pile of papers before looking up and seeing Ben for the first time. Ben gave him a friendly nod and was surprised to see a startled look of recognition cross the man's features. It was gone almost as soon as it appeared, and Ben wondered if he'd imagined it.

"Are you being helped, sir?"the man asked.

"Yes, thank you," Ben said, coming to his feet as he saw Rachel reappear. "I'm waiting for Rachel."

This time there was no mistaking the change in the blond man's expression. His eyes hardened, and he watched Rachel's approach with something akin to possessiveness.

"I'm taking an early lunch," Rachel told the receptionist as she passed her desk.

The woman nodded, but the man gave her a cynical look. "Nice to know you're now accepting lunch dates, Rachel," he said.

Ben saw the color rise in Rachel's cheeks, and he stepped forward, placing a protective hand on her back.

"Only if the guy's car costs less than $30,000, he buys his clothes off the rack, and he polishes his own shoes," Ben said. "Otherwise, there's not a chance."

Then, ignoring both the blond guy's venomous look and the receptionist's muffled laughter, he guided Rachel out the door.

"Ugh! Sorry about that," Rachel said, barely suppressing a shudder as the door closed behind them.

"Who was that idiot?" Ben asked, instinctively reaching for her hand as they walked toward the staircase.

"Karl Trost," Rachel said. "He's Senator Sheldon's personal secretary."

"He looks kind of familiar, but I can't think where I might have seen him before. For a second, I thought he knew me too, but that could just be another identical-twin issue."

"You may have seen each other in Hawaii," Rachel said. "He was staying at the Grand Wailea and could have been in the lobby when you were there."

"Maybe," Ben said. "Is he always that obnoxious?"

"No. Sometimes he's extremely charming. But to be honest, that creeps me out even more."

"I knew you were smart," he said with a grin.

Rachel shook her head slightly. "On the subject of smart," she said, "how did you know all those things about Karl?"

Ben laughed. "I recognize a designer suit and a spit-polish when I see them, and the car was just a lucky guess."

He felt her grip on his hand tighten. "Thanks," she said quietly.

"Anytime," he replied.

Chapter 27

THEY ATE AT A SMALL café a couple of blocks from the Senate office building. It was early enough that they'd beaten most of the lunch crowd and were able to choose a quiet booth near the back of the room. The café had a rustic feel with natural wood furniture and sage-green painted walls. Framed photographs of wildflowers decorated the room, and sprigs of fresh forget-me-nots sat in short, squat pottery vases on each table. The ambiance was restful, and as the delicious homemade soup and rolls worked their magic, Rachel felt the stress she'd been under since she got home begin to lift.

"Feeling better?" Ben asked.

Rachel grimaced. "Is it that obvious?"

"Only because I know the relaxed Rachel of the Islands," he said in a teasing tone. "Don't get me wrong; the professional Rachel of Washington, DC, takes my breath away, but she seems to be carrying a heavier load."

Rachel lowered her head, embarrassed that she was so transparent.

"Did I say something wrong?" Concern filled Ben's voice.

"No," she said with a sigh. "I just need to get used to how perceptive you are."

He gave a rueful smile. "Sorry. Chalk it up to journalistic training." He met her eyes. "Would it help to talk about it?"

"Probably," Rachel said. "But tell me about the investigation first. How are things going?"

Ben raised a questioning eyebrow but must have sensed she wasn't going to change her mind because, after waiting only a moment, he gave an acquiescent nod. "When I first got back, I met with a couple of FBI agents who showed me a copy of a paper the Dicksons found in Jed's safe. We believe Bill Nichols, the broker from Sterne and Lowe who died the same day as Jed, sent it to him."

"You think this has something to do with the Wall Street mystery Jed e-mailed you about?" Rachel asked.

Ben nodded. "If the dates on the paper mean what we think they mean, someone out there is buying and selling stocks a little too perfectly. It looks a lot like an insider trading job, but we have no proof, just hunches."

He pulled a folded paper out of the inside pocket of his coat, opened it up, and set it on the table. "The crazy thing is, even though this list was printed on Sterne and Lowe letterhead and included a note from Bill, there's no record of it anywhere in Bill's office, and none of the other brokers know anything about it."

"Do you think someone stole Bill Nichols's copy?"

"That's the only thing I can figure," Ben said. "So yesterday I spent the day reviewing the Sterne and Lowe office surveillance video for the day Bill Nichols died."

"Because you think the same guy who stole the papers may have killed him," she said.

Ben paused. "Remember when I told you you were smart?" he said. "I wasn't kidding."

Not wanting to dwell on how much Ben's praise meant to her, Rachel pointed to the paper he'd placed on the table. "Is that Jed's list? Can I look at it?"

At his nod, she turned the paper so she could more easily read the words and numbers. Ben got up from the other side of the table and slid onto the bench beside her.

"This," he said, pointing to a long row of names, "is the list of companies." He then pointed at a row of numbers that ran parallel to the company names. "If our assumptions are correct, these are the dates stock was purchased in each of the companies. Only some of them have a second date, and we think those may indicate when the stocks were sold."

He leaned back against the padded booth wall. "If we're right, every single one of those stocks was purchased at its lowest price and sold at its highest. Millions of dollars could be involved."

Rachel studied the paper before her. Was it true? Would someone really kill for the money this list of companies represented? The thought both sickened and frightened her. She read the names. Some were familiar; others were not. But none of them meant much to her until she reached the ones at the bottom of the list. At that point, her heart started pounding so hard she could barely think clearly. She reread the last three names again and checked the dates beside them. The stock for all three companies had been purchased on the same day, about six weeks ago. None of them had selling dates, and with sinking surety, Rachel knew why. "Ben!" Even she could hear the panic in her voice. "Ben, the last three companies on the list—they're ones Senator Sheldon was negotiating for in Hawaii. They all signed ten-year contracts with healthcare providers in Japan. They're going to go from relative obscurity to household names virtually overnight."

Ben snatched the paper from her shaking hands. "These?" he said, pointing at the three names. "Are you sure?"

She nodded. "In the evenings in Maui, after I put Zoe to bed, I'd read over the treaties that Senator Sheldon was working on. I saw the company names over and over again as the details of the contracts were hammered out."

"Do you recognize any of these other companies?" he asked urgently.

"No. But I've only been on Senator Sheldon's staff for a year, and if it weren't for my last-minute invitation to Hawaii, I wouldn't have known these either."

"How many people in his office would be privy to that information?" Ben asked.

Rachel shrugged. "Senator Sheldon, Karl, and perhaps the two aides, Devin Shupe and Trevor McDonald. I don't think the intern, Derek Jackson, would have any reason to know, and the receptionist, Kelly Barnum, would only find out if she was asked to type up the paperwork. It seems like Karl takes care of almost all the classified material."

She reached for the paper again, and Ben set it down between them. "Look at these other dates though," she said, pointing to the top of the paper with an unsteady finger. "It doesn't make sense. These stocks were purchased five years ago, but Senator Sheldon's only been in office for two years, and none of his office staff were with him before that point."

"What did Senator Sheldon do before he was elected to the Senate?" Ben asked.

"He was the lieutenant governor of Arizona," she said.

Ben pulled out his cell phone. "I'm going to call the FBI to see what they can do with this lead," he said.

Rachel nodded and watched numbly as Ben recounted their conversation to the man on the other end of the phone.

"They're going to look into who would have access to information on the negotiations ahead of time and see if they can find a similar scenario with any of the other stock purchases," he told her after he disconnected.

Rachel gazed down at the paper before her. It seemed impossible that someone she worked with could be involved in all this. But a week ago, she would have thought it impossible that she would be questioning her place in Washington politics too. It was as though something she'd never considered movable had suddenly shifted, and she was having a hard time coming to grips with it.

"Hey." Ben's voice was gentle. "Are you okay?"

Rachel looked up and realized that a couple of tears had escaped and were rolling down her cheeks. She started to nod, but halfway through, she changed her mind and shook her head. Wordlessly, he put his arms around her, and she buried her face in his broad shoulder and cried.

When she pulled back, Ben passed her a couple of unused paper napkins, and with a whispered word of thanks, she accepted them and wiped away the last of her tears. "This is all Zoe's fault," she said with a shaky laugh.

"Zoe's?" Ben looked startled.

Rachel nodded. "After spending time with her in Hawaii I . . . I don't know how to explain it, but suddenly, the career I've been planning on for so long seems all wrong. In one week, I went from a girl whose primary goal in life was working her way up the political ladder to one who doesn't even want to go into the office anymore. And now, on top of my own doubts, there's this." She pointed to the incriminating paper. "Have I been living in a bubble? Or have I been off base all this time? I've admired Senator Sheldon's political work for years, but in Hawaii, I saw what it costs him. Those experiences I had with Zoe could have been his and Whitney's. They missed out on something they can never reclaim. I don't want that to be me."

Ben placed his finger under Rachel's chin and turned her tortured face toward his. "Hey, even if someone in Sheldon's office is involved, there are still lots of good, honest people working in politics who just want to improve things in this country. That's an honorable thing, and if you decide to stick it out, you'll be one of those people. But I understand where you're coming from. You're looking at the guy who's traveled abroad so much during the last few years, he's run out of blank pages in his passport twice. That's been my life. I've loved it, and I'm proud of the work I've done. But last week Zoe got to me too. I don't want to be gone all the time anymore. I want to be there for Zoe, and I'm starting to realize how much I need her too."

"You have to get her back, Ben," Rachel said. "Leaving her with the Sheldons at the airport . . . It was the worst . . ." She swallowed hard. "It was the worst . . ." Her tears started again, and she couldn't continue. Lowering her head to her hands, she covered her face.

"What happened?" Ben's voice was grim. "What happened at the airport?"

She shook her head without looking up.

"Rachel, listen to me," he said, and she heard the desperation in his voice. "Last night Detective Roman called. He went to see Jed's lawyer, and in a nutshell, the lawyer confessed to telling Whitney about Zoe's trust fund and agreed to testify against her if we go to court over custody. I talked to my lawyer friend, Zach Bennett, this morning. With this new revelation about Whitney's illegal interaction with Jed's lawyer, he thinks it's possible the Sheldons will agree to take care of this out of court. He's agreed to help and is doing everything he can to expedite our end of it, but if there's something else I need to know about Zoe and the Sheldons, you've got to tell me."

The image of Zoe sobbing in the car seat had haunted Rachel for twenty-four hours. It had kept her awake that night, and she didn't want to carry the burden of keeping Whitney's shameful act a secret anymore. She used a napkin to dry her tears again and turned to look at Ben. "Promise me you won't do anything rash—anything that might mess up having Zoe with you permanently," Rachel said, forcing herself to meet his concerned brown eyes without dropping her gaze.

"You have my word," he said, squeezing her hand gently.

Rachel took a shuddering breath. "Zoe was overtired. She fell asleep on my shoulder as we walked to the cars, and I put her in the car seat before she really knew what was going on. When she woke up, it was like Big Beach revisited, but this time she was screaming for me, not you."

The look on Ben's face told Rachel she didn't need to say more. He knew how awful it had been. "I tried to calm her, but nothing seemed to help. Then Whitney took over." Rachel's voice dropped to a whisper. "She yelled something at Zoe, leaned into the car, and slapped her hard across the face. Then she marched around to the other side of the vehicle and got in."

Ben's hand let go of hers and curled into a tight fist. "She hit Zoe across the face?" His voice was hoarse.

Rachel nodded miserably and continued. "I told Senator Sheldon I'd take Zoe home with me until they found a full-time nanny, but he insisted that Zoe needed to go home with her mother. He promised he wouldn't let Whitney hit Zoe again and made sure to remind me of all the confidentiality papers I signed when I joined his staff."

"His wife abused a child in front of him, and he threatened you with your job?" There was no hiding Ben's fury or disgust. "I can't believe this! Is everything really about public image to him?"

"I don't know," Rachel said unhappily. "I don't feel like I know anything anymore."

"Well, I'll tell you what I know," Ben said, pulling his cell phone out once more. "I don't care what I have to do to make it happen, Zach's getting on the next available flight into DC, and he's going with me to talk to the Sheldons today."

Chapter 28

IT HAD STARTED TO SNOW. Ben and Rachel hurried up the stairs of the Senate office building, past security, and into the lobby. After shaking off the snow clinging to his hair and coat, Ben led Rachel beneath the nearest archway, away from the other people coming and going through the vast rotunda. She turned to face him, tension obvious in her blue eyes.

"It'll be okay," he said. "Remember, as far as everyone else in your office is concerned, nothing has changed. You just went to lunch with some guy who came into town unexpectedly. Nothing too threatening about that."

A small smile played across her lips. "I'm not sure if Karl would agree."

Ben rolled his eyes. "You're right. After our last interaction, I don't suppose I qualify as one of his favorite people, but he asked for it when he insulted you like that."

Rachel gave his hand a gentle squeeze. "Every girl should have a superhero like you to defend her."

He raised an eyebrow. "Does being a superhero involve wearing tights? I don't do tights."

When Rachel laughed, he drew her into his arms. "I love it when your smile reaches your eyes," he said. "Just so you know."

She wrapped her arms around his neck. "And I love it when you fly into town to take me to lunch," she responded. "Just so you know."

This time it was Ben who smiled. Then he bent down and gave her a gentle kiss. "Call me when you get off work," he said, reluctantly releasing her.

"I will," she said, stepping back. "I have to pick up the office mail before the senator's afternoon meetings, so I'd better go. Please let me know when there's any news."

He nodded and watched as she turned and hurried down the hall toward the mailroom.

Ben waited until Rachel was out of sight, then headed around the rotunda toward the main doors. Two men, deep in conversation, crossed the wide lobby ahead of him, and as they drew nearer, he realized one of them was Karl Trost. Not wanting his reappearance in the Senate office building to raise the guy's hackles further, Ben hung back in the arch's shadow until the men passed by.

He was still bothered by the feeling that he should know Karl from somewhere. There was something so familiar about the way he walked, even the way he carried the manila folder tucked under his arm. From his concealed alcove, Ben studied the guy, racking his brain for some connection. He watched as Karl turned his head and raised his hand in greeting to another passerby, and then, in the moment Karl turned back, Ben knew. He'd seen that exact gesture before—on the security tape in Bill Nichols's office.

Swallowing the bile rising in his throat, Ben pulled out his cell phone and moved briskly in the opposite direction from the one the two men had taken. He scrolled down his list of contacts until he reached Agent Leavitt, then he hit the call button.

The FBI agent answered on the first ring. "Agent Leavitt."

Ben took a steadying breath. "I've got a positive ID on the blond guy no one recognized on the security tape yesterday," he said. "He's Senator Sheldon's personal secretary, Karl Trost."

Agent Leavitt let out a low whistle. "How sure are you?" he asked.

"One hundred percent," Ben replied.

"That's good enough for me," the FBI agent said. "After your last call, we started narrowing down the list of suspects in Sheldon's office. This Trost guy was one we homed in on, and when Perez started running a background check, he hit some red flags right off the bat. Before working for Sheldon, he was an aide to the former governor of California. Trost was there when the California Association of Winegrape Growers met with the state legislature to determine state laws on the type of fertilizers used by crop dusters."

"Let me guess," Ben said. "The ag companies on Jed's list benefited from the decision."

"Yep. Big time. And we're now looking into a connection between a contract signed between Nellis Airforce Base and a company on the list that makes ammunition. It went into effect while Trost was an intern for the former senator of Nevada." Agent Leavitt paused. "Bottom line, if things keep moving as fast as they have been, we'll have an arrest warrant issued before the end of the day. Until then, keep out of his way. You look way too much like your brother."

"It's too late for that," Ben said. "He saw me about an hour ago."

"Did he act like he recognized you?"

"I'm not sure; he may have."

Agent Leavitt swore. "I've got to make some phone calls. I'll get back with you."

As soon as Agent Leavitt disconnected, Ben tried Rachel's number, but the call rolled straight through to her voice mail. Tamping down his fear for her safety, he sent her a text message. Then, hoping he was doing the right thing, he slipped out of the building as quickly and unobtrusively as possible.

* * *

Rachel entered the office carrying a box of mail and placed one pile of letters on the corner of the receptionist's desk. Kelly, who was talking on the phone, gave her a brief nod of acknowledgment before redirecting her attention to her call. The remaining letters needed to go to Karl, so Rachel walked over to his office door and knocked. When there was no reply, she opened the door and went in. As usual, Karl's office was immaculate. The books on the bookshelf were organized in order of descending height; the files on the table were lined up perfectly, with no miscellaneous papers lying askew; the chair was tidily tucked underneath the desk; and despite Karl's recent absence, there wasn't a single brown leaf on the lone green plant. Careful not to disturb any of the other paperwork on the desk, Rachel set the pile of mail right next to a file labeled *Investments* before making a hasty retreat from the antiseptic office. She was closing the door behind her when Karl entered the front office. The moment he saw her, his expression hardened, and he headed straight toward her. "What were you doing in my office?" he asked through gritted teeth.

"Delivering the mail," Rachel said, not sure why he should be so upset about something she did almost every day. "I put it on your desk."

"And what else did you do while you were in there?" he asked.

Rachel took an instinctive step back when she saw the menacing look in his eyes. "I don't know what you're talking about, Karl," she said. "I went in; I put the mail on your desk; I left." She lifted the empty mailbox in her hand. "That's it."

"From now on, if I'm not there, leave the mail with Kelly," he ordered before pushing past her, opening his office door, and shutting it firmly behind him.

Her stomach churning with tension, Rachel looked over to see Kelly staring at her.

"What was that all about?" Kelly asked.

"I have no idea," Rachel said. "But it looks like you're getting all the mail from now on."

Kelly gave an irritated frown. "For the number of times I cover for other staffers' mess-ups, I deserve a pay raise," she said.

Rachel felt her cheeks color at Kelly's thinly veiled personal affront, but before she could respond, a door opened behind her, and Senator Sheldon appeared. "Rachel, may I have a word?" he said.

With a sinking heart, she stepped over to the senator's office and braced herself for yet another reprimand.

"Whitney just called," he said. "It appears that we have a function to attend this evening and have no babysitter. Would you be willing to stay with Zoe for a few hours?"

Relief flooded through her. "I'd love to."

"Excellent," he said. "You'll probably have to leave the office early so you can be at our townhouse by six. Do you need directions?"

Rachel shook her head. "No. I've been there before for the office Christmas party."

"That's right," the senator said. "Well then, I'll see you at six."

The senator obviously considered the conversation over, so Rachel hurried back to the relative privacy of her table behind the filing cabinets and pulled her cell phone out of her purse. There was a missed call and a text message from Ben.

Stay away from Karl.

She thought of her recent interaction with the senator's secretary and gave a grim smile. *Don't worry. I will,* she texted back. Then she added her news. *Seeing Zoe tonight :) Will leave work early to be at the Sheldons' by 6:00 p.m.*

* * *

Ben wandered through the News History room at the Newseum, his eyes scanning the newspaper headlines that had originally screamed the nation's breaking news and now recorded its history. To see so many memorable incidents in world history documented in one room was fascinating. From the bombing of Pearl Harbor to the assassination of JFK, from the fall of the Berlin Wall to the death of Elvis Presley, the events were immortalized in print, and it was a sobering reminder of the importance of good, honest journalism.

He'd hoped that visiting one of his favorite museums in DC would help take his mind off the torturous waiting game, but despite his interest in the exhibits, his mind was elsewhere. Zach had promised to head to the airport as soon as his last meeting was over and would bring with him whatever documents he'd already gathered to present to the Sheldons. Seeing as Ben had yet to hear from him, however, it appeared that the meeting was running late. He could only hope that there would still be a flight available by the time Zach reached JFK.

There'd also been no word from Agent Leavitt. Ben knew the FBI agent's attention was focused exclusively on whatever needed to be done to bring in Karl Trost. Until that happened, Ben prayed that his cryptic text message to Rachel would be sufficient warning for her to avoid all contact with the guy. He wasn't sure she'd be able to act naturally if she knew how quickly evidence was mounting against the senator's secretary. And it was vital that she maintain her normal office interactions. He didn't want to think about what Karl might do if he became even remotely suspicious that he would soon be facing multiple criminal charges, including murder and insider trading.

Ben entered one of the museum's theater rooms, took a seat beside a group of French tourists, and looked up at the huge screen displaying old newsreels from one of the Apollo landings on the moon. Despite the dated, crackling audio transmission, the stress in the men's voices at NASA as they communicated with the astronauts was palpable, and as Ben felt his own tension mount, he knew he couldn't sit there any longer.

Startling the elderly woman beside him, he rose abruptly, slid past the few people sitting between him and the exit, and headed for the elevator. By the time he reached the main doors, his coat and gloves were on. Then his cell phone rang. Tearing off one glove, he hit the answer button. "Ben Cooper."

"Ben, Detective Roman. Our jailbird's starting to sing. Just heard from the Vegas PD. Eddie Belton's given us a first name—Karl. Based on the fact that the FBI could supply us with a last name, I guess they already had this Karl guy on the radar."

Ben's stomach churned. "Yeah. You've just confirmed the number-one suspect."

"It sounds like the pieces of the puzzle are finally coming together," Detective Roman said with satisfaction. "We're putting out a warrant for his arrest, but remember, until the FBI has this punk in custody, you stay clear of him!"

"I'll try."

"Trying's not good enough. Do it."

Slipping his phone back into his pocket, Ben paused at one of the museum's large windows to look left down Constitution Avenue toward the Russell Senate Office Building. Then using every ounce of self-control he possessed, he stepped out of the museum, lowered his head against the continuing sleet, and turned right.

As he walked, anxiety over Rachel's well-being ate at him like a starving beast. Knowing that the woman he was falling in love with was less than half a mile away with a man who had likely orchestrated his brother's death made him want to barge into Sheldon's office and take matters into his own hands. But he knew that this was not the time to let his heart rule his head. For Jed's sake, Ben had to listen to Detective Roman and let the authorities do their job; he had to put his faith in them and in God that Rachel would be kept safe. In the meantime, he would find Zoe.

He reached his rental car, unlocked it, and jumped inside. A few well-placed calls earlier that morning had given him Senator Sheldon's residential address in DC. Turning on the engine, Ben took out his phone and transferred the address to the car's onboard GPS. Clutching the steering wheel, he waited three more minutes for the windshield defroster to do its job, then he pulled into traffic and headed north.

Ben slowed the car as he navigated the narrow road. The sleet had stopped, but a sloppy, watery mess remained on the sidewalks, and the roads were wet. The large townhouses were well maintained and most of the cars parked along the roadside were new, upper-end models. There was a general air of affluence to the neighborhood. He searched the house numbers, looking for the one he needed. And finally, he saw it at the very end of the row on the left-hand side, with an ancient oak tree shading the large front window.

As he pulled up in front of the house, Ben's cell phone chimed twice in succession, notifying him of incoming texts. He took his phone out of his pocket and glanced at the screen. The first one was from Rachel.

Leaving the office. Will call you from the Sheldons' so you can talk to Zoe.
The second was from Zach.
Boarded aircraft. Should arrive at Dulles in 45 mins.

Ben breathed a sigh of relief. Rachel would be with Zoe and away from Karl. And Zach would be here tonight. With a long, last look at the Sheldons' townhouse, he pulled away from the curb and headed for the airport.

Chapter 29

AT RACHEL'S KNOCK, SENATOR SHELDON opened the door. He had left the office half an hour before her and had obviously used that time to change into a formal tux.

"Thank you for coming, Rachel," he said as she entered the townhouse. "Zoe is in the family room."

He started to lead her down the hall toward the rear of the house when Whitney appeared at the top of the stairs. "Oh, good. You're here," she said, making her entrance down the stairs in a low-cut, full-length burgundy gown. Shimmering sequins and diamond jewelry sparkled as she took her place beside her husband and tucked her hand under his arm. "We should go, honey," she said, handing him some kind of fur stole to put over her shoulders. "The driver's waiting, and it wouldn't do to be late to a White House event."

Senator Sheldon used his free hand to straighten his bowtie and threw Rachel an apologetic look. "I'm sure Zoe will be pleased to see you," he said. "Go on through. We probably won't be back until eleven or twelve."

More than happy to escape Whitney's smug expression and cloying perfume, Rachel nodded and turned to walk down the hall, relieved to hear the front door slam shut seconds before she reached the arched entrance to the kitchen and family room. She paused to get her bearings. To the left was a spacious kitchen, complete with a bar, marble countertops, cherry wood cupboards, and state-of-the-art stainless steel appliances. Glass french doors led to a patio outside, and a dark cherrywood kitchen table and four chairs were positioned between the kitchen work area and the family room to the right.

A lavish display of yellow roses sat on the table, with a matching arrangement on the mantelpiece above the family room's fireplace.

Multicolored area rugs covered portions of the wooden floor, and the colors were echoed in three large, impressionistic oil paintings hanging on the walls. Two tan leather sofas, replete with a variety of throw cushions, faced a large, flat-screen TV that was currently showing *Dora the Explorer*. Pushed up against the TV was a narrow coffee table, and kneeling at the coffee table, peering up at the television, was Zoe.

Rachel stepped into the room and realized that the noise of the television program had masked her arrival. She watched the little girl push her half-eaten TV dinner aside and pick up the stuffed dolphin sitting beside her. Rachel's throat constricted as she watched Zoe lean forward to get a little nearer to the television screen.

"Zoe!" she said, moving farther into the room.

Immediately, Zoe swung around and scrambled to her feet. "Wachul?"

Rachel moved close enough to be within Zoe's range of sight and held out her arms. With a cry, Zoe ran to her, wrapping her small arms around Rachel's neck as Rachel tightened hers around the little girl's waist. "I missed you so much," Rachel said.

Zoe didn't reply. She just buried her face in Rachel's shoulder and hugged her. Holding her close, Rachel stepped over to the nearest sofa and sat down with Zoe on her knee. She raised one hand and gently stroked the little girl's hair until she felt her begin to relax.

"How is Dolphin? Has he been behaving well?" Rachel asked.

Zoe raised her head high enough to look back at the coffee table, where her toy lay abandoned. "Where is he?" she asked.

"I think he's watching *Dora*," Rachel reassured her. "Do you want to go get him?"

Zoe nodded and wiggled off Rachel's knee. When Zoe was a little closer to the table, she spotted the toy, picked it up, and ran back to Rachel.

"Is Uncle Ben coming now?" she asked hopefully, automatically making the association between Rachel and Ben.

"Not yet," Rachel said. "But maybe after we get your pj's on, we could call him on the phone."

"Yeah!" Zoe hopped up and down with excitement.

Rachel laughed. "Come on, silly goose," she said, offering Zoe her hand. "Show me where your room is, and we'll find your pajamas."

Zoe led Rachel up the stairs to a small guest room on the opposite side of the house to the master suite. The only indication that it was where Zoe had been sleeping was the presence of her open suitcase on one of the two twin beds and her fish book from the aquarium lying on the other bed.

Rachel knelt beside the case and pulled out a pair of pink flannel pajamas that had been too warm for Zoe to wear in Hawaii. "Let's try these," she said.

Zoe danced over to her, and Rachel carefully lifted the little girl's glasses off before tugging her Disney princess sweatshirt over her head. As the sweatshirt fell to the carpet, Rachel drew a sharp breath. Finger-shaped purple bruises ringed Zoe's left upper arm, leaving little doubt about what had caused the injury.

Very gently, Rachel reached out and touched the bruises. "Does your arm hurt?" she asked.

Zoe turned to face her, her large brown eyes straining to focus without her glasses. "She was holding too tight. I said I needed a Band-Aid, but she said no."

Trying not to let her emotions get the best of her, Rachel gently kissed Zoe's forehead before helping her into her pajamas. Her hands were shaking again, but this time, she recognized her fury and how to direct it. Whitney was not going to get away with abusing Zoe again. Before the night was over, she would use her phone to photograph and record the marks on the little girl's arm.

When Zoe finished washing and changing, they made their way back downstairs to the family room, where Rachel had left her purse. Rachel took her cell phone out and kicked off her shoes, and with Zoe curled up beside her on the sofa, she dialed Ben's number. It rang four times before Ben answered.

"Hi, Ben. It's Rachel, and I have a little girl sitting right next to me who'd like to talk to you." Rachel smiled at Zoe, who was squirming with excitement.

"Is that right?" Ben asked. "Is her name Peanut?"

Rachel turned to Zoe. "He wants to know if your name's Peanut?"

"No!" Zoe squealed with laughter. "My name's Zoe."

"Did you hear that, Uncle Ben?" Rachel said, even though Ben's chuckles already told her that he had.

"Zach and I are on our way back from the airport. I think we're within ten minutes of the Sheldons' house," he told her. "Any idea when they'll be home?"

"Sometime between eleven and twelve."

"Hmm. I'll ask Zach how he wants to play this, but in the meantime, let me talk to Zoe."

Rachel smiled at Zoe and handed her the phone. "Your turn," she said.

As Zoe's little fingers grasped the phone, a gust of cold air fluttered through the room, followed by the sound of a door closing. Startled, Rachel looked up as footsteps sounded in the hall. She rose to her feet, turning to face the unexpected arrival.

"Karl!" she said as he walked into the family room. "What are you doing here?"

"Spare me the innocent act, Rachel," Karl said. "We both know what's been going on, and I think you know what has to happen next."

* * *

Dread shot through Ben when he heard Rachel greet Karl. But the dread skyrocketed into full-blown panic when Karl's words were followed by a loud crash and then nothing at all. To Ben's right, a red pickup changed lanes unexpectedly, cutting in front of him. He stomped on the brake and swerved left, narrowly missing a white sedan and eliciting several angry honks from other drivers.

"Whoa!" Zach grabbed the armrest on the door. "What's going on?"

Ben tossed Zach his cell phone and glanced in the rearview mirror. "Scroll down until you find Agent Leavitt's number. Push dial, then hand it back. And do it fast!"

Zach didn't ask questions and had the phone back in Ben's hand in no time.

"Leavitt."

"Rachel and Zoe are alone at the Sheldons' townhouse. Karl Trost just showed up, and he knows we're onto him."

"I have two men on his tail," Agent Leavitt said.

"Then get them inside the house." Ben's voice was rising. "Right now!"

A tiny gap in the steady stream of traffic opened up, and Ben seized it, moving right, then right again until he was on the soft shoulder of the Beltway. He turned on his hazard lights, and with his foot on the accelerator, he tore past the slower-moving vehicles to his left toward the closest off-ramp.

"You are so getting a ticket for this," Zach muttered between clenched teeth, his hold on the armrest resembling a death grip.

Ben ignored him, swung right at the light, and sped on toward the next intersection. With another glance in his rearview mirror, he cut through a Walgreens parking lot and barreled out onto the perpendicular road that led to the Sheldons' neighborhood. Up ahead, a large delivery truck swung wide, turning into the parking lot of a grocery store. Ben swerved around it, missing the base of a lamppost by inches and receiving at least three honks from irate drivers who had to brake hard to avoid collision. Zach's breathing became a series of unsteady gasps.

"The two people I care about the most are alone in a house with the guy who murdered my brother," Ben said as the tires squealed their protest at his speed around the next corner. "The more cops I attract, the better."

Chapter 30

Karl moved toward Rachel one deliberate step at a time. As he passed the kitchen table, he swiped at one of the chairs, sending it crashing to the ground. On the sofa, Zoe had dropped the phone and was now whimpering.

"It's okay, Zoe," Rachel said, feigning a calm she didn't feel and forcing herself to maintain eye contact with Karl while she spoke. "I need you and Dolphin to go upstairs while Karl and I talk."

"I d-don't want to go upstairs," Zoe said.

Karl's lip curled up in derision. "Once a brat, always a brat. Doesn't look like you've managed to teach her obedience any better than Whitney did."

"She's frightened, Karl," Rachel said. "You're frightening her."

"I haven't done anything yet," he said, now so close she could see the beads of sweat on his forehead. He thrust his right hand into his pocket. "I haven't even pulled out my gun." He withdrew his hand from his pocket and raised his arm until the small handgun was aimed directly at Rachel.

Rachel took a steadying breath, praying that Zoe couldn't see the weapon. "Zoe, please go upstairs," she tried again. "If you hide, I'll come find you in a few minutes."

Karl gave a mirthless laugh. "Well, what d'you know? The good little Mormon girl tells lies. Pretty sure you won't be going anywhere in a few minutes."

Rachel balled her fists, refusing to respond to his taunts or to allow him the satisfaction of seeing her fear. "Why are you doing this, Karl?"

Anger flashed across his face. "Why?" he growled. "I'll tell you why." He stepped forward, seized Rachel's blouse with his free hand, and pulled her toward him. With his face inches from hers, he continued. "Because I'm not going to let you or that cocky boyfriend of yours ruin everything I've worked for."

He shoved her hard, and she stumbled backward, her blouse tearing as she fell against the coffee table, her legs buckling as the metal frame hit her behind the knees.

Struggling to keep her balance, she was unprepared for Karl's second rough push that sent her tumbling to the ground. As her hip impacted with the wooden floor, the pain left her gasping for breath, and from the other side of the room, she heard Zoe start to cry. Before she could raise her head, however, Karl stepped closer and stood over her, gun still in hand.

"You could've experienced the high life with me, Rachel." For a fraction of a second, remorse tinged his voice, but it disappeared behind an even greater surge of anger. "But you didn't think I was good enough, did you?"

Rachel struggled to her feet. "What do you mean, Karl?"

"You really want to know how big a mistake you made?" he said, his eyes glinting wildly. "Then I'll tell you. How does a villa in the south of France, a private boat berthed at Cape Cod, and millions of dollars in offshore accounts sound?" He raised his eyebrows, arrogance filling his voice. "That loser, Cooper, can't offer you anything like that, can he?"

Rachel stared at him. "Ben?" she said. "What does Ben have to do with this?"

"Why don't you tell me?" he said, his expression hardening.

Rachel raised her hand to her head as though the action would clear her turbulent thoughts. Zoe was still crying somewhere in the vicinity of the sofa, but Rachel didn't dare look in that direction. Somehow, she knew she had to keep her focus on Karl—on what he was saying and what he was doing.

"I'm afraid I don't understand," she said.

Karl snorted. "Don't pretend with me, Rachel. What exactly did he want you to give him? A full copy of my portfolio or just the amount of money involved?"

Rachel's mind raced. What was he talking about? "Your portfolio?"

"That's right," he said, tightening his hold on the gun. "The one Cooper had you check out when you oh-so-conveniently delivered the mail to my office today."

As the memory of placing Karl's pile of letters beside a folder labeled *Investments* returned, Rachel felt the blood drain from her face. An investment portfolio, buying and selling of stocks, millions of dollars in offshore accounts—all at once, pieces of the puzzle fell into place with terrifying clarity. Someone in Senator Sheldon's office was behind an insider-trading scheme that had already caused the deaths of two people. And now Rachel knew with sickening clarity who the perpetrator was.

When Ben had come to the office to take her to lunch, Karl must have recognized him as Jed's brother. Karl obviously didn't believe in coincidence. In his sick mind, Rachel's uninvited entrance into his office afterward merely confirmed her involvement in whatever plot he imagined Ben was hatching against him.

Through the mind-numbing mist of panic and fear that now threatened to engulf her, Rachel clung to one clear thought. She had to keep Karl talking. Her only hope of escaping alive and of protecting Zoe was to stall long enough for help to arrive.

She risked a glance at Zoe. Still in tears, the little girl had climbed down from the sofa and was frantically scanning the room. Offering up a silent prayer that since Zoe had never gotten on the phone, Ben would know that something was wrong, she turned back to Karl. "I didn't look at your portfolio, Karl."

"And that," he said, aiming his gun at her chest, "is your second and final lie, Rachel Hamilton."

* * *

Directing a warning honk at a young woman crossing the road with a dog, but making no effort to slow down, Ben flew past as she ran for the curb, skidding to a stop behind a navy-blue Chevy Malibu about ten yards from the Sheldons' front door. He guessed it had taken him about five minutes to get there from the time he'd lost contact with Rachel and Zoe. Praying he'd been fast enough, he yanked the car door open. Two men in suits were racing up the path to the Sheldons' townhouse, and behind him, he heard the strident wail of sirens. Without waiting for Zach, Ben took off running.

By the time he reached the Sheldons' front door, one of the men had disappeared around the side of the house. At Ben's approach, the remaining man pulled a gun.

"Ben Cooper," Ben said, pausing only long enough to catch his breath. "My girlfriend and niece are inside." He wasn't sure when Rachel had become his girlfriend; he only knew that he might never fully recover if he lost her now.

The man lowered his gun. "Agent Miller. Leavitt said you might show up."

"You're the guys who were tailing Trost?"

The stocky, dark-haired agent frowned. "Yeah. Until a knuckleheaded teenager rear-ended someone in an intersection right in front of us. We got here as fast as we could." Agent Miller tilted his head, putting his finger over his earpiece as he listened intently. "Roger that," he said before looking back at Ben. "Agent Larson's round back. He has a visual on Trost through the french doors that lead to the kitchen. Trost's holding a woman at gunpoint, but there's no sign of the child."

Ben's heart rate went into double time. Rachel was still alive, but where was Zoe? "We've got to get in there," he said, a sense of urgency surging through him. "Trost could—"

Agent Miller raised his hand to stop Ben, listening again as his earpiece came to life. "Larson's spotted the child on the other side of the room, and Trost's getting violent." He positioned himself in front of the door, his gun trained on the lock. "Larson and I are going in." He glanced at Ben. "You're staying here."

"If you think I'm going to just—" Ben began.

Agent Miller silenced him with a glare. "I don't have time to argue with you, Cooper. Stand back!"

Ben took three steps to the left and, with mounting anxiety, watched the FBI agent's slight but regular head motion as the countdown came through his earpiece. At the third faint nod, Agent Miller pulled the trigger, blowing a hole in the door where the lock was and sending slivers of wood flying. From somewhere else in the house, another gunshot, Zoe's scream, and the crash of shattering glass reached them. In one fluid motion, the agent gave the damaged lock a solid kick, and with a crack of splintering wood, the door gave way. Then he ran down the hall toward the rear of the house, with Ben right behind him.

Glass from the french doors littered the kitchen and family room, and on the floor beside the coffee table, two men were grappling with each other, both fighting for control of a small handgun. Agent Miller raced across the room toward the wrestling men.

Ben was at Rachel's side before Agent Miller knew he'd entered the room. Blood was everywhere, turning her blouse dark red and staining the floor for several feet. Zoe lay curled up in a little ball beside her, sobbing uncontrollably, her pink pajamas also covered in blood.

Ignoring the grunts, shouts, and thuds behind him, Ben dropped to his knees. *Please, Heavenly Father, let her live*, he prayed as he placed his fingers on her neck, searching for a pulse. At his touch, her eyelids fluttered open.

"Rachel!" His voice came out in a hoarse rasp.

"Ben," she whispered. "Help . . . help Zoe. She's so scared."

He took her hand, squeezing it gently. "Hang on, Rachel," he said as the sound of running feet announced the arrival of the paramedics. At Ben's shout, two of them headed straight toward him and took positions on either side of Rachel. Within seconds, they'd torn the sleeve off her blouse and were working to stem the steady flow of blood coming from a bullet hole in her upper arm. Ben reached for Zoe.

Behind him, more men raced into the room. Ben turned his head. Three police officers had taken positions beside Agent Miller, their guns trained on the wrestling men. Karl's leg swung wide, clipping the leg of the coffee table and bringing it crashing down inches from Agent Larson's head. Ignoring the distraction, the FBI agent slid to the left, forcing Karl to follow his move.

"Give it up, Trost," Agent Miller shouted.

Agent Larson cut Karl's vitriolic response short when he suddenly rolled to the right and launched himself onto his opponent, pinning Karl by the shoulders before finally silencing him with a solid right hook to the jaw. With a loud thump, Karl's head fell back against the wooden floor, and Agent Miller sprang into action, dropping to his knees and securing handcuffs onto Karl's wrists before the stunned man had a chance to move. As the resounding click filled the room, Agent Miller looked up, gave his partner an approving nod, and pulled out his phone.

One of the police officers hurried out of the room, and Ben turned his attention back to Rachel and Zoe. A paramedic was applying pressure to Rachel's wound, and though Rachel's eyes were closed, she was moaning softly. Zoe was clinging to Ben, shaking uncontrollably. Ben gently pried his coat lapels out of Zoe's clenched fists and searched for any sign of injury on his niece.

"The little girl saved the woman's life."

Ben looked up as Agent Larson came to his feet. The FBI agent, built like a heavyweight boxer and looking none the worse for having wrestled Karl Trost into submission only minutes before, brushed the broken glass off his pants.

"What do you mean?"

"I was through the glass door before Trost pulled the trigger, but I didn't reach him in time to prevent him from shooting. The little girl ran into him, knocked him off balance. The shot went wide."

Ben tightened his grip on his niece. As bad as this was, things could have been so much worse. "Are you hurt, Zoe?" he asked.

Still sobbing, Zoe raised a bare foot, which was scored by half a dozen angry cuts, the largest one with a shard of glass still protruding from the corner. Another paramedic ran in carrying an IV bag. He handed it off to one of the men working on Rachel and turned to Ben. "How's the girl?"

Ben lifted Zoe's foot. "She has slivers of glass in her foot, but as far as I can tell, that's it. She's covered in blood, but it must be Rachel's."

The paramedic knelt down beside them and drew one of the open medical bags a little closer. "Let me take a look at it."

Despite having to work around Zoe's extra screams and kicks, with Ben's help, the paramedic had her foot glass-free and bandaged in minutes. When he finished, he pulled a sucker out of his pocket and handed it to the tearful child.

"For being brave," he said with a smile.

Zoe wiped her nose on her sleeve and gave a big sniff. "I think I need another one."

"Zoe, you don't need more than one sucker," Ben told her.

"No." Zoe shook her head vehemently. "Not a sucker. A Band-Aid."

"Why do you need another Band-Aid?" the paramedic asked.

Zoe wiggled free of Ben's arms and pulled on the sleeve of her pajamas. "I have another owie," she said.

Concerned that he'd missed another injury, Ben helped Zoe pull her arm free of her pajama top and stared in horror at the finger-shaped bruises on her upper arm.

The paramedic handed Ben a Disney princess Band-Aid. "Any idea where those came from?" he asked grimly.

"Yeah." Ben spoke through gritted teeth.

"You understand I have to add this to my medical report," the paramedic said.

Ben nodded. "Do it. It'll be one more way of preventing her from getting near Zoe again."

The paramedic gave Ben a long, hard look and must have been satisfied with what he saw because he gave a curt nod and started packing his bag.

"I demand to know what is going on here." At the commanding voice, the chaos in the room stilled for a moment before the crackly voice of a distant dispatcher on someone's CB radio broke the silence.

Senator Sheldon, dressed in formal wear and flanked by his wife and two police officers, stood in the entrance of the family room, surveying the area with a mixture of fury and horror.

Chapter 31

BEN WATCHED AGENT MILLER HURRIEDLY end his call and slip the phone back into his pocket.

"Who's in charge here?" Senator Sheldon said. "I got an emergency call from my security system company telling me that we'd had a break in, and I drove home to find half the emergency service vehicles in Chevy Chase parked outside my house."

Agent Miller stepped forward and extended his hand to the senator. Flashing his ID, he introduced himself. "Agent Greg Miller, FBI, Senator Sheldon. I'm sorry to inform you that your home is currently the scene of an attempted murder."

"A . . . a . . . murder?" The senator's face blanched, and he looked around the room with new awareness, focusing on the bloody floor and the paramedics surrounding a stretcher.

"What happened?"

Agent Larson pulled the handcuffed man to his feet. With disheveled hair and eyes that flashed with hatred, Karl directed a string of obscenities at the FBI agent before wiping his bloody nose against the shoulder of his silk shirt.

"You're in enough trouble as it is," Agent Larson growled, grasping Karl firmly by the arm and forcing him to move toward the door. "I'd keep my mouth shut if I were you."

"Karl, what is going on?" Senator Sheldon's shock was evident on his face and in his voice, but Karl didn't even look at him. He kept his eyes forward as Agent Larson nodded at one of the police officers to join him in escorting Karl out of the house.

"Agent Miller, explain this to me," Senator Sheldon said.

The FBI agent didn't mince words. "Karl Trost's wanted by the state of Utah for murder. But he's currently under arrest for attempted murder and insider trading."

The senator looked at the FBI agent as though he were hearing things. "You have something to back up these allegations, I assume?"

"Yes, sir."

The paramedics lifted Rachel onto the stretcher and rose to their feet. Ben moved to stand beside her, the sight of her pale face beneath the oxygen mask making his heart constrict. He was grateful that Zoe had been spared seeing Rachel in this frightening state. From the moment the paramedic had left them, Zoe had buried her face in Ben's chest as though willing the nightmare around her to disappear. Her regular breathing now indicated that she'd escaped into sleep.

A movement at the hall entrance caught his attention, and he saw Zach slip into the room and make his way around the sofa to where he stood.

"Sorry," Zach said. "It took me ages to get one of the police officers out there to let me in. The press is gathering, and even the 'I'm an attorney, and I need to reach my client' argument took some doing." He looked over at Rachel and then back at Ben, concern etched across his face. "Is she going to be okay?"

Ben let out a long breath. "I think so. She was shot in the arm. She's lost a lot of blood, but at least the bullet didn't hit any vital organs."

Zach gave him a sympathetic look but stepped back as Senator Sheldon approached the stretcher.

"Rachel? He shot Rachel?" His stricken look spoke volumes.

"I'm sorry, sir," the paramedic at the head of the stretcher said, "but we need to get Miss Hamilton to the hospital."

Without another word, Senator Sheldon stepped aside so the paramedics could pass by.

Ben tapped the shoulder of the paramedic who had worked on Zoe's foot. "Which hospital?"

"Holy Cross," he said.

"I'll meet the ambulance there."

The paramedic nodded and hurried after the stretcher.

"I don't believe I know you," Senator Sheldon said, addressing Ben.

Ben extended a hand, keeping the other one firmly around Zoe. "Ben Cooper," he said. "I'm Zoe's uncle." From across the room, he heard

Whitney's sharp intake of breath as she looked past all the medical and law enforcement personnel in the room and saw him for the first time. With a clack of heels, she marched across the wooden floor. Ignoring her approach, Ben turned to Zach. "And this is my attorney, Zach Bennett."

The senator shook Zach's hand, but his attention remained on Ben. "You say you're Zoe's uncle?"

"Yes. Jed was my twin brother. I was in Afghanistan on assignment when Jed passed away, and by the time I returned, Whitney had absconded with Zoe. I'm here to take her home."

"Absconded?" Whitney had reached them and was livid. "You can put Zoe down right now, Ben Cooper. She's my daughter. I have every right to claim her."

"No, Whitney, you do not." There was no mistaking the steel in Ben's voice or the tightening of his grip on his niece. "You relinquished custody rights to Jed when you left him, and you've had no interest in Zoe since then. I'm listed as Zoe's legal guardian on Jed's will, and quite apart from the fact that I love Zoe, I intend to honor my brother's wishes and care for his daughter."

"You can't tell me that any court will rule in favor of Zoe being in the care of an unmarried uncle who spends the majority of his life traipsing around the world over a married biological mother with a secure home," Whitney said, her arched eyebrows daring him to defy her.

"Perhaps not," Zach broke in. "But the court may feel differently if it were to learn that the biological mother was physically abusive and wanted custody solely because it gave her access to her daughter's substantial trust fund—especially if the deceased father's lawyer illegally revealed to her the details of that loosely worded trust fund."

"You have no proof of that," Whitney said, her face white, her fingers clenched.

"Actually," Zach said, drawing a piece of paper out of his briefcase, "we do. Mr. Blaine Thompson, attorney-at-law, has given us a signed full confession of his interaction with you before and after the death of his client Jed Cooper."

Senator Sheldon gave Zach a piercing look. "You mean to tell me my wife knew that custody of Zoe gave her access to Zoe's trust fund and that she knew guardianship of both the child and the money had been willed to Jed's brother?"

"That's right," Zach said.

The senator swung to face his wife. "Why did you tell me there was no one else willing to take Zoe?"

Whitney folded her arms. "Because I wanted her and knew you wouldn't let me keep her if you knew."

"For goodness' sake, Whitney! She's not a dog; she's a child."

"A child that comes with $2.5 million," Whitney said. "Think of how much that money would help with your next campaign."

Senator Sheldon looked as though he was going to be sick. "The way things stand right now, there'll probably never be another campaign," he said stiffly. "In fact, I may not even survive this term. In case you hadn't noticed, my personal secretary has just been arrested for murder and insider trading."

"But, honey," Whitney began. "Don't you see that—"

"What I see," the senator interrupted icily, "is that if I don't start following my conscience right now, I'll lose what little credibility I have left. If you decide to contest Jed's will for custody of Zoe, I will testify against you, citing among other things specific examples of your neglectful and physically abusive treatment of her. And that, in case you have any doubts on the matter, should fuel the media for some time and will likely put an end to all your aspirations for elite social standing."

Before Whitney could utter another word, the senator turned to Ben and extended his hand again. "I'm glad to know Zoe has at least one family member who will give her the love she deserves."

"Thank you, Senator," Ben said.

Then Senator Sheldon shook Zach's hand and, in a constrained voice, said, "I hope to never see you in court, Mr. Bennett." Then he turned on his heel and walked away.

Whitney, her perfect features contorted by an expression of pure loathing and with fury burning in her eyes, took one step toward Ben before swinging her arm back and slapping him across the face. "This is the last time a Cooper will mess up my life," she hissed. "I never ever want to see you again."

In his arms, Zoe stirred, but Whitney didn't even glance her way. With one last venomous look at Ben, she strutted back across the room and disappeared into the hall. Ignoring his stinging cheek, Ben raised his hand to his niece's small head, stroking her hair until her even breathing returned. "Good-bye, Whitney," he said softly, the words ringing with releasing finality.

Chapter 32

DAYLIGHT WAS JUST BEGINNING TO filter through the closed blinds of Rachel's hospital room when Zoe scrambled off the makeshift bed in the corner and clambered onto Ben's knee.

"Hi, Uncle Ben."

With a groan, Ben rolled his shoulders, trying to work out the ache that came from spending the night in the uncomfortable chair.

"Is it morning time yet?" Zoe asked.

Ben glanced at the clock on the wall. Six thirteen felt indecently early to be called morning, but technically, it was. "I guess so," he said.

"Is Wachul going to wake up now?"

Ben looked over at Rachel lying on the nearby hospital bed. She was still too pale, but after receiving three pints of blood and coming out of surgery successfully the night before, she was off the oxygen mask and her vital signs were good.

"I don't know, Peanut." He was as anxious as Zoe to see Rachel's blue eyes and bright smile again. "Hopefully soon."

His young niece snuggled closer, and Ben lifted the thin hospital blanket up and over her shoulders, loving having her near. He didn't want to think about how close he'd come to losing both Rachel and Zoe. The vision of Rachel lying on the Sheldons' family room floor covered in blood would be a recurring nightmare for a long time to come, and he could still hardly believe he'd walked out of the Sheldons' home with Zoe, knowing that she would never have to go back.

"Is Grampa Bert making me breakfast today?"

Ben chuckled. He'd called the Dicksons from the hospital the night before to tell them Jed's murderer had been found and apprehended and that Zoe was coming home. Dorothy had been unable to restrain her tears. Both she and Bert had talked to Zoe on the phone, and Zoe was as excited as they were for their reunion.

"Grandpa Bert will make you breakfast as soon as you get home," he said.

"Can we go home today?"

"I don't think so," Ben said. "We need to make sure Rachel's okay first."

"When she's better, can Wachul come too?"

"I would love it if Rachel came home with us," he said. "But she lives here, and her work is here."

"No." Zoe's head popped up, and she looked as though she was going to burst into tears. "Wachul doesn't go to work. She's 'posed to stay with me."

"She'll be with you for a few more days," Ben said, not wanting Zoe to cling to unrealistic expectations.

"No, forever," Zoe cried, pushing herself off Ben's knee and hobbling over to the hospital bed on her bandaged foot.

Before Ben knew what was happening, Zoe had climbed up the side of the bed and was crawling over the blankets.

"No, Zoe." Ben jumped to his feet as Zoe lay down beside Rachel and began patting Rachel's cheek.

* * *

Rachel was vaguely aware of voices. It seemed like she should recognize them, but she struggled to make out the words. Her mouth felt like sandpaper, and her whole body hurt—especially her arm. The pain began at her elbow and throbbed up through her shoulder, making it hard to think.

A child's voice. Zoe's voice. She recognized it now.

"Stay with me forever, Wachul," she said. "Please stay forever."

"Okay." Rachel mouthed the word, but no sound came. She tried again. "Okay." Still nothing. A tear born of frustration rolled down her cheek. "Okay."

"Uncle Ben, she said okay." The bed moved violently beneath her, and Rachel moaned as the pain in her arm intensified.

"Hold still, Zoe." Rachel heard Ben's voice.

"Ben," she whispered.

"I'm right here," he said, and she felt a gentle finger wipe the tear from her face as her eyelids finally fluttered open.

Two pairs of brown eyes looked down at her, full of concern and caring.

"She's awake!" Zoe wiggled closer, beaming.

Rachel smothered a groan as the shaking of the bed vibrated up her arm.

"Off, Zoe," Ben said, lifting the little girl up and placing her on the floor beside him.

"But why?"

"Because you're hurting Rachel. She has a bad owie on her arm, and every time you move the bed, it hurts."

"Like my owie?" she said, raising her bandaged foot.

"Even bigger than yours."

Zoe's mouth formed a tiny *O*, and she moved closer to peer at Rachel's arm.

Ben gently stroked Rachel's head, running his fingers through her hair. "How are you feeling?"

"Sore," she said, her voice cracking. "And thirsty."

He walked over to the small sink, filled a paper cup with water, and, after raising the head of the bed, he held it to her lips. "Better?" he asked as she pushed the cup away.

She nodded and looked down at the heavy bandage wrapped around her left arm. "It was Karl," she said quietly.

"I'm so sorry, Rachel." Ben ran a hand across his haggard face. "If he hadn't seen me with you . . . Once we knew . . . I never should have let you stay at the office."

"Ben, this is not your fault." She reached out her hand to him. "I wasn't even at the office when it happened. And if you hadn't come when you did . . ." She shuddered at the memory of Karl's menacing approach across the Sheldons' family room. "It was like something inside him had snapped. He was . . . He was . . ."

"He was desperate." Ben finished for her.

"Yes," she said. "But I don't understand. What made him do it?"

Ben wrapped his fingers around hers. "Last night one of the FBI agents told me a little about Karl's background. He grew up in Vegas with a single mom who worked at one casino after another, losing everything she earned before making it home. It must have been a pretty miserable existence, and he vowed he'd get out, make it big, and never want for anything again." Ben looked at Rachel. "He was smart, managed to get a scholarship to the University of Nevada, Las Vegas, and from there, he got an internship with a senator from Nevada. That position taught him the power of information. Suddenly, he had the inside scoop on companies that were about to land huge contracts—and the insider trading began."

Rachel shook her head, pity filling her heart for Karl's bad start.

"He was good, and it wasn't long before his financial empire was so big he had to start hiding it in real estate purchases or offshore accounts," Ben continued. "I don't know what tipped Bill Nichols off—we may never know—but once Jed was involved, Karl knew he had to get rid of them before they went public with their suspicions, or he risked losing everything.

"We think he personally administered some kind of lethal drug to Bill, but a guy named Eddie Belton—someone Karl grew up with who followed a more obvious life of crime and was willing to do pretty much anything for enough money—helped with Jed's accident."

"And because Karl saw me with you and thought I'd figured out what he was doing, I was the next target," Rachel said.

Ben nodded. "He was always dropping off or picking up paperwork at the senator's house, so he had a key, and he knew you'd be alone. It was a perfect setup." He paused, momentarily reliving the terror he'd experienced in the car when he hadn't known if he would make it to the Sheldons' home in time. "If we hadn't been on the phone when he entered the house . . ." He took a deep breath, his eyes holding hers. "I never want to come that close to losing you again."

"Is it breakfast time yet?" Zoe's voice came from the floor at the foot of the bed, where she'd been amusing herself by stacking paper cups.

Rachel could barely suppress a smile at Ben's long-suffering sigh.

"It's Big Beach revisited," he said with a groan.

"But she's with you, and she's safe," Rachel said. Then more hesitantly she asked, "Did you talk to Whitney?"

"She and Senator Sheldon showed up about the time you headed to the hospital. I was glad Zach was there to back me up, but once the senator learned what Whitney had done, it was pretty much over. He told her if she went to court to contest Jed's will, he'd testify against her himself and cite her neglect and abuse."

Rachel's eyes widened. "He said that?"

"Yep. And he left nobody—including Whitney—with any doubt that he'd follow through."

"Wow!" Rachel had a pretty good idea of what that action would do to a man of Senator Sheldon's standing, and she was grateful to know that the moral backbone she'd recently started to question was still present.

"To say Whitney was ticked would be an understatement," Ben said. "But if I have anything to do with it, Zoe will never have to see her again."

Tears of relief and gratitude pricked Rachel's eyes. Although her own future was uncertain, at least she would know Zoe was safe and with people who loved her.

"Uncle Ben, I'm hungry!"

Rachel choked back a giggle as Ben rolled his eyes. "I'd better take her down to the cafeteria before the requests get any louder."

"Okay," she said. "Pretty sure I'll still be here when you get back."

"You'd better be," he said. Then leaning across the bed, he kissed her gently on the lips before pulling away slightly and resting his forehead against hers. "I love you, Rachel Hamilton," he whispered.

Forcing herself to breathe, she watched as Ben moved to the end of the bed and picked up Zoe.

"Come on, hopalong," he said. "We'll be faster if I carry you."

"I'm not hopalong," Zoe said, swinging her bandaged foot back and forth. "I'm—"

"I know, I know. You're starving!"

"No!" Zoe squealed.

With a grin, Ben reached for the door. "We'll see you in a few minutes," he said, looking back at Rachel. "Try not to miss us too much."

"Okay," she said, and a little more quietly, she added, "I love you too, Ben."

Ben froze, and at the look he gave her, a hundred butterflies began fluttering in her stomach. Before she could catch her breath, he'd crossed the tiny room, dumped Zoe on the end of the bed, and was beside her, cradling her face in his hands. He held her gaze for just a few seconds before lowering his lips to hers again. And the butterflies took flight.

Chapter 33

BEN WATCHED ZOE CHASE THE last remaining Cheerios around her bowl in the hospital cafeteria and knew he had work to do. Still dressed in her borrowed child-size hospital gown, Zoe needed clothes. He wasn't about to go back to the Sheldons' house to pick up her suitcase, but she needed more than the bloodstained pajamas, blanket, and stuffed dolphin she'd brought with her.

Along with that, he needed to call his office. His boss had been understanding about his absence a week ago, but now he'd have to ask for extra time to get Zoe settled into her Utah home and figure out a long-term plan for being there himself. If necessary, he'd have to resign from *Our World* and look for another job that required less traveling.

And then there was Rachel. Knowing now that his deep feelings for her were reciprocated made the thought of parting even more unbearable. But the fact remained that her work, her home, and her life were here in DC. She'd already endured traumatic injury because of her association with him; he wasn't about to ask her to sacrifice anything more. He didn't know how to surmount their looming separation, but he knew he had to try. Praying for inspiration, he cleared his and Zoe's dirty dishes, picked up Zoe, and headed back upstairs.

When they arrived at Rachel's room, the doctor was in with her. Staying out in the hall, Ben asked a passing nurse if she'd retrieve Zoe's blanket and his coat and tell Rachel he'd be back within an hour. When the nurse brought everything out, Ben wrapped Zoe as warmly as possible, carried her down to his rental car, and drove half a mile to the nearest Walmart for his first foray to the little girls' clothing department.

* * *

Rachel lay back against the pillow on the hospital bed and glanced at the clock for the third time in three minutes. She'd had a positive visit with the doctor. Miraculously, although the bullet had punctured muscle tissue at relatively close range, it hadn't done any damage to bone or tendons, which meant that a full recovery was possible as long as she didn't do anything too strenuous for a few weeks.

She'd also been able to speak with her parents on the phone. Someone from the FBI had contacted them the night before, and they were already making plans to fly to DC. Reassuring them that she was okay had been difficult, and it had taken some time to convince her mother that an expensive, last-minute flight to see her was unnecessary.

During their conversation, Rachel's mom had repeatedly urged her to return home to Arizona to recuperate, but even though accepting her mother's offer held some appeal, it didn't feel right. Nothing felt right—except being with Ben and Zoe. And they'd be leaving for Utah very soon. She closed her eyes. She didn't want to think about her life here after they left. They'd been gone ten minutes longer than Ben had told the nurse, and already, Rachel missed them.

Reaching for the remote, she clicked on the television and scrolled through the channels until she reached CNN. A reporter was standing on a flooded street in the outskirts of Manila and was describing the devastation caused by a recent tsunami. She watched for a few minutes until the sound of Zoe's voice in the hall reached her.

"This door? Is this the right door?"

Rachel clicked the mute button as the door opened and Zoe tumbled in, fully clothed and clutching a bunch of gerbera daisies. Right behind her, Ben entered carrying several Walmart bags.

"Look, Wachul! These are for you," Zoe said with excitement. She pulled herself onto the bed one-handed and crawled forward, crushing a couple of blossoms along the way.

"Careful, Zoe," Ben said as Zoe got closer to Rachel.

Rachel reached out to take the proffered flowers. "Thank you, Zoe," she said, giving the little girl a kiss on her cheek. "They're beautiful."

Zoe beamed. "And look at my new shoes." She lay on her back and lifted both legs in the air to display a pair of puffy Disney princess snow boots.

"Wow! They're awesome," Rachel said, risking a glance at Ben, who grinned and shrugged.

"They were the ones she wanted, and they have enough padding in the sole for her to walk without hurting her heel. I figured it was a win-win."

"They look great," Rachel said, trying not to smile at how the snow boots finished off Zoe's pink and purple frilly ensemble. "I'm glad you let her choose."

Ben pulled a large, wooden Tinkerbell jigsaw puzzle out of one of the bags and handed it to his niece. "Here's your puzzle, Zoe. How about you sit on your bed and work on it for a few minutes." He lifted her off Rachel's bed and onto the small one in the corner of the room, opened the puzzle box, and spread the pieces out in front of her. Zoe picked up the pieces, studying them one by one, and Ben moved to sit on the edge of the hospital bed beside Rachel. "What did the doctor say?" he asked, taking the flowers and setting them on the bedside table before reaching for her hand.

"He's given me a prescription for pain medicine and instructions not to lift anything for a while, and he told me I can go home tonight."

Ben's face lit up. "They're releasing you already? That's great!"

She nodded, wishing she could feel as happy. The sooner she was released, the sooner she'd go back to her lonely apartment and Ben and Zoe would leave. "I spoke to my mom and dad on the phone," she told him. "I think I managed to persuade them that I'm going to be okay."

Her attempt at being upbeat was failing. Turning away from his perceptive eyes, Rachel fought to hide her misery. Across the room, the silent television flickered to a new picture, and she gasped as she recognized Senator Sheldon standing in the rotunda of the Russell Senate Office Building. Ben reached for the remote and turned up the volume.

They sat listening quietly as the senator was interviewed about the shooting in his home, the injury to one of his staff members, and the arrest of his personal secretary. Ever the statesman, he expressed shock and concern along with a promise to get to the bottom of the alleged illegal activity. Evading the trickier questions masterfully, he soon excused himself for a meeting and left having told the audience hardly anything of any substance.

"I don't want to go back," Rachel whispered as the reporter continued pontificating on what they knew and what they didn't.

Ben ran his finger down her cheek. "By the time you've healed well enough to return, this media frenzy will be a thing of the past."

Rachel shook her head. "I told you before all this happened that I was having serious doubts about my place in the political arena. The thought of stepping back into that office, continuing on with the menial work I was doing before, makes me feel sick."

Carefully avoiding her bulky bandage, Ben slid his arm around her and drew her close. She rested her head on his shoulder, fighting tears. "Working for Senator Sheldon has been my focus for so long, I feel like I've broken free of my moorings and I'm lost at sea."

"Have you thought through your options?" he asked. "Would you like to work in someone else's office or go a different direction? Is there something that sounds better than anything else?"

She hesitated, not sure if she had the courage to tell him the truth.

"Rachel?" He moved back slightly so he could see her face. "Tell me."

Color flooded her cheeks, and she lowered her head, shaking it slightly. "At the moment, the only thing that feels right is being with you and Zoe."

He stilled. Wondering if she'd made a fool of herself, Rachel looked up. Hope shone in his eyes, and he reached for both of her hands. "Hear me out on this, okay?" At her nod, he continued. "I need to take Zoe back to Utah as soon as possible. She needs the stability of being back in her own home, and being with Dorothy and Bert will be good for both Zoe and the Dicksons. I also need to make a job change—either a reassignment within *Our World* or a new position somewhere else, something that involves less travel and enables me to be based out of Utah most of the time. Until then, though, I'm obligated to finish up current assignments, including the article on Afghanistan, and spend some time in the New York office.

"Because of the accident, Dorothy is pretty much immobile—and will be for weeks, maybe months. She and Bert can't look after Zoe without help. I can be there at first but not long enough. Would you . . . would you consider going out there with us? Taking care of Zoe like you did in Hawaii and staying on when I have to leave? It would be a full-time job, and I'd pay you accordingly. I know you're injured, but maybe with all of us, we can make it work." He took a deep breath. "I'd be lying if I told you this wasn't personal. I want the opportunity to spend more time with you, Rachel. But you'd be giving up a lot to move to Utah, and you've already sacrificed enough for me and for Zoe. I only want you to do this if you feel that it's the best thing for you."

Rachel stared at him, trying to take in all that he'd just said. "You really think Dorothy and Bert would be okay with me being there?"

"Are you kidding me?" Ben said. "You'd be an answer to their prayers—and mine. I knew I'd need to find extra help, and there's no one Zoe or I would rather have at the house, and I guarantee you'll win over the Dicksons within minutes of your arrival."

A glowing warmth began in her chest and slowly suffused throughout her body. She could walk away from her position in Senator Sheldon's office knowing that she'd done all she needed to do and her time there was over. Her desire to make a difference still burned, but it was illuminating a very different path—a path she didn't have to walk alone. And it felt right. "And you'll help me persuade my parents that this is a good idea?"

His eyes twinkled. "Have I ever told you I was my high school's debate champion?"

Rachel laughed. "No. But it doesn't surprise me."

Ben tightened his grip on her hands. "It's a big decision, Rachel. Are you sure you want to do this?"

"Yes," she said, feeling truly happy for the first time since she'd woken up. "I'm sure."

Chapter 34

Four Months Later

TWILIGHT WAS FALLING AS BEN drove his car up the circular driveway and came to a halt beside Bert's truck in front of the large log home. It was hard to believe how much had changed in four months. Gone were the barren trees, deep snowdrifts, and bitter, icy conditions. In their place, green grass and wildflowers covered the ground, and shimmering aspen leaves danced in the warm breeze.

Grabbing his carry-on bag from the backseat, Ben got out of the car and stood gazing at the house as the last brilliant orange rays of the setting sun reflected off the windows. There wasn't a day that went by that he didn't miss Jed, but he was grateful that the sense of mourning that had hung over the house months ago was mostly gone, replaced by a feeling of homecoming.

And it truly was a homecoming this time. He was returning from his last assignment as an international correspondent. His apartment in New York had been sublet, and his belongings had been moved to his new home in Utah. In two weeks, he would take over as *Our World's* North America division managing editor—a promotion that had taken him by surprise but could not have come at a better time. Although traveling would still be part of his job, it would be limited in distance and duration. For the most part, he would be in Utah with his family.

Quickening his pace, he hurried up the stairs to the front door. As he entered, Turbo ran to greet him, giving an excited bark and sliding across the tile in his usual out-of-control manner. Ben rubbed his head affectionately. He was a crazy dog, but returning home wouldn't be the same without him. Moments later, Bert shuffled into the hall.

"You're back," he said, a welcoming smile crossing his craggy features. "We weren't expectin' you till tomorrow."

"I managed to catch an earlier flight," Ben said.

"Ah, couldn't wait to get back to the women in your life, is that it?"

"Something like that," Ben said with a grin.

Bert chuckled. "Thought as much." He started shuffling back toward the living room. "Well, come on, then. Mustn't keep those ladies waitin' any longer."

Ben followed Bert into the living room, where Dorothy was sitting in an armchair, reading a book. Her cane lay on the floor beside the chair, but her cast was gone, and only a few scars remained on the side of her face. She looked up as he walked in.

"Ben, welcome home!"

"Thanks, Dorothy." Ben walked over to her and leaned down to kiss her wrinkled cheek. "How are you?"

"Getting stronger all the time," she said cheerfully. "I even made some strawberry jam a couple of days ago. Was managing just fine until Rachel shooed me out of the kitchen, saying I'd been on my feet too long." She pursed her lips. "It's a good thing I love that girl, or I'd have been quite offended. Shooing me out of my own kitchen like that."

Ben laughed. "Where is Rachel?"

"She just went to put Zoe to bed. If you go down there now, you might catch them before Zoe goes to sleep."

Leaving his bag in the living room, Ben headed down the hall toward Zoe's bedroom. The door was ajar, and he peeked in, the Tinkerbell nightlight illuminating just enough of the room for him to make out Rachel kneeling beside Zoe at her bed. He waited as Zoe finished her simple prayer and watched as she climbed into bed. Burrowing under the covers, she drew one arm out and draped it around Rachel's neck. Rachel moved closer.

"What song shall we sing tonight?" Rachel asked.

"Um, how 'bout, the birds and the roses?"

As Rachel began softly singing the Primary song "My Heavenly Father Loves Me," Zoe joined in. Ben stood spellbound until the song was over and Rachel leaned over to kiss Zoe's cheek. "Good night, Zoe. Sleep well. Uncle Ben should be here tomorrow."

"Good night, Wachul," came Zoe's sleepy reply.

Then Rachel got to her feet and walked quietly to the door.

Ben stepped away from the door and waited for Rachel to close it behind her before moving out of the shadows.

"Oh!" Rachel jumped, but the shock on her face immediately melted into a radiant smile. "Ben! When did you get here?"

"About ten minutes ago," he said.

She stepped toward him, and he opened his arms, a trace of her perfume reaching him as he drew her close. "I missed you so much," she whispered.

"I missed you more," he said fervently, and then he kissed her.

* * *

The evening passed quickly. Rachel sat next to Ben on the sofa as he told them all about his recent trip to South Africa. Bert wanted to know about the wild animals he'd seen, and Dorothy was curious about the food. When he told them of his close encounters with wild elephants and hippos, Rachel was doubly grateful that he was home safely and that his new assignment would be less life-threatening. She could tell he was ready and eager to take on the challenges of his editorial position at *Our World*, and she was looking forward to having him around more.

It was late by the time Dorothy and Bert excused themselves for bed. Ben rubbed his hand across his face, and Rachel saw the fatigue in his eyes.

"You must be exhausted," she said, getting to her feet and reaching down to him. "I'll turn off the lights, and you go get some sleep."

Ben took her hand, but instead of rising, he pulled her back to the sofa. "I will," he said. "But first I want to give you something—something I brought back from South Africa."

"What is it?" she asked as she took a seat again.

He gave an enigmatic smile, slid his hand into his pocket, and withdrew a small, black-velvet drawstring bag. As he placed it gently in her hand, she read the name written in elegant silver script on one corner of the bag and recognized it immediately.

"De Beers," she said so quietly she thought the pounding of her heart would drown it out. She was holding something from one of the most prestigious diamond companies in the world.

Ben nodded. "One of my interviews took place at the Venetia Diamond Mine that De Beers operates. Most of the raw diamonds are sent out of the country to be cut, but some of them go to Johannesburg. The guy I was visiting was more than happy to show me the few they have on display. I asked him if I could buy one to take home to the woman I want to marry, and he let me choose from his collection."

"The . . . the woman you want to marry?"

Taking the bag from her trembling hand, Ben untied the drawstring and carefully shook its contents onto Rachel's palm. A stunning, square-cut diamond, its multiple facets sparkling in the living room lights, blinked up at her.

Rachel gazed down at it, a lump forming in her throat and tears forming in her eyes. "It's so beautiful," she whispered.

"I thought perhaps you'd like to choose a setting for it," he said.

Overwhelmed, she looked up at him. He reached out, gently running his finger down her cheek. "All those weeks ago when you were in the hospital after the shooting, Zoe was the one who first woke you. Do you remember?"

"Yes," Rachel said, a small smile forming at the memory. "She was up on the bed, patting my cheek."

"Can you remember what she was saying?"

Slowly, Rachel nodded. "She asked me to stay with her forever."

Ben took her hand, his emotion-filled eyes not leaving hers. "And you said okay," he said softly. "Ever since then, I've prayed that one day I'd have the opportunity to ask you the same question—and that maybe, if I was luckier than I deserve, you'd give me the same answer." His grip tightened a little. "Marry me, Rachel. Say that you'll stay with me forever."

The tears that had been gathering in Rachel's eyes finally spilled over. "Okay," she said, a beaming smile breaking through her tears. "A thousand okays."

An answering smile lit Ben's face. "A thousand okays?"

"A million okays," Rachel said, slipping her hands around his neck, her heart overflowing with happiness. "I will marry you."

Ben's arms wrapped around her waist, and he drew her closer. "I love you, Rachel Hamilton."

"I love you too, Ben Cooper."

Then Ben kissed her, and with joyful certainty, Rachel knew this was where she was meant to be; this was where she belonged.

About the Author

SIAN ANN BESSEY WAS BORN in Cambridge, England, and grew up on the island of Anglesey off the north coast of Wales. She left Wales to attend Brigham Young University and graduated with a bachelor's degree in communications.

Traveling has given Sian a deep appreciation for a world full of diverse cultures. Through her writing, she introduces her readers to some of the locations she has come to love.

Sian is the author of several LDS novels and children's books. She has also written articles for the *New Era*, *Ensign*, and *Liahona* magazines. She and her husband, Kent, currently reside in Rexburg, Idaho. They are the parents of five children and the grandparents of two beautiful little girls and two handsome little boys.